MINE TO TAKE

USA Today Bestselling Author
JENNIFER SUCEVIC

Mine to Take

Copyright© 2024 by Jennifer Sucevic

Published by Tangled Hearts LLC

All rights reserved. No part of this book may be reproduced in any form or by any electronic or mechanical means, including information storage and retrieval systems, without written permission from the author, except for the use of brief quotations in a book review.

This is a work of fiction. Names, characters, businesses, palaces, events, locales, and incidents are either the products of the author's imagination or used in a fictitious manner. Any resemblance to actual persons, living or dead, or actual events is purely coincidental.

Cover Design by Mary Ruth Baloy at MR Creations

Special Edition & Illustrated Cover by Claudia Lymari at Tease Designs

Editing by Evelyn Summers at Pinpoint Editing

Proofreading by Shauna Stevenson at Ink Machine Editing

Interior Formatting by Silla Webb at Masque Publishing

MAVERICK

McKINNON 28

WILDCATS

1

I lift the bottle to my lips and take a swig of cold beer as my gaze skims over the crowd. Music pumps, the bass vibrating in my bones. People are dancing and cutting loose on a Friday night.

We won our game yesterday.

Afterward, we all headed to Slap Shotz to celebrate with rounds of shots and karaoke. It's the unofficial home of the Western Wildcats hockey team.

There's barely time to revel in our victory before we have to prepare for our next game against the East Town University Rattlers.

That's one we abso-fucking-lutely need to win.

Even thinking about their left wing, River Thompson, pisses me off. I crack the muscles in my neck to loosen the mounting tension. The rivalry between us dates back to high school. He's a right wing and always looking to score. I'm a defenseman and always shutting him the fuck down.

On more than one occasion, we've come to blows on the ice.

Aw, hell...who am I trying to kid?

It's unusual if we *don't* get into a brawl and end up in the box.

I'm knocked from the tangle of those thoughts when slender hands glide their way up my chest, and I find myself staring down at the dark-haired beauty beaming up at me.

"Hey, Mav. I've been looking all over for you."

I lift the bottle to my lips again and take another drink. "Looks like you found me."

Her grin intensifies. "Lucky me."

Jenna Montgomery.

She's one of the Wildcats' biggest fans, if you know what I mean.

I flick another glance around the room.

It gets snagged by Ryder and Juliette playing kissy face.

My nose scrunches.

They really need to warn people before engaging in PDA.

Ugh.

Even though they've been together for a couple of months, I'm still trying to wrap my brain around the fact that my best friend and sister are now an item.

Should I have seen it coming from a million miles away?

Probably.

I've always sensed the tension that vibrated in the air when they were in the same room together. It's been that way since middle school. I'd just assumed they hated each other.

Joke's on me—turns out the opposite was true.

When my chest tightens, I shove those thoughts from my head.

Not that I'd admit it to anyone else, but I miss the way things used to be before they started dating. Ryder was usually down for anything. We'd chill out and play a little NHL or Madden on the Xbox. Sometimes we'd head to the bars after practice. Or we'd get a lift in.

Now he spends all his spare time with Juliette.

Hey, it's not like I begrudge their happiness.

I really don't.

I just wish it weren't at my expense.

A sigh escapes me.

And now I sound like the world's biggest pussy.

Exactly what I didn't want.

Unable to watch them make out for another second, my gaze settles on Wolf and Fallyn. Another couple who recently got together.

Or maybe a more accurate description would be that they were just hitched in Vegas.

Yeah...

Mind completely blown.

Who the fuck gets married when they're twenty-two?

Especially someone who has the hockey world by the balls.

I shake my head.

The answer to that question would be Wolf Westerville—future NHL goalie for Boston.

And then there's Ford and Carina, Riggs and Stella, Madden and Viola, and last, but certainly not least, our newest couple on the block —Colby and Britt.

Christ, the guy can't keep his damn hands off her.

Turns out, they secretly tied the knot in Vegas as well.

It wasn't all that long ago when these guys were single and ready to mingle.

Or get laid by groupies.

Now, however?

It's me, Bridger, and Hayes.

We're the last ones standing.

"Maverick?"

I really hate all these maudlin thoughts trying to weigh me down. There's been too many of them lately.

I stare into Jenna's green eyes. "Yeah?"

She presses closer until I feel the rounded softness of her breasts against my chest. "You seem tense. I know exactly what will help with that."

I'm sure she does.

Jenna's superpower is that she's capable of making you forget your own name.

Maybe that's exactly what I need.

To forget all this bullshit pressing in at the edges.

When I don't pounce on the offer, she stretches onto the tips of her toes and nips my lower lip with sharp white teeth.

"Trust me, I'll make it worth your while," she adds in a husky voice that's chock-full of promise.

And just like that, my decision is made.

I jerk my head in a tight nod. "Sure, let's go."

A sly smile lifts the corners of her pink-slicked lips before she grabs my hand and drags me toward the staircase. On the way across the living room, Hayes catches my eye and smirks. His hands are full with two eager bunnies.

Now that Colby has officially retired his dick, Hayes is drowning in pussy. By the look on his face, he couldn't be more thrilled with the predicament.

And Bridger?

He's off moping in a corner by his lonesome.

I haven't seen him drink or hook up since the mass texts became a bone of contention with his old man, the chancellor of the university. They've put a serious crimp in his social life. Bridger employed a couple of friends to help figure out who's behind the messages, but they haven't been able to get to the bottom of this Scooby Doo mystery.

Yet.

I feel bad for the guy.

Whoever's intent on making his life hell must have a serious hard-on for the dude, because it hasn't let up. Just the other day, another one surfaced. Within five minutes, his father was blowing up his phone. Bridger ended up dumping his uneaten lunch in the trash and storming off to his office.

I raise my beer to him as Jenna drags me up the staircase. Once we hit the second-floor landing, we take a right and pass by two closed doors before she wraps her fingers around a knob and shoves it open.

It's not the first time my room has been graced by Jenna's presence, but it has been a hot minute.

I'll fully admit that I went a little crazy in the pussy department freshman year.

How could I not?

I had all the freedom I craved, and girls were throwing themselves at me as if I were already a superstar on the ice. Ryder and I were going out all the time. Sophomore year turned out to be more of the same.

Hockey and girls.

In that order.

Now I'm almost done with my third year and my business classes have become more of a challenge. I have to work harder just to keep my head above water.

Maybe it's for the best that Ryder is preoccupied with Juliette and I've lost my partner in crime. I'm forced to sit my ass at home and plow my way through all the required reading.

As soon as I cross the threshold, Jenna slams the door shut and leans against it. The expression on her face is nothing short of gleeful.

"I've been dying to get you alone for weeks," she admits.

Barely do I have enough time to set the bottle of beer on my desk before she flings herself at me. Her fingers slip beneath the hem of my T-shirt to gather up the cotton material and drag it over my head.

This girl doesn't have a coy bone in her body. It's straight down to business.

Gotta appreciate that.

"You are so damn gorgeous." Her palms slide upward, stroking over bare flesh. "All that hard, chiseled muscle." A fine tremble racks her body. "And for tonight, it's mine."

The way she eats me up with hungry eyes should be sexy.

Instead, it leaves me feeling slightly uncomfortable.

Hollow.

Like I'm nothing more than a piece of meat.

"Ivy is going to be so jealous when I tell her." She flashes a triumphant smile. "And I'm going to share every tiny detail for her to savor."

Hmmm...

I'm not sure how I feel about that.

Do I catch wind of the rumors that float around campus concerning my...appetites?

Yup. It would be hard not to.

I was amused by the stories freshman year.

Now, however?

Not so much.

The last thing I'm interested in is being a notch on some girl's bedpost.

You'd be surprised by how mercenary some of these chicks can be or the way they like to compare notes.

Without looking, she tosses the T-shirt over her shoulder. It hits the bottle of beer on my desk, knocking it to the floor. Golden liquid bubbles up from the long neck and spills everywhere.

I swear under my breath as my mood takes a swift nosedive.

With a giggle, she swings around and picks up the glass container before setting it on the desk. Her gaze gets snagged by the English paper I tossed there a few days ago.

"Just leave it," I say with a grunt.

Trying to lose myself in this girl was a mistake, and I should have realized it sooner. Instead, I forced something that wasn't there to begin with.

There used to be a time in the not-so-distant past when hooking up and having non-discriminant sex was fun. A way to blow off steam for a couple of hours and relieve the stress that would build to a breaking point inside me.

It hasn't felt that easy in a while.

Jenna stares at the paper before glancing over her shoulder to meet my gaze. "Linstrom is your professor and you still got a D minus?" Disbelief threads its way through her voice. "All you have to do is show up and you're guaranteed a C."

Embarrassment slams into me as flames lick at my cheeks.

She flips the page to glance at the second one. "Have you ever heard of a little thing called spellcheck?"

I swipe at the paper, only wanting to snatch it from her. At the last moment, Jenna shifts so that it's just out of reach and my fingers claw the air.

"Give it to me," I growl. My teeth are clenched so tightly that my molars ache. It takes effort to keep from lashing out and jumping down her throat.

I fucking hate when people read my papers or see my grades. In elementary school, it was an endless source of embarrassment. After all these years, that feeling has never subsided. It doesn't matter if there's an explanation for it. I'm sure as shit not about to share that with Jenna.

She waves me away. "Just give me a minute and let me read this."

"I asked you to give it back. So how about you just do it?"

"Are all your classes going this well?"

That question sends another tidal wave of humiliation crashing over me as I clamp my lips together, refusing to give her an answer. It's just easier to go numb and block out the shame that tries to eat me alive.

When I remain silent, she tosses the paper onto the desk before swinging around to face me.

"That's all right. I doubt the university gives a damn if you pass your classes." A smile tips the corners of her lips. "Not when you're busy winning championships for them." She gives me a little wink. "Personally speaking, I don't mind my hockey players a little slow on the uptake. Just as long as they know how to wield their sticks."

My chest constricts as the comment circles around in my brain. I didn't think it was possible to be any more pissed off.

It takes effort to force out the question and not lose my shit. "Excuse me?"

She shrugs. "I'm just saying that the only thing that really matters is that you're going to the NHL."

Her bluntness is enough to steal the air from my lungs.

"The only thing that really matters is that you're going to the NHL."

The muscles in my belly clench as even more heat stings my cheeks until it feels like they're on fire.

When I continue to stare, she moves closer and twines her arms around my neck.

Like hell that's going to happen now.

My fingers shackle her wrists before prying them loose as I take a giant step in retreat. This girl can go fuck herself, because I sure as hell won't be doing it.

Not tonight or any other night in the future.

"You need to leave," I growl.

I wince, hating the hurt that bleeds into my voice.

She blinks in confusion. "What?"

I speak carefully so there's no chance of her misinterpreting what I'm about to say. "You need to leave. This is no longer happening."

Her eyes widen as her face scrunches. "Are you serious?"

"As a heart attack." I point toward the door. "Get out."

Her teeth scrape against her lower lip. "Look, I'm sorry. I was joking around. I didn't mean to hurt your feelings."

"You didn't." Huge fucking lie. "I'm just not in the mood anymore."

Actually, I was never in the mood, but, unlike her, I keep that little tidbit to myself.

"Oh." There's an awkward pause as guilt flashes across her expression. "I guess I could help rewrite your paper. I mean, it would take a lot of work, but—"

This girl is off her rocker if she thinks I'd accept a damn thing from her.

My voice grows colder. It's a wonder she doesn't get frostbitten. "Do me a favor and close the door on your way out."

Unable to stomach the sight of Jenna, I swing toward the window.

It's only when the lock clicks into place that the thick tension filling my shoulder blades loosens and I become more aware of the music that pulses through the floorboards from downstairs.

There's no way in hell I'm returning to the party.

Although, that decision has nothing to do with the chick I just kicked out.

I'm sure she assumes I'm just another lazy jock coasting by on his athletic prowess, marking time until he can get picked up by a professional team.

And maybe there's some truth to that.

Given the choice, I'd already be playing in the NHL. Instead of applying at Western, I would have played a year or two of juniors and then entered the draft. Instead, my parents insisted I needed a degree first.

Trust me, I fought that tooth and nail.

But after Mom was diagnosed with breast cancer, I didn't have the heart to argue with her. I would have moved heaven and earth to give her whatever she wanted.

So, here I am—in my junior year at Western.

Unlike my sister, academics have never come easy to me.

Juliette is the resident brainiac of the family.

I, unfortunately, take after my father and was diagnosed with dyslexia in early elementary school. It's my fucking cross to bear.

As I drop onto the queen-sized bed and stare up at the ceiling, my mind circles back to the shitty English grade Jenna got such a kick out of.

It takes effort to force out the stalled breath trapped in my lungs.

If I don't get it up, my ass will get benched, and with playoffs right around the corner, that's the last thing I can afford.

Sure, I'm here to get an education.

But even more importantly, I'm at Western to play hockey.

And if I can't do that, what's the fucking point?

POCKETFUL OF SUNSHINE

WILLOW & MAVERICK

01:10   04:10

WILLOW

LEUKEMIA

2

"Exactly how did I let you talk me into this?" my bestie asks as we navigate the crowded corridor.

"Because you love me." I flash an overly sweet smile in her direction.

With a scowl, she flattens her lips before grumbling, "Well, you got me there."

Holland and I became fast friends back in elementary school. She's my sister from another mister. The yin to my yang. Whenever I've needed her, she's been there. I'd like to think that I've done the same, but at this point, she's definitely put in more time.

She's a true friend in every sense of the word.

And there's nothing I wouldn't do in return for her.

Holland gives off major don't-fuck-with-me vibes. But beneath her hard, crunchy exterior lies a soft, nougat filling. Although, if you said that to her, she'd probably take a chunk out of your backside with her teeth.

But she can't fool me. We've been friends long enough that every so often, she'll drop the mask and allow her vulnerability to take center stage. I love that she's comfortable enough to give me those rare and precious glimpses of the real Holland.

"Added bonus, you enjoy watching River play."

A devilish smile lifts the corners of her lips. "Actually, what I enjoy is watching your brother knock grown men on their asses. There's something immensely satisfying about it. Especially when he does it to one player in particular." She glances at me. "Which is the real reason I agreed to this outing."

I knock my thinner shoulder into hers. When she meets my eyes, I waggle my brows. "It wouldn't be the worst start to a relationship."

She snorts. "I'm sorry, have you totally lost your mind? I have zero interest in hockey players and even less in your brother."

"Are you sure about that?"

Her tone turns steely. "One hundred percent."

My brain tumbles back to our childhood. "You might not realize this, but I've always secretly hoped you two would fall in love and get married. Then we'd truly be sisters."

"What are you talking about? That's never been a secret. You used to leave sticky notes on my books with our names surrounded by little hearts."

For years, I tried nudging them in each other's direction with no luck. Neither seem interested in the other. River treats Holland like the sister he never wanted or asked for.

"Plus, your brother is a total bonehead."

I loop my arm through hers and draw her curvy body closer before adding in a cajoling voice, "Just think, if you play your cards right, he could be *your* bonehead."

"Hard pass. I'm focused on finishing up college and getting the hell out of here. In that order." There's a pause before she mutters, "And Marcus left a lasting impression. One that has been singed into my soul."

It's not often that my friend dredges up her ex.

"That was years ago," I say carefully.

I hate that he hurt her so much. Holland has always been a master at keeping her emotions tightly contained. I can hardly blame her with the way she grew up. I'm just glad our house was something of a refuge for her.

She jerks her shoulders and brushes off the comment. "Once burned, twice shy and all that bullshit."

"I'm just saying that you should be open to the idea of love if it presents itself. That's all."

"Maybe after college, once I'm a boss-ass bitch," she concedes.

That reluctantly given admittance feels like a major victory.

When my phone vibrates in my pocket, I slip my hand inside and fish it out before glancing at the screen.

"Let me guess—it's Becks."

Even though I try not to let it affect me, everything inside me deflates. "Yup."

"She wants to make sure you've taken all the necessary precautions this evening."

"Right again."

"You realize that woman would put you in a bubble if it were socially acceptable?"

"Don't give her any ideas," I grumble.

A smile trembles on her lips. "Oh, I'm pretty sure she's already investigated it. Must not have been feasible."

I hate to admit just how spot-on Holland is in her assessment of the situation.

"How hilarious would it be if you showed up in a biohazard suit?"

I glare. "She'd be thrilled."

"Yeah, probably. The woman is a total nutjob." She glances at me. "Sorry, but it's true."

"I'm aware," I say with a reluctant sigh.

We follow the swiftly moving crowd until finding our seat section. Even though I'm a student at Western, the only time I attend their games is when my brother's team is playing the Wildcats. My twin has been involved in the sport since kindergarten, so I grew up watching it. More times than not, Holland was dragged along to keep me company.

As soon as we enter the arena, I glance around, searching for my parents. Mom pops to her feet and waves erratically. The people surrounding her swivel in her direction and stare. Somehow, they managed to secure amazing seats right up against the plexiglass.

"Oh good, there's Becks," Holland mutters. "I've missed her. What's it been? Seventy-two hours since she stopped by our place to do a deep clean?"

I shake my head at the nickname. "You know she hates when you call her that, right?'

She flashes a grin. "Why do you think I do it?"

Even though I shake my head, I can't help but be amused by my bestie. She does and says things that I would never dream of.

It would be difficult not to admire her spunk.

I return the wave, hoping Mom will settle down.

"Think she got here early and sanitized our entire section?"

"Probably."

It would be amusing if it weren't true.

My mother has always been nervous by nature. My diagnosis in high school only amplified those tendencies.

Once we make our way to the seats, Dad rises to his feet and pulls me in for a warm embrace. He's way more chill than Mom. After a handful of seconds, she elbows him out of the way to do the same. Her grip borders on bone crushing. When the embrace stretches a few seconds too long, I pat her back. Only then does she draw away enough to study my face, as if looking for telltale signs of fatigue or illness.

"How are you feeling, sweetie? I hope you've been taking those new immunity boosters I bought. When I didn't hear from you yesterday, I was concerned."

I bite back the sigh that sits perched on the tip of my tongue, and paste a smile in place. "I feel great. I told you when you stopped by the other day that I'd be busy with classes and the tutoring center."

Her brows pinch at the mention of my job on campus. "You're just asking to pick up an illness working there. All those germs... I really hope you're taking the necessary precautions. Washing your hands, using sanitizer, wearing a mask, and social distancing when possible. And when you return home from school, make sure you're changing right away and throwing your dirty clothes into the laundry."

"Mom..."

"I'm serious!" Her voice rises as fear flickers in her eyes.

"We talked to Dr. Edwards about it at my last appointment, remember? He agreed that it was fine. I'm not putting myself at risk."

She presses her lips together before muttering, "I still don't like it."

"She's fine, Becks. Willow hasn't even caught so much as a cold this semester."

Mom turns glaring eyes on my roommate, and her voice flattens. "Oh, I didn't notice you there, Holland."

My roommate grins. "It's nice to see you too."

After all these years, my mother has finally learned to tolerate Holland because I love her so fiercely and refuse to listen to one bad word she has to say about her or her family. What Mom can't deny is that she's been a steadfast friend through everything.

As far as Mom's concerned, it's Holland's only saving grace.

"I'm being careful. Promise," I say, cutting into their conversation before it can spiral out of control and ruin the evening.

It's happened before.

We're here to support River, not talk about me.

It won't be long before she launches into a spiel about me going into elementary education and how many germs children carry. She'll probably end up stroking out when I begin my student teaching placement next year.

Or she'll show up every day armed with a can of disinfectant, sanitizing wipes, and masks.

I wouldn't put it past the woman.

Just as I'm about to drop down onto the seat, she says, "Wait! Let me wipe down the chair again."

"Mom," I groan. "That's not necessary."

She meets my beseeching gaze with a determined look of her own. "It'll only take a second."

Embarrassment claws at my cheeks as she pulls out a travel-size pouch of wipes and scrubs the plastic and metal. A few people seated in the row above us stare as she grabs a small bottle of spray and then disinfects it.

The alcohol scent, masked by something that can only be described as artificially floral, stings my nostrils.

Once she tucks away her cleaning supplies, she waves toward the seat. "Now it's ready."

"Thanks."

"No problem, sweetie. Do you want to wear a mask?" She glances around with a frown. "There are so many people packed in here."

"If the germs don't kill her," Holland mutters beneath her breath, "your smothering will."

By the way Mom narrows her eyes, she heard the comment loud and clear.

Before either one can take another swipe, the lights in the arena are dimmed as the music volume is raised, cutting off the possibility of further conversation.

When the players from the East Town Rattlers are announced, we whistle and cheer as River's name reverberates throughout the arena. Then it's time for the home team players to be introduced. I glance around as the fans cheer and applaud until the noise becomes deafening. The Jumbotron gives their fans a close-up shot as each player takes to the ice with a wave.

Since transferring to the university in the fall, I haven't paid much attention to the athletes on campus. Although, it would be impossible not to be aware of them. Hockey and football are by far the most popular sports at Western. Each team generates a ton of revenue for the school, and they have more groupies than they know what to do with.

It's been the same for my brother in both high school and college.

It only takes one glance to notice a few girls in the visiting team's section holding up signs with my brother's name and number scrawled across the white posterboard.

That's reason number one as to why I would never get involved with an athlete.

River is the other.

My twin would have a conniption if I looked twice at one of his teammates. He's always been quick to run off any of the guys who show even a hint of interest.

His behavior is almost as overbearing as my mother's.

Last year, I reached my breaking point and brought up the idea of switching universities. Holland encouraged it and offered to be my roommate. Even though both my mother and brother objected to the move, I transferred last summer and started at Western in the fall.

So far, it's been one of the best decisions I've ever made.

I only wish I'd done it sooner.

There's freedom in the people I meet not knowing who I am or my backstory.

I'm knocked from the tangle of my thoughts when the puck gets dropped at center ice and the players explode into action. I unzip my jacket, revealing my brother's jersey.

His dream is to play professional hockey.

When River was a junior in high school, he reached out to Brody McKinnon, who owns a sports management agency, in hopes of representation. The former NHL player turned him down, saying that they weren't taking on any new clients.

My brother was crushed.

Especially since his son is Maverick McKinnon. They played on opposite teams in high school, and it's the same in college. Over the years, it's turned into something of a rivalry.

A none-too-friendly one.

I blink back to the action on the ice when one of River's teammates makes a quick pass to him. As soon as the puck lands on the end of his stick, my brother takes off, maneuvering around players as they attempt to swarm.

Energy buzzes through the arena as Western's fans shout for River to be shut down. A look of intensity settles on my brother's face as he darts across the ice. I leap to my feet and cheer when he skates closer to the goal. He's one of the top scorers on his team. Just as he veers toward us to avoid a defenseman, another player slams him into the boards. My eyes widen as my hands fly to my mouth. The sound of the collision reverberates throughout the vast space as I stare at the defenseman who just took out my brother.

Our gazes lock for a heartbeat.

And then another.

Time stands still as icy air gets clogged in my throat. The cheering crowd fades as I stare into eyes that can only be described as the color of rich mocha.

When his gaze drops to my jersey, the loss of eye contact is instantaneous. His lips twist into a scowl. That's all it takes for my heart to explode into action, racing beneath my breast as my brother scrambles to his feet and plows a gloved hand into Maverick McKinnon's wide chest.

My knees weaken now that the intensity of his stare is no longer drilling into me.

Players from both teams descend, trying to pull Maverick and River away from one another. I don't have to hear the words that fall from my brother's lips to know that he's pissed off. Frustration wafts off him in thick, suffocating waves.

Mom shakes her head and scowls. "I've said it before and I'll say it again—that McKinnon boy is an animal."

"Damn," Holland mutters. "I was hoping more of a fight would break out. Maybe a little bloodshed to break up the monotony."

Mom shoots her another glare as my gaze slices to my twin's rival. His teammates have their arms wrapped around him as the ref blows his whistle, ending the possibility of a brawl breaking out.

When Maverick's hard-edged stare slices to me for a second time, my fingers rise to play with the silver W pendant that hangs loosely around my neck. River wears a matching one with his initial. He bought them for us after my diagnosis, and there's never been a day that I haven't worn the delicate piece of jewelry. It's become a good-luck charm.

As the game gets back underway, anticipation crackles in the air like an impending storm. Instead of keeping my attention focused on my brother the way I should, I find myself staring at the handsome defenseman.

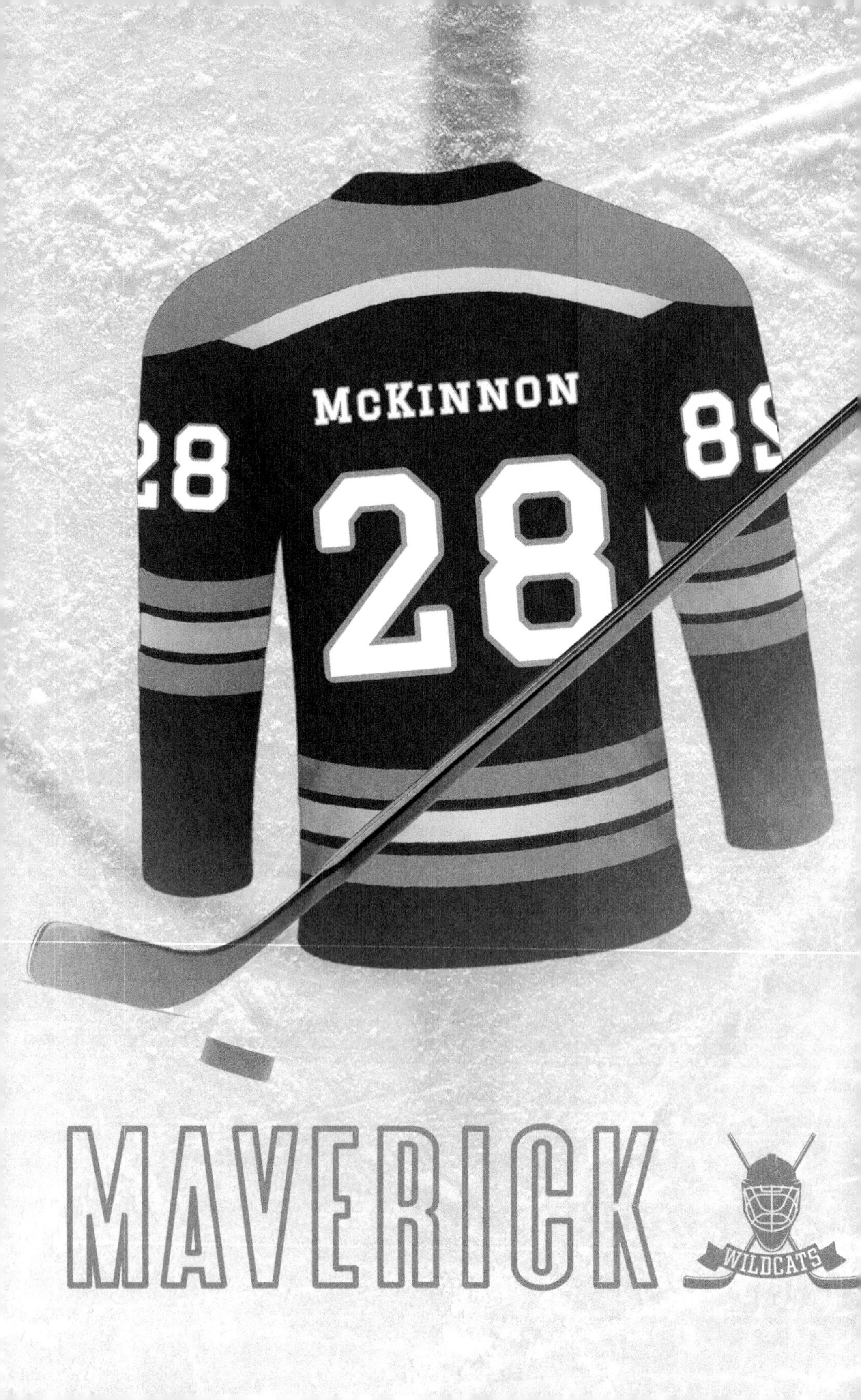
McKINNON
28
28
MAVERICK
WILDCATS

3

I glance at the clock on the scoreboard. We're midway through the third period and the game is tied. The energy in the arena feels like a living, breathing entity. It's always like this when we play the Rattlers. East Town University is only forty-five minutes away, so it's an easy trip for their fans to make. One side of the arena is a sea of orange and black, while the other is white and light blue. This is our team's biggest conference rival, and both sets of fans are rabid for a win.

If we don't pull one off tonight, there'll be hell to pay.

And yet...

As much as we have riding on the line, I can't stop thinking about the pretty blonde in the stands near the glass and the way our gazes caught as I checked River Thompson into the boards.

Fuck, but taking him out like that in the first period had been a pure pleasure.

The guy's been out for payback ever since.

Bring it on, asshole.

Bring.

It.

On.

I'm sure he was pissed that I made him look like a pussy in front of his girl.

My heart stutters for a handful of seconds before pounding into overdrive.

Is that what she is? His girl?

The thought burrows beneath my skin like an incurable rash. I send another look her way, only to find her watching me.

Good.

I want her attention focused on me the entire time she's wearing Thompson's jersey.

Even though I don't know who she is or what her name is, I want to tear the damn thing from her body.

My hands clench in my gloves in order to stop myself from crawling over the plexiglass and doing exactly that.

I glance at her again.

She's like a ray of sunshine with the way her golden hair tumbles around her shoulders. I'm having a difficult time concentrating on the reason we're here.

The game.

I swear under my breath as River manages to get around me and score a goal.

Motherfucker.

The girl wearing his jersey leaps to her feet and claps. Happiness radiates from her in intoxicating waves. It infuriates me that she's cheering for the one guy I can't fucking stand.

When her gaze flicks to mine again, her eyes widen.

A shoulder bumps mine, and I reluctantly break eye contact only to find Ryder McAdams frowning at me.

"You okay, man? It's not like you to let Thompson fake you out like that."

Fuck.

He's right.

I'm distracted when I should be laser focused on getting my job done, and that's never happened before.

Hockey has been my number one priority since I was old enough to lace up my own Bauers. I'm so damn close to making all my dreams come true. After this season wraps up, I just have to make it through senior year and then I'll be free to sign my contract with Boston. Hell, if I could convince my parents to let me do it early, I'd quit school in a heartbeat and head straight to the NHL.

Although, I won't hold my breath for that.

Every time I mention the possibility, they shoot it down, refusing to discuss the situation. I'm not sure why it's so damn important I earn a degree. After I'm done playing hockey, I'll end up working for my father's sports agency.

I blink back to the present. "Yeah, I'm fine."

It's carefully that he searches my eyes.

Apparently satisfied with what he finds, he claps me on the shoulder. "Good. Let's shut these guys down. If we don't, we'll never hear the end of it."

With a nod, we take our positions at the blue line as Hayes gets ready for the faceoff. As soon as the puck gets dropped, Hayes knocks it to Colby McNichols, who races up the ice before passing it to Ford Hamilton. It goes back and forth as defensemen swarm. At every turn, the Rattlers attempt to regain possession before Ford scores through the five hole. In true Ford fashion, he grins at the stands, and I know he's looking straight at his girlfriend.

The game is now tied with less than two minutes on the clock.

The energy in the arena turns frenetic. Under normal circumstances, I'm able to block out the screaming fans and focus solely on the job that needs to get done.

That's not the case this evening.

And it has everything to do with the hot little blonde.

It's impossible to shake the heat of her gaze as I skate across the ice.

This time, when the puck is dropped, Hayes loses the faceoff. The Rattler's right wing scoops it up and takes off. From the corner of my eye, I keep an eye on River. I know his teammate will pass to him, and I'll be damned if I allow him to score for a second time.

I skate closer, making sure to keep him in my periphery. I'm not giving him one damn inch. The wing with the puck glances at their center, as if he'll pass to him. Just as I back off, he flicks his wrist in the other direction.

To River.

I swear under my breath, realizing that he managed to get away from me while I was focused on the other player.

My blades dig into the ice as I take off, attempting to catch him, but it's too damn late. I'm not even close enough for a back check.

He swoops in front of the net before Ryder can get there and scores another goal.

Fuck.

Fuck.

Fuck.

The horn blasts throughout the arena before echoing in my ears. River grins around his mouthguard as he points to the girl in the stands.

When his gaze settles on mine, he smirks. "Better luck next time, McKinnon. Looks like Sabrina wasn't the only thing I stole from you."

My vision goes red as I slam him against the boards for a second time.

River gets knocked off his skates and hits the ice with a thud. Even though the sound is satisfying as hell, it does nothing to assuage my fury. He scrambles to his feet before taking a swing.

Now I'm the one who's smiling.

Until his gloved fist connects with my helmet and sends my head careening to the left. My teeth snap, sinking into the mouthguard as I lunge.

A whistle gets blown as players from both teams pry us apart.

"You're a fucking asshole!" River growls.

I do the only thing I can and grin.

One of the refs stabs a finger in my direction. "In the box you go, McKinnon." Then he looks at River. "You too."

"What?" His incredulous voice escalates. "He started it!"

"Doesn't matter," the other ref says before skating away.

The Rattlers coach has a few choice words with the refs, arms flailing, but it doesn't change the outcome.

I glance at the blonde on my way to the penalty box.

Her wide eyes stay pinned to me the entire way.

It's exactly where I want them.

POCKETFUL OF SUNSHINE
WILLOW & MAVERICK
01:10 04:10

WILLOW

LEUKEMIA

4

"Are you sure I can't convince you to stick around and wait for River?" I cajole Holland.

She gives me an are-you-cray-cray look. "Consider yourself lucky that I came to watch the game at all." She sends a sidelong glance toward my mother. "You know there's only so much of Becks I can handle, and I've reached my quota for the year."

My gaze reluctantly resettles on Mom. She's still foaming at the mouth that River was sent to the penalty box at the end of the game for a fight he didn't provoke.

"Oh, come on. She's not *that* bad." Even as I say the words, I know they're a lie.

Holland snorts. "Um, yeah, she is. And we both know it. At some point, you'll need to have a come-to-Jesus meeting with her. The woman has to cut the cord and take a giant step in retreat. For both of your sakes."

My shoulders sink under the heavy weight of her comment. Holland isn't telling me anything I haven't secretly mulled over a million times before. The more I try to spread my wings, the harder Mom doubles down and hovers, refusing to hand over the reins to my own life. It makes me want to scream.

When I fail to respond, she says, "I'll see you back at the townhouse, all right?"

I nod. "Yup."

With one final wave, Holland takes off, navigating her way through the thick crowd. After she disappears around the corner, I join my parents to wait for my brother. Other than the fight at the end of the third period, he had an amazing game.

We chat about school and the tutoring center until River walks out of the visiting team's locker room, freshly showered. A grin flashes across his face when he sees us.

Dad claps him on the shoulder. "You had a great game."

"Thanks. Coach said there were a few scouts in the stands." His eyes darken. "Hopefully that jackass McKinnon didn't ruin it for me."

That's enough to wipe the smile from Mom's face. "Every time you two play against each other, there are issues. Why can't he just let—"

"You were on fire," I cut in before the conversation can go off the rails. We all know why Maverick McKinnon has a bone to pick with River. Even if Mom doesn't want to acknowledge it. "I'm sure they were impressed."

My twin's expression softens. His first love has always been hockey, and I can't imagine that ever changing. "Thanks, sis. Glad you were able to make it."

"I wouldn't have missed it for the world."

"Are you hungry?" Dad asks. "We can get some dinner before heading back home."

River shakes his head. "Nah, a few of the guys were talking about grabbing something to eat. You don't mind if I go with them, do you?"

"Of course not." Mom glances at her watch. "If we hurry, we can catch the news."

River flicks a glance my way. "Any interest in coming out to celebrate with us?"

I blink, thrown off by the unexpected offer. He usually doesn't invite me out to party with his teammates.

"Really?"

He pops a shoulder as if it's no big deal. "Sure, why not?"

I mull it over for a few seconds before nodding. "Okay. Yeah, that sounds fun."

As soon as I agree, Mom frowns. "I don't know if that's such a good idea."

"Don't worry. I'll keep an eye on her. She'll be fine," River adds.

Even though she technically doesn't have a say in what I do, Mom chews her lower lip with indecision.

"Rebecca, let the kids have fun. They'll be fine. River will watch out for his sister. He always does."

Irritation pricks at me.

"I don't need anyone to watch out for me." I huff. "I'm almost twenty-one."

Dad waves off my comment, attempting to make light of it. "I know, I know."

This isn't the first time we've had this conversation. Unfortunately, it won't be the last either. Holland's words ring unwantedly in my ears. My parents really do need to cut the cord before I get strangled by it.

We all say our goodbyes before they head out and we're joined by a few of River's teammates. When we were younger, I knew all the guys my brother played hockey with. We attended the same school and they'd stop by the house after practice and in the summer. I've only met the players on River's college team a handful of times.

It's easy to see that everyone is flying high from the win. There are lots of smiles, laughter, and good-natured ribbing.

"Let's grab something to eat and then hit up a bar or two," a tall guy with rich brown, wavy hair says.

After everyone agrees, he flicks mossy-green colored eyes in my direction before doing a double take and upping the wattage of his smile. "Well, hello there."

The greeting barely makes it past his teeth before River growls, "Back off, Higgins. That's my sister."

Tension fills my muscles as I wait for the inevitable but pray that this time will be different.

"She had fucking cancer."

It's like dropping a bomb in the middle of an unsuspecting town.

Air leaks painfully from my lungs as the happy chatter of seconds ago dies a quick death and the guys closest to us turn and stare like I'm a circus oddity. Heat scalds my cheeks as pity floods their eyes. As soon as I meet their gazes, they shift and glance away as if I'm contagious.

The cute guy who'd been flirting seconds ago looks properly chastised by my brother's comment. He drags a hand through his damp strands and mumbles, "Oh. Sorry about that. I didn't know."

After most of his teammates turn away, I ball my hand and punch River in the bicep.

Not that he feels it.

When pain shoots through my fist, I shake it out and glare. "Did you seriously just blurt that out in front of everyone?"

With a frown, he jerks his shoulders. "What? What did I do?"

I narrow my eyes.

I love my brother, but sometimes, I just want to kill him.

Slowly.

With my bare hands.

This is one of those times.

It's the main reason I decided to transfer after my sophomore year. I was tired of him hovering, outing my diagnosis before people could get to know me as a person, not a medical condition.

"You know exactly what you did," I grumble, opening my purse and rifling through it for my keys.

Deep down, I knew this was a mistake.

When I pull them from the bag, River blurts, "I'm sorry, okay? I didn't mean to say it."

I pause with them clasped tightly in my hand. "If this is what the rest of the night will be like, then I'm just going to head home now and skip the embarrassment."

"I'm sorry, Willow. I'm just..." His voice trails off. "Protective of you. I want everyone to understand that you're off-limits."

Even though I don't want it to, everything softens inside me. It's always been impossible for me to stay mad at River. "There was no need to humiliate me in order to get your point across."

"You're right. It was a shitty thing to do. Please don't leave. I want you to come out and celebrate with us."

It takes a minute or so for my muscles to loosen.

When I remain silent, he gives me sad, puppy-dog eyes. The ones I can never say no to. "Do you forgive me?"

"I don't know," I mutter, trying to hold on to the last wisps of my anger. "If I hear cancer or leukemia come out of your mouth one more time tonight, I won't talk to you for a month. Maybe longer."

He holds up his hand with a solemn promise. "I won't say another word about it. I swear."

"Fine."

River throws a muscular arm around my shoulders before hauling me close. "We're going to have a blast!"

The group moves en masse to the exit at the front of the building. Now that all cancer talk has screeched to a halt, the mood once again turns celebratory.

Some of the Wildcats players are still hanging around as we reach the lobby. A shiver skates down my spine when my gaze is snagged by a dark, brooding one. Even without a jersey that has his name stamped across the back of it, I know exactly who this guy is.

During the game, I'd tried telling myself that the little zips I'd felt every time our eyes locked were a figment of my imagination.

That's no longer possible.

His eyes narrow as he pins me in place with a hard-edged stare.

The connection is only severed when one of the girls who'd been holding a sign with River's name scrawled across it slams into his chest and twines her arms around his neck before pressing her lips against his.

I hate referring to any girl as a flavor of the week, but that's been River's track record for the past few years. There's absolutely no point in me getting to know them. They're here and gone before I can blink. There hasn't been anyone of significance since he and Sabrina parted ways freshman year of college.

I'm just about to untangle myself from my brother when he slips his other arm around the overenthusiastic girl as we head to the exit.

Unable to help myself, I sneak another glance at the hot hockey player. Our eyes collide for the umpteenth time tonight, and my feet stutter at the disgust stamped across his expression. It's written in the hard glint that now fills his icy depths and the curl of his upper lip.

My heart kicks up into overdrive as River tugs me along before smirking at Maverick.

"Tough loss, McKinnon. Better luck next time."

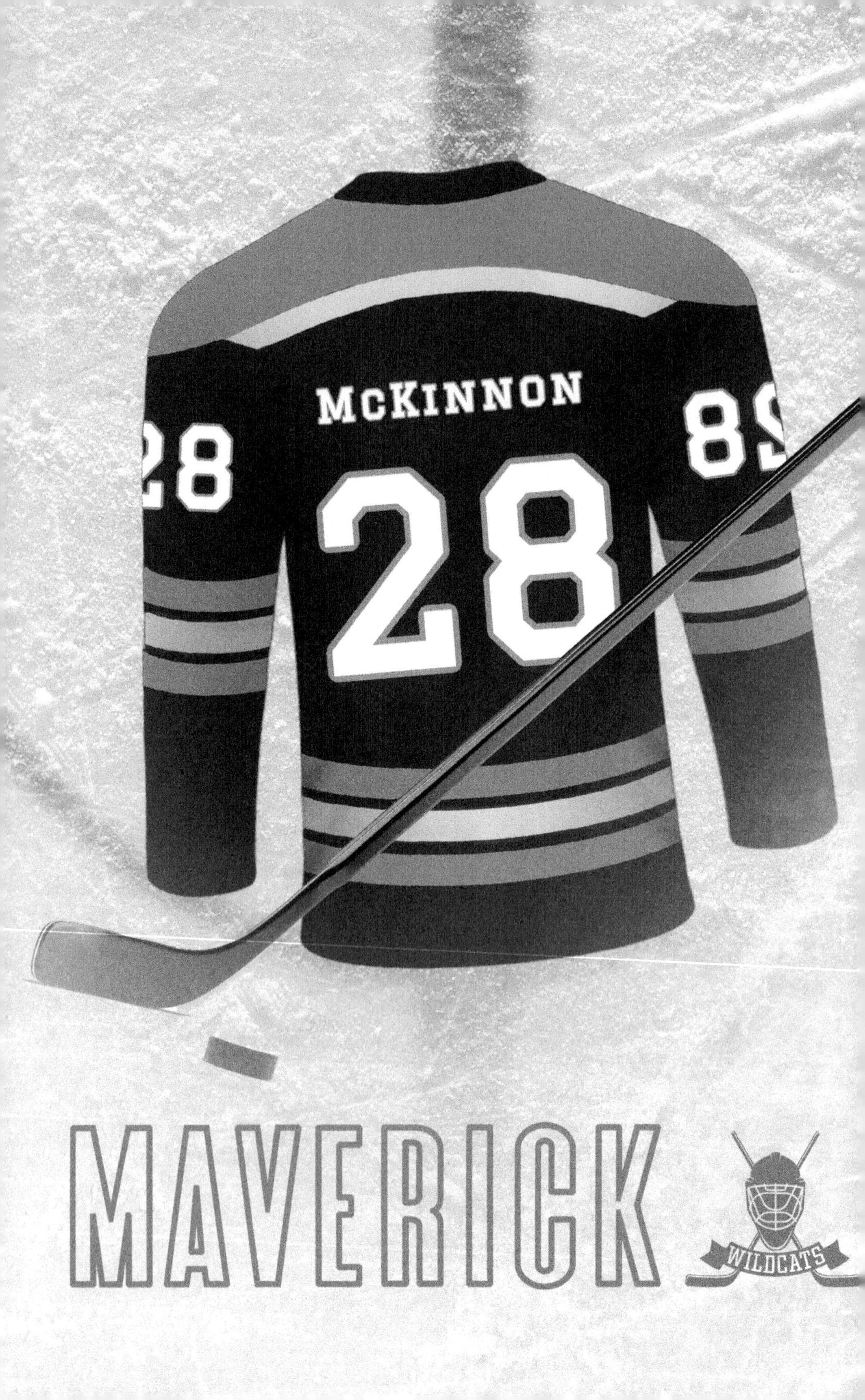

McKINNON
28
28
89
MAVERICK
WILDCATS

5

There's only one way to describe the mood at Slap Shotz, and that's somber. Frustration and anger hang heavy in the air. This isn't the first game we've lost this season, but let's just say it's not a regular occurrence.

The fact that it happened against our biggest conference rival only adds salt to the wound.

No one is taking it well. A few guys are drowning their sorrows in glasses of cheap beer. Others are rehashing the game play by play, trying to figure out where it all went to shit.

Plus, no one's looking forward to the next practice. Coach will rip us a new one, all the while putting us through the wringer. It wouldn't surprise me if a few of the younger players throw in the towel afterward and quit the team.

That thought sinks to the bottom of my belly like a heavy stone, where it settles uncomfortably.

No doubt about it—we're definitely going to get the shit kicked out of us.

And I have the sneaking suspicion that I'll get the brunt of it.

I was distracted and allowed my emotions to get the better of me.

Realizing how my future will play out, I down the rest of my beer and decide to head home. I caught a ride to the arena and then the bar with Hayes and Bridger.

I flick a glance in their direction.

Neither look very happy, so it's doubtful they'll stick around for long.

As I set the empty glass on the bar, the back door swings open and a dozen guys saunter in with grins plastered across their smug faces.

My gaze narrows as I catch sight of River fucking Thompson.

You have to be seriously shitting me right now.

What the fuck are these clowns doing here?

At *our* bar?

The place where *we* always hang out?

Everyone knows that Slap Shotz unofficially belongs to the Western Wildcats.

My gaze slides to the girl glued to his side, and every muscle tenses, going on high alert.

Blondie.

After she walked out of the arena, I never expected to see her again. As soon as our gazes collide, her eyes widen as she stutters to a stop. The douche at her side sends a questioning look her way.

It's tempting to bare my teeth and knock him away from her.

How is it possible that she's even more beautiful than I remembered?

River leans down and murmurs something in her ear. She rips her attention away from me long enough to meet his questioning gaze. A potent concoction of anger and jealousy bursts to life inside me as he drapes his arm around her again.

The visceral reaction I'm having to this girl is almost enough to give me pause. I search my memories, unable to remember a time when I've felt anything like it.

And that includes with Sabrina.

Until this moment, I didn't think it was possible to feel more.

After Mom's cancer diagnosis in high school, I've done everything within my power not to feel anything too deeply. Those months of chemo were a dark period for everyone in the family. The fear and uncertainty that she could be ripped from our lives sat at the bottom of my belly like a heavy, unmovable weight. It's not something I want to go through again.

I'm knocked from the tangle of those thoughts when Bridger leaps to his feet. I've known the guy for almost three years, and he's never been a hothead. If anything, he's the levelheaded one who tries to maintain peace in the kingdom. But he's been dealing with a lot of shit these past couple months. It wouldn't take much to shove him over the edge.

"What the fuck are you doing here, Thompson?" he barks.

River straightens to his full height, which is a few inches over six feet. "Good to see you too, Sanderson." He shrugs. "Just thought we'd stick around town and celebrate our win. Or, you know, the shit stomping we gave you."

Ryder, Ford, and Wolf move to flank our teammate. Madden and Riggs aren't far behind.

Bridger stiffens, the muscles in his jaw ticking. "It would probably be in your best interest to find somewhere else to do that."

River glances around the dark space. "Nah, here's good. Last I checked, you didn't own the place."

"That's right, they don't," Sully says, raising his voice to be heard over the music, "but I do. And I don't want any trouble, or I'll toss every single one of you out on your asses."

Gerry, one of the bouncers, makes his presence known by cracking his knuckles and folding burly arms across his chest. The sleeves of his black T-shirt strain against the bulging biceps.

He's one dude I wouldn't want to fuck with.

If these guys have any brains whatsoever, they won't either.

"Are we gonna have any problems tonight?" the older man asks, voice turning hard.

River cocks his head. "Not from us."

Bridger glances at Sully. "You won't get any from us either."

The bar owner gives hard stares to both warring factions. "Good. Glad to hear it. Now, what can I get you to drink?"

Some of the crackling tension blanketing the atmosphere dissipates as the Rattlers make their way to the stretch of bar and my teammates continue to glare at their rivals as if waiting for them to step one toe out of line.

If that happens, all hell will break loose.

Another wave of jealousy crashes over me as River steers blondie toward the bar. My molars grind as they order a round of drinks and hoist their glasses in the air, toasting their win.

I can't help but shake my head at their arrogance.

It's like they're begging to get their asses kicked.

No matter what I think of River, the guy has some major balls waltzing in here and rubbing their victory in our faces.

For as long as I can remember, tension has simmered between us.

And then in high school, he stole my girl.

The fact that she left me for the one guy I've always considered my rival stung more than actually losing her.

She could have broken up with me for anyone.

Anyone but River fucking Thompson.

I can't take my eyes off the blonde as the bartender hands her a brown bottle of beer. The moment she lifts it to her lips, River nips it from her grasp. My brows shoot up as he guzzles the entire contents before setting it down on the stretch of bar. With a frown, he gives his head a slight shake.

Are you fucking kidding me?

What a dick.

That thought is further solidified when the girl who'd attacked him at the arena wraps her arms around his neck and smothers him in sloppy kisses. My gaze slices back to his girlfriend, waiting to see how this scene will unfold.

Will she go after the chick sucking River's face?

It certainly wouldn't be the first catfight I've witnessed.

Most of the girlfriends understand that they need to be on high alert and beat the groupies off with a stick.

It comes with the territory of dating a hockey player.

Puck bunnies, on the other hand?

They don't mind sliding into bed with someone else's man.

And they certainly don't mind sharing them either.

When distaste flashes across blondie's face and she swivels away from the mauling still taking place, I realize she's not a girlfriend after all.

Huh.

I wouldn't have pegged her for a groupie.

Guess I was wrong.

My muscles tense when one of River's teammates sidles up to her. A hesitant smile quirks her lips as she tucks a stray lock of golden hair behind her ear.

Fuck.

Even her ears are adorable.

When the guy grins and steps closer, invading her personal space, I take an unconscious step in their direction. I recognize the hungry expression written across his face. It's one that says he's looking to get lucky.

Before I can take another step, River breaks away from the girl and scowls at his teammate before pulling blondie closer. He gets in the player's face, pointing to her again and saying something. The other guy gives her a sidelong glance before shaking his head and taking a giant step in retreat, as if he can't get away fast enough.

If I didn't realize it before, I do now—River Thompson is a grade-A dick.

He says something to the blonde before resuming his make out session with the girl, who looks as if she's trying to swallow him whole.

I'm curious as to what this chick's next move will be.

If I were her, I'd haul off and deck him.

Maybe a few times.

Instead, she presses her lips together and heads for the exit at the back of the bar.

It's not a conscious decision on my part to take off after her.

It just happens.

POCKETFUL OF SUNSHINE
WILLOW & MAVERICK
01:10
04:10
WILLOW
LEUKEMIA
SURVIVOR

6

When will I learn?

I knew tagging along with my brother tonight was a mistake. If I'd been smart, I would have listened to my intuition. Instead of interrupting River, I shoot him a text on the way to the exit and let him know that I'm heading home.

At some point, I need to sit down and have a serious convo with him about keeping my private information private. Part of me is irritated, but a bigger part is sad that my family can't seem to move on.

I refuse to live in a bubble.

I spent enough time in high school sitting on the sidelines and watching everyone around me live their best lives.

I won't do it any longer.

The cool evening breeze slaps at my cheeks as I shove through the back door of the bar. It's a relief to leave behind all the suffocating tension simmering inside. I have the sneaking suspicion that River knew exactly what he was doing when he casually suggested the place.

I glance up at the dark sky.

The night is cold and clear. Pinpoints of light glitter brightly from up above. It's tempting to stop and search out the Little and Big Dippers. My love for star gazing and astronomy was born during my battle with leukemia. There were days when I was so fatigued that I couldn't do anything more than lie in bed and read. It gave me something to focus on and explore from the comfort of our home. Dad bought me a telescope and we'd search out the constellations at night. If I didn't have the physical strength, he would carry me out to the back porch. We followed any astronomical event that happened and would stay up until the wee hours of the morning to experience them.

Marveling at the vastness of the universe and the infinite number of galaxies helped put everything I was struggling with into perspective. In the grand scheme of things, my life and problems were insignificant.

Instead of giving in to the urge, I burrow into the collar of my jacket and hurry toward my Ford Bronco. It was a present from my parents on my eighteenth birthday. In true Mom fashion, she made sure it had all the safety bells and whistles.

When I'm a few feet away from the vehicle, I slip the key fob from my pocket and click the locks. As soon as the beep rings throughout the air, swift-moving footsteps snag my attention. My heartrate kicks up as I swing around, ready to confront a possible attacker.

I'm thrown off when I come face-to-face with Maverick McKinnon.

Even though he hit the plexiglass in front of me, I'm struck by his masculine beauty without the barrier between us. His hair is so inky in hue that it's nearly black. Under the illumination of lights scattered throughout the parking lot, his eyes appear just as deep and dark. His face is angular with chiseled cheekbones and a strong, straight nose that fits his profile perfectly. Scruff covers both chin and cheek.

That's all it takes for arousal to slam into me with the force of a tsunami.

This guy is way too good looking.

Our proximity leaves me feeling strangely tongue tied.

The heavy silence that has fallen over us continues to stretch as our gazes remain locked. It's like we're both too busy eating the other one up with our eyes to say a word.

It's almost a relief when he jerks his head toward the exit I'd rushed through minutes ago.

"You just gonna walk out on your boyfriend?"

I blink, thrown off by the gruff question. Out of everything I expected him to say, that wasn't it. "Boyfriend?"

A mixture of heat and anger sparks to life in his eyes. "Yeah, River. He's your boyfriend, right?"

It takes a handful of seconds to process the question. My brain feels muzzy, and it has everything to do with this handsome guy standing no more than a foot or two away from me.

That's when I realize he's inching closer, swallowing up the space between us.

"He won't miss me."

My guess is that he's still sucking face with the girl at the bar.

When he's close enough for me to inhale a big breath of his cologne, I take a hasty step in retreat. And then another. On the third, my spine hits the side of the Bronco as I flatten against the door.

A predatory expression leaps to life in his eyes. "Are you afraid of me?"

I lift my chin, attempting to brazen out the situation. "Of course not. Is there a reason I should be?"

When his lips spread into a slow smile, my belly pinches before dropping to my feet.

With our gazes locked, he bridges the distance between us until I have to crane my neck to maintain eye contact. It wouldn't take much to drown within his fathomless depths. It's an unsettling thought that should scare the crap out of me.

Oddly enough, it doesn't.

My heart slams against my chest, beating a mad rhythm. When my tongue darts out to moisten my dry lips, his attention drops to the movement. Arousal sparks in his eyes as he slants them upward again to meet mine.

I remain silent as he steps close enough for the steely strength of his chest to press against the tips of my breasts.

"You didn't answer the question. Are you with River? Or are you a bunny who gets off on sleeping with any hockey player?"

My eyes widen as understanding slams into me.

Wait a minute...

He thinks I'm a groupie?

Just as I open my mouth to fire off a denial, his warm breath ghosts across my lips. It's a dizzying sensation that scatters my brain cells into a million directions and makes holding on to rational thought an impossibility. Another millimeter and we would be touching.

Kissing.

Is his mouth as soft as it looks?

I'm dying to find out.

Another wave of shock crashes over me when he nips my bottom lip with sharp teeth. A rush of air gets clogged at the back of my throat as we remain locked in silent battle. He gives it a slight tug before relinquishing his hold.

"Come home with me, and I'll show you what it feels like to get fucked by a real hockey player."

Before I can attempt to make sense of my out-of-control thoughts and emotions, his mouth crashes into mine as one hand snakes around the nape of my neck to hold me in place. Not once does it occur to me to fight the grip or untangle myself from him.

The only things I'm cognizant of are the fireworks exploding within every cell of my being and the way my body vibrates with need...and wonderment.

The velvety softness of his tongue plunges deep inside my mouth to tangle with my own. It isn't until my fingers curl into the soft material of his hoodie that I realize I'm holding on for dear life.

His mouth is a force to be reckoned with.

Dominant.

Possessive.

And I love it.

I desperately want more of it.

No one has ever kissed me like this.

It makes me realize how starved I am for this kind of affection.

I have no idea how long we stand embracing in the parking lot with the silvery moonlight filtering down on us.

He pulls away just enough to search my eyes.

The heat filling them is enough to singe me alive.

"What's it going to be, sunshine?"

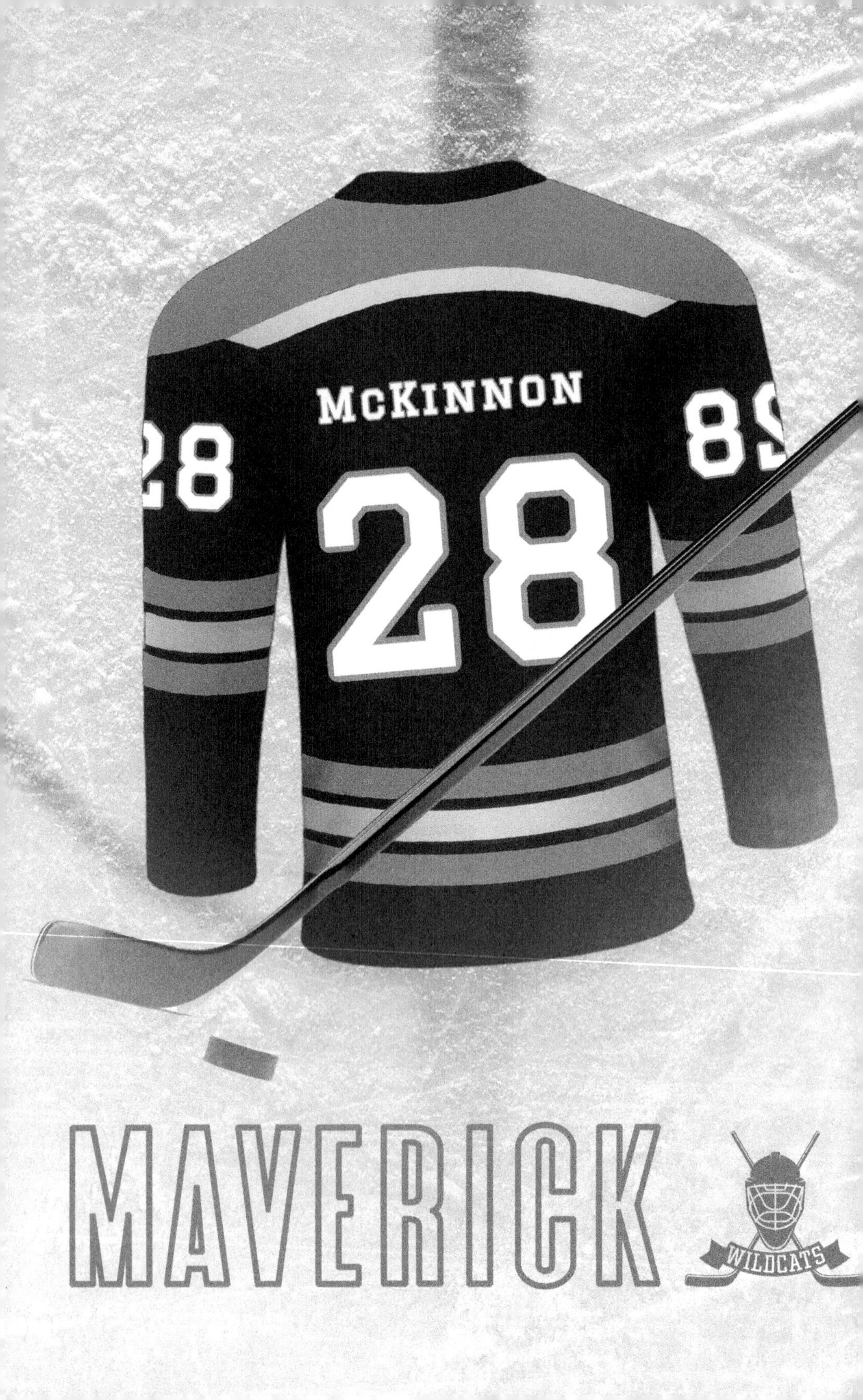
McKINNON
28
MAVERICK
WILDCATS

1

Impatience vibrates through every thickly corded muscle as I wait for her response.

For one night, I want to know that this girl is mine. That I can play with her body any way I want, all the while fucking her senseless.

A couple of hours spent between the sheets will more than likely do the trick and evict her from my brain.

That's the way it's always been. There's no reason to think the pretty blonde will be any different.

When she remains silent, desperation flares to life within me.

I need this to happen.

Especially now that I've gotten a small taste of her.

Somehow, she's even sweeter than I imagined.

I'd lay odds that she's just as delicious everywhere.

My cock stiffens at the idea of licking every inch of her delectable little body.

Unable to resist the lure of her mouth, I nip her pouty lower lip and give it a slight tug, hoping it's enough to wake her from the daze that's fallen over her.

"I need an answer, sunshine."

With a blink, her expression transforms, as if she's once again aware of her surroundings.

She jerks her head in a tight nod. "Okay."

The relief that crashes over me is almost enough to weaken my knees.

This shitty night will end a hell of a lot better than it started.

She clears her throat as color seeps into her cheeks, as if she's embarrassed by the situation. Almost as if she doesn't have much experience in this department.

The feigned innocence is a nice touch.

"I'll follow you back to your place," she murmurs, glancing away.

Hell no.

Like I'm going to give her a chance to rethink her decision.

I refuse to let this girl out of my sight for one damn second.

"I didn't bring my truck, so I'll ride with you." My gaze scours hers. "Is that cool?"

She sucks her lower lip between her teeth before chewing it as her brows pinch. This girl is definitely adorable. It's easy to see why she's a fan favorite with the East Town team.

Only wanting to put her at ease, I smirk and force my muscles to loosen. "I'm not an axe murderer, if that's your concern."

Her response is swift as she tilts her head. "Isn't that exactly the kind of thing an axe murderer would say?"

Unexpected laughter gurgles up inside me before I tamp it down. "Probably."

So she's got a sense of humor.

Even better.

I nod toward her Bronco. "Ready to do this?"

She sucks in a deep breath before gradually exhaling. "Yeah."

I reach around her for the handle. The movement brings us into closer proximity. Not once do I break eye contact. In fact, I'm finding it difficult to look away. Even in the shadowy darkness that surrounds us, her blue eyes hold me captive.

"You're gonna have to move, sunshine." As much as I want to get out of here and get her alone, I'm loathe to distance myself from her. The heat of her body pressed against mine feels too damn good. The way her delicate scent permeates my senses makes me lightheaded.

That's all it takes for her to slip out of my arms. The loss of her warmth is abrupt and devastating. I remind myself that my hands will be back on her soon enough.

I pop open the driver's side door and extend my arm, only wanting to hasten things along. I've always been patient when it came to the fairer sex.

But that's not how I feel with her.

Her cautious gaze stays fastened to mine as she slides into the front seat and pushes the ignition. I can't help but notice the way her fingers tremble as the vehicle roars to life. With a slam of the door, I hustle around the front of the Bronco and settle on the seat beside her.

Charged energy crackles in the small cabin as she navigates the vehicle out of the parking space. "You'll have to give me directions."

Easy enough.

"Once you pull out of the lot, take a left at the next light and head toward campus."

My gaze flickers from her face to her hands, only to notice that they're locked around the wheel in a death grip.

The question is out of my mouth before I can stop it. "Are you nervous?"

She glances at me before refocusing on the ribbon of road beyond the windshield.

The silence that stretches between us makes me wonder if she'll bother to answer the question.

"A little bit," she admits.

The urge to put this girl at ease spirals through me, and I reach out to stroke my fingers along her jeans-clad thigh. There's something both delicate and strong about this girl. It's a fascinating combination.

"What's your name?" I ask, shifting toward her.

An odd expression flashes across her face. "I think it's better if we keep this strictly about sex."

Disappointment and irritation flare to life inside me. I didn't realize how much I wanted to know it until she refused to give it.

It takes effort to keep my tone light. "Fair enough. Guess we'll just stick with sunshine."

With her golden blonde hair and bright blue eyes that are the color of a clear summer day, it certainly fits. From the whiff I got of her, she smells like strawberries and cream.

Fucking addictive.

I just want to gobble her up before delving back in for more.

As we come to the next street, I point. "Take a right and we're the fourth house on the left."

After slowing to a stop along the curb in front of the dilapidated blue Victorian, she cuts the engine and stares at it through the windshield.

Fear and anxiety spiral through me. We're so damn close to sealing the deal. It's all I can think about.

It takes effort to keep my tone casual. "Having second thoughts?"

Her gaze slides to mine. "No."

Thank fuck.

I would have been rocking a massive case of blue balls otherwise. It's doubtful any other girl would have been able to alleviate the need this one has sparked to life inside me.

I want this hot little blonde.

She's the only one who'll do.

I shake that disturbing thought loose before it can take root.

With my fingers still wrapped around her thigh, I give it a gentle squeeze. "I'll make it good for you."

I almost wince.

When was the last time I had to cajole a girl into sleeping with me?

The answer to that question is never.

She studies my face before nodding. With a jerk of her fingers, she pops open the door and steps out. The crunch of snow fills the silence that has settled around us as I do the same. It takes no more than a handful of seconds before I catch up to her on the concrete path that cuts through the front lawn. Air gets clogged in my lungs at the way the silvery moonlight slants down on the loose strands of her hair as they bounce around her shoulders and down her back.

Even in the darkness of the night, she's like bright sunshine illuminating the way.

My hand slips around her waist as we head up the rickety front porch stairs.

The warm weight of her pressed against my body feels good.

Right.

Almost as if we've come home together a million times before and this is nothing out of the ordinary.

There's an ease between us that shouldn't be there.

I don't understand it.

It's only when I slip the key into the lock that I realize that her fingers aren't the only ones shaking with pent-up nerves. I clear my throat, only wanting to draw her attention away from them so she doesn't notice. Throwing the door open, I steer her toward the staircase and then the second floor. Every step that brings us closer to my room has my heart jackhammering harder until it thuds painfully in my chest.

When was the last time I felt this kind of anticipation thrum through my veins? The need to lay my hands on her is all I can focus on. In this moment, nothing else matters.

Not even the possibility that she belongs to River fucking Thompson.

By the time I step over the threshold into my room, my skin is buzzing with adrenaline.

One twist of the lock and I'm ready to pounce.

POCKETFUL OF SUNSHINE

WILLOW & MAVERICK

01:10 — 04:10

WILLOW

LEUKEMIA

8

Hunger burns brightly from his dark eyes as he stares at me like I'm the only thing he's cognizant of. Like he plans on swallowing me whole in one tasty bite. It's doubtful anyone has ever looked at me with so much pent-up intensity.

Longing.

Desire.

It's a heady sensation.

An addictive one.

Everywhere his gaze caresses tingles with newfound awareness as electricity pulses in the air around us. It wouldn't surprise me in the least if the room burst into flames and I combusted with it.

He cocks his head. "Are you ready for me, sunshine?"

Anticipation dances down my spine. I don't think I've ever felt more ready for anything in my life than this man.

For this precise moment in time.

I didn't realize it until now.

"Yes."

His lips lift into a ghost of a smile as he shoves away from the door. Once he's on the move, there's no more holding back. I feel it in the shift of the atmosphere.

I've given my consent.

I'm here.

This is happening.

And I wouldn't want it any other way.

His large hands drift over my cheeks until he's able to cup the sides of my head. He angles my face upward so his mouth can crash onto mine. When his tongue sweeps across the seam of my lips, I open and allow him entrance. It never occurs to me not to. The second they part, he's delving inside and dragging me beneath the surface of the ocean where breathing becomes impossible.

Unnecessary.

"So fucking sweet," he whispers before diving back in for more.

Even though his mouth grows demanding, his lips remain just as soft as I imagined when I caught sight of him on the ice. It's weird to think that it was only hours ago. It seems more like days or weeks.

His palms fall away, dropping to the zipper of my jacket.

"This needs to go," he mutters.

As soon as the words are released, the sound of metal grinding against metal fills the room and then the black jacket is shoved away from my shoulders before it falls to the carpet beneath my feet.

His mahogany-colored eyes turn stormy as he stares at my jersey. Before I realize what's happening, it's yanked up my body and over my head. He glares at the scratchy white and blue material wadded in his hands before flicking a hard stare in my direction.

"After I'm finished with you tonight, you'll never look twice at that jersey again," he grits between clenched teeth before tossing it away like garbage.

I can't imagine what would happen if he discovered that I'm not the puck bunny he assumes, but River Thompson's sister instead.

Would he stare at me with the same kind of hatred he reserves for my twin?

That thought is enough to send a shudder of unease skittering through me. My nipples tighten into hard little points beneath the light-blue cami stretched across my breasts. His attention zeros in on the gentle swells and his previous desire returns full force.

"You're like a beautifully wrapped gift on Christmas morning. I just want to tear the paper away until I can see what's waiting beneath for me to play with."

Arousal pools at the bottom of my belly as I lift my chin and say something I never thought I would. "Then what are you waiting for?"

Anticipation floods my system until there's a good chance I'll drown in it.

A growl vibrates from deep within his chest as his fingers grip the hem of the cami and drag it up my torso. Seconds later, it meets the same fate as both the jersey and jacket. A lacy pale-pink bra covers my breasts. The gorgeous material is sheer and reveals far more than it conceals. Unlike Holland, I'm not overly generous in the cleavage department. When you don't need a lot of support, it's easy to wear pretty little undergarments.

By the appreciative expression on his face, he's in full agreement with that decision.

"Fuck. I seriously hope you're wearing matching panties."

"There's only one way to find out." The comment that shoots out of my mouth takes me by surprise.

I have no idea who the brazen girl standing in front of this stranger is, but I like her.

A lot.

That's the only incentive he needs to get to the bottom of the mystery. The button of my jeans is popped and the zipper lowered. He wraps his hands around the waistband and shoves the thick denim down until it puddles around my ankles and I'm able to kick my way free.

He drags a hand down his face as his heated gaze roves over every inch of me, as if committing the image to memory.

"Way better than any Christmas present I've ever received."

Laughter bubbles up in my throat. I've never felt so sexy in my life.

The way Maverick stares at me makes me feel daring.

Better than that, he makes me feel alive.

For tonight, I want to forget about my reality and live in the moment, where nothing but the feelings Maverick McKinnon has managed to rouse within me matter.

His hand snakes out to nab my fingers before he tows me toward him until my mouth can once again collide with his. His fingers strum along my spine as they dip lower to palm my nearly naked ass. He squeezes the firm flesh before dragging me even closer. With barely any effort at all, he hoists me up so my legs can tangle around his trim waist.

With our mouths fused, I'm barely aware that he's swung us around and has walked us toward the queen-sized bed until I'm lowered to the mattress. He severs the connection before straightening to his full height and staring down at me. The longer his gaze roams over my bare skin, the more heat sparks from his eyes.

"You look good in my bed, sunshine. I might just have to keep you there indefinitely."

If only that were possible.

Unfortunately, much like Cinderella, once this interlude is over, I need to vanish into thin air.

Never to be heard from again.

I shove that thought from my head and squirm beneath the intensity of his stare, only wanting to feel his mouth and hands on me again as he drags his thick Wildcats sweatshirt over his head. The navy T-shirt beneath soon follows, leaving him bare chested. My mouth turns cottony as my gaze roves over perfectly chiseled pecs and washboard abdominals.

The man is ridiculously beautiful.

Strong and solid.

That's all it takes for my panties to flood with heat.

Not that there have been many guys in my past, but Maverick puts them all to shame. Next to him, they seem more like adolescent boys than grown men.

He flicks the button of his jeans and tugs the zipper before shoving the denim down powerfully built legs until he's standing before me in black boxer briefs that hug his thighs. The mattress sinks beneath his heavy weight as he kneels on the bed and crawls up my body until he's able to hover over me. His muscles bunch and flex as he cages me in with his strength.

"Still good with this?" he asks from between clenched teeth.

I nod. "Yes."

I would be devastated if this didn't happen. We haven't even done anything yet and already it's turning out to be the hottest night of my life.

His lips lift into a relieved smile before slanting over mine. The velvety softness of his tongue licks at me. Just when I think he'll lose all control and delve in for more, his teeth scrape along my jaw before he nips at the point of my chin.

Only wanting more of the dizzying sensation, I bare my throat. That's all the sign he needs to lick and kiss his way down to my collarbone. The slide of his bigger, harder body against my softer one is nothing short of delicious.

It's enough to make my eyes cross as a hum escapes from my lips.

Those thoughts scatter in a million directions when he makes his way to my breasts and his teeth scrape over one stiffened peak as he draws it into his mouth and sucks it through the delicate lace garment. My spine arches off the mattress in response as I press closer. Every tug of his lips sends a flood of pleasure rushing through me. Just when I think I'll come undone, he releases the tip before giving the same ardent attention to the other one. My arms rise, twining around his head so my fingers can tunnel through the thick strands of his hair.

Once the nipple has popped free from his mouth, he straightens to kneel above me. His hands settle on the slender band that encircles my ribcage. A second later, he unhooks the clasp and the stretchy material springs free. The straps slide down my shoulders as he plucks the bra away.

His gaze roves over my naked breasts.

They're still tingling from his previous attention.

"They look even better than they taste."

Lowering himself down again, he sucks one bare tip into his mouth. Sensation spirals through me, rushing through my veins until it feels like too much for the confines of my skin. Any second, I'll splinter apart. A gasp escapes from me when he nips the stiff little point with sharp teeth before kissing and licking it.

He works his way down my body, adoring every inch, until he reaches the elastic band of my panties. I inhale a sharp breath when he buries his nose against my slit and inhales a lungful of air.

There's no way he doesn't feel the dampness of the material.

"This must be what heaven smells like," he growls.

The low scrape of his words sends another round of arousal detonating at the bottom of my belly.

His fingers slip beneath the waistband before dragging the thin fabric down my hips and thighs until I'm completely bared to his sight.

When I shift, only wanting to close my legs, he flattens his palms against my inner thighs and presses them farther apart.

His gaze never deviates from my exposed core.

My heart pounds a steady tattoo beneath the intensity of his sharp gaze.

The look of appreciation that settles on his face is the only reason I don't fight the hold.

"So fucking gorgeous." One hand trails along my center, his thumb caressing the delicate flesh. Sensation ripples throughout my being before echoing in my fingertips and toes.

When he strums me for a second time, the pleasure is nearly enough to make my eyes roll back in my head.

I've had boyfriends before, but they never teased out these kinds of exquisite sensations. They never made me want to give myself over to them or come undone.

He's barely touched me and I'm ready to burst out of my skin.

With my legs spread wide, he shoulders his way between my thighs. His gaze holds mine captive as he lowers his face and swipes at me with his tongue.

A whimper works its way loose from my throat.

"Tell me, sunshine… Do you enjoy having your pussy licked?"

The dirty question has heat rushing to my cheeks and leaves me squirming. His grip tightens around my thighs to hold me in place as he leisurely strokes one thick finger along my slit.

Another low moan escapes from me, breaking the silence of the room.

I couldn't rein it in if I tried.

Maverick leans forward and traces the same path his finger traveled seconds ago with his tongue.

Pure bliss.

I want to die with the pleasure that rushes in and bombards my senses. Or maybe what I really want to do is spread my thighs impossibly wide in order to feel more of the velvety softness stroking over me and darting inside.

He grazes the top of my slit rather than probing deeper with his tongue. My fingers thread through his inky black hair as he presses butterfly-like kisses against my damp flesh. All I want is for him to bury his face between my legs and ravage me instead of giving me chaste pecks.

It's pure torture.

"Please. I need more."

Instead of giving me what I want, he takes another long lap that has my core clenching.

"You didn't answer the question."

When I remain silent, he nibbles at my clit.

The sound that leaves my lips is garbled and unintelligible.

He chuckles, and his warm breath ghosts over me. That's all it takes for goose bumps to break out across my body.

His eyes stay pinned to mine from between my legs. "You must really hate it if you can't even bother to respond." He stabs his tongue deep inside my body. "I should stop."

If that happens, I'll probably die. Nothing in all my life has ever felt this amazing.

"No!" I blurt.

It feels like my body is burning up from the inside out.

His gaze sears into mine as he licks from the bottom of my slit to the top of my clit, another deep laugh rumbling up from him. The throaty sound of it dances across my flesh as he holds me in place.

"Then answer the question."

"I like it," I admit. "A lot."

Way more than that.

He continues to caress me with his tongue. "What exactly do you like?"

He presses a kiss against my inner thigh before dragging his teeth against it. As good as it feels, it's not where I want his mouth. The gleam that fills his eyes tells me he knows exactly what I'm so desperate for.

"What you're doing?" I ask on a tortured groan.

"Come on, sunshine. You can do better than that." His teeth sink into the flesh he'd been kissing.

"I like when you lick my pussy," I gasp.

"Good girl."

With that, the flat of his tongue slides over me.

Pleasure gathers in my core like an impending storm. Any second, it'll break loose and destroy everything in its path.

Including me.

And I've never craved anything more.

When he nibbles at my clit, I fall to pieces as wave after wave crashes over me, dragging me to the bottom of the ocean. I don't care if I ever surface again. The pleasure overwhelming my system is so much more than I was prepared for.

He continues to stroke me until every last spasm has been wrung from my body.

With a final press of his lips, he growls, "Did you enjoy that, sunshine?"

"Yes."

"Good. Know what I'm going to do next?"

I shake my head, unable to imagine anything else feeling this spectacular.

"Fuck you senseless."

Oh god.

It's not a threat. More like a delicious promise.

He straightens before shackling his fingers around my ankles and dragging me to the edge of the mattress.

"Spread your legs nice and wide. Show me exactly how wet that little cunt is for me."

Even though I just came—hard—more wetness smudges my inner thighs.

I've never been with anyone like Maverick before. Someone so commanding yet giving. Able to whip me into a frenzy with such ease.

Without further prompting, my thighs fall open. As the air within the room wafts over my flesh, I've never felt more exposed than I do at this moment.

By the same token, I've never felt so alive.

My heart slams against my ribcage as blood sizzles through my veins and arousal pools in my core.

And I feel...*sexy*.

Desired.

By a man like Maverick McKinnon, who can have any girl he wants with the crook of his finger.

Even though the room is bathed in shadows, it would be impossible not to see the stark hunger written across every line of his face as he stares down at me, eating me up with his eyes. Pent-up tension vibrates in every straining muscle as it attempts to break loose.

He wraps his hand around his thick cock before sliding it up and down the long shaft. His pupils dilate as he leisurely strokes himself.

"Tell me who that pretty pink pussy belongs to for the night."

I gulp and blurt, "You."

His eyes flare with heat as more moisture gathers at my center.

"To use anyway I want?"

I nod.

He tilts his head and smirks. "Use your words, sunshine."

Arousal detonates at the bottom of my belly.

"Yes, to use any way you want."

A smile curves his lips as he fondles his hard length. "Mmm. There are so many delicious ways I'm going to have you."

The thought is as dizzying as it is intriguing.

My gaze stays locked on the way he fists his erection.

"You like to watch?" He continues jacking himself off. "Here's a little secret I'll only share with you—I like to watch too. There's nothing sexier than a woman giving herself pleasure."

I can't rip my attention away from him as his grip intensifies, turning the head of his cock a mottled purplish hue.

My core throbs with newfound awareness until it becomes painful.

I don't realize that I'm cupping my own breasts, squeezing the softness, until a whimper escapes from me.

"Pinch those sweet titties," he growls.

I don't think twice about following the directive as I tweak the small buds until they're unbearably hard.

"Fuck." He strokes his hand along his length. "You're so damn sexy."

That's the ironic thing—I've never felt sexy before this moment.

But Maverick knows nothing about me.

I can be anyone I want.

To him, I'm not Willow Thompson.

Sick girl.

Cancer survivor.

I'm a woman living out her sexual desires and discovering new ones.

The deep scrape of his voice, along with the need that fills his expression, gives me the courage to take this further. To do something I've only done under the cover of darkness without any witnesses.

One hand drifts down my chest, past my ribcage, and to my belly before sliding lower to the vee between my legs. My fingers glide over my drenched lips, circling the entrance before dipping inside the heat.

It's so tempting to close my eyes and forget about the man devouring me with a ravenous expression.

But then I would miss all the delicious things he's doing to himself. And there's no way I'll allow that to happen. The way he strokes his thick cock is the sexiest thing I've ever seen.

"As much as I'm enjoying watching you play with your pussy, it'll make me come, and that's not how I want it to happen."

He saunters around the bed to the nightstand and then yanks out the drawer before rifling through the contents. It's on the tip of my tongue to ask what he's doing when he pulls out a square foil package.

A condom.

I can't believe I didn't think about protection.

Not even once.

He rips it open with his teeth before taking out the latex and sheathing himself in it. Once the rubber covers his thick length, he takes up position between my legs and brings the head to my opening, stroking the tip against my delicate lips. But it's not nearly enough to satisfy me. Unable to control myself, I wriggle, only wanting him to sink deep inside me.

Instead of giving me what I'm silently begging for, he remains in control. "Damn, but you're so wet. Your cunt is crying for me, isn't it?"

"Yes," I groan. It's the truth. I've never been this aroused in my life.

He rubs the length against me before tapping the tip against my clit. That's all it takes for a gasp to escape from me as sensation ripples throughout my body. Each time he slaps that tiny bundle of nerves with his erection, it pushes me closer to the edge until I'm dancing on it.

Before I can beg him to fuck me, he presses the head against my entrance. The way he continues to take his sweet damn time drives me insane. All I want to do is impale myself on his thick shaft and be done with it already.

He refuses to give me anything more than the tip.

His hips flex as he thrusts with tiny movements. With each piston-like action, my muscles tighten around him. Sweat breaks out across his brow as he clenches his teeth. Just when I think he'll bury his length inside me and give us what we're both desperate for, he pulls out.

"Please," I gasp. "I need more."

"I know exactly what you need." With gritted teeth, he buries himself deep inside my heat with one swift stroke.

A scream tears from my mouth at the fullness now seated inside me.

It's almost too much to bear.

He gives me a moment to adjust, to breathe, before arching his hips and slipping almost all the way out. Just as I'm on the verge of begging for more, he propels back inside until his pelvis can grind against my own. Each time he slides home, a moan escapes from me. The steady rhythm sends me climbing higher until there's nowhere left to go but down.

"Fuck, sunshine," he growls as his gaze stays pinned to mine. "There's no way I'll last much longer with the way your pussy is strangling my cock."

The feel of him pummeling me is sheer poetry in motion.

Utter bliss.

It doesn't take long for a second orgasm to streak through me. I can't stop the cries that fall from my lips. With a groan, he follows me over.

My body spasms around his, milking every drop from his cock until he gives one last shudder before collapsing on top of me. His warm breath feathers against the delicate hollow of my neck.

I don't think I've ever felt so satiated in my life.

What just took place between us is nothing short of earth shattering.

Maverick pulls out and straightens to his full height. He stares at me before slipping the condom off his softening cock and dropping it into the trash can near his desk. As he turns away, the heat of his gaze disappears. That's all it takes for reality to slam into me full force.

Oh god…

I just slept with the one guy my brother can't stand.

I need to grab my clothes and get the hell out of here. Plus, it's doubtful he wants the hookup he brought home hanging around and making things uncomfortable.

Just as I sit up and scoot to the edge of the mattress, he swivels around and grinds to a halt.

"Where do you think you're going?"

I tuck an errant strand of hair behind my ear. I'm sure it's mussed from his fingers tunneling through it. I probably look like a disaster.

"I was going to take off."

He shakes his head. "Now, why would you want to do a thing like that when we're just getting started?"

POCKETFUL OF SUNSHINE

WILLOW & MAVERICK

01:10　　　　　　　　　　　　04:10

WILLOW

LEUKEMIA SURVIVOR

9

It's the bright stream of sunlight filtering in through the window that has me surfacing from a deep sleep full of strange dreams that feature the very sexy Maverick McKinnon. I'm almost reluctant to fully wake and leave them behind.

The moment my eyelids flutter open, I blink and realize that I'm not safely tucked in my own bed.

It's carefully that I turn my head and stare at the sacked-out male slumbering soundly no more than a foot from where I lay.

A rush of breath escapes from me.

Apparently, those sexy dreams featuring the hot hockey player weren't fantasies playing out after all. Memories flood my consciousness, and in an instant, the murkiness becomes crystal clear.

My eyes widen as one hand drifts to my mouth to cover it.

While I've had boyfriends in the past, this is the first time I've gone home with a virtual stranger.

For the first time after having sex, my body feels well loved by a man who understands exactly what he's doing, teasing out all sorts of pleasure. Most of the guys I've been with treat me like I'm made of spun glass that could break if they don't take the utmost care with me.

Maverick was the complete opposite.

It really is a shame that this was a onetime thing.

I wouldn't mind experiencing that again.

It's so tempting to roll closer and study him more thoroughly while he's unaware of the perusal, but I'm afraid to move a single muscle.

Afraid I'll wake him.

Last night, I'd gotten away with concealing my identity. I'm not so sure it would work in the harsh light of dawn after what happened between these very sheets.

Air leaks from my lungs as my gaze roves over every inch of exposed sun-kissed skin. Even in sleep, while fully relaxed, he's formidable, with hard, sculpted muscles. There's nothing soft about him.

All right, maybe that's not true.

His lips are ridiculously plush.

And the way he'd used them to nibble at me...

When arousal pools in my core like warmed honey, I shut down that train of thought before any flickering flames can catch fire and burn the house down. I have far more pressing matters at hand than lying here and eating Maverick McKinnon up with my eyes.

Like escaping before he wakes up and figures out my identity.

The last thing I need is what happened between us getting back to my brother.

I wince.

Any desire within me is doused by those thoughts.

The smartest thing I can do is get moving before my choices from last night bite me in the ass.

Actually, that already happened.

Several times, if I recall correctly.

And I enjoyed every second of it.

It's carefully that I slide to the edge of the mattress before slipping off and dropping to the carpet. My heart riots painfully against my ribcage as I pause and listen for his deep, even breaths before exhaling a shaky one of my own. I peek over the edge of the mattress, only to find him in the same position as moments ago with one brawny arm thrown over his eyes and his lips parted slightly. Even though half his face is shielded from view, I'm struck all over again by how handsome he is.

It takes effort to rip my gaze away and glance around for my clothes. A small smile touches my lips as I locate my panties, bra, cami, jersey, and jeans strewn around the room. I crawl to each piece and tug them on. When I'm dressed, I pick up my shoes and jacket before tiptoeing to the closed door.

As I cross the threshold, I throw one last glance over my shoulder. The sight of him sprawled out on the queen-sized bed is enough to have regret pricking at me. For just a heartbeat or two, I wonder if I'm making a mistake by sneaking away like this.

It was just a one-night stand, right?

He's not interested in more.

And even if he was, he and River despise each other.

Before those thoughts can take root and cause confusion, I shake them loose and force myself into the hallway. As soon as the lock clicks into place, shuttering the hot hockey player inside his room, a rush of breath escapes from me.

What I need to do is leave this delicious interlude where it belongs—in the past.

And no one will ever be the wiser.

I slip my Vans onto my feet before slinking down the hallway.

It's still early. If I'm lucky, everyone will still be sacked out. Maybe the team wasn't celebrating a victory last night at the bar, but they were still belting back drinks, attempting to drown their sorrows.

Relief blooms inside me when I reach the first floor and the front door comes into view. Just as I congratulate myself on making a clean getaway, someone clears their throat from behind me.

With a high-pitched yelp, I nearly jump out of my skin before spinning around and locking gazes with Hayes Van Doren.

"Well, well, well...can't say I ever expected to find Willow Thompson sneaking out of the hockey house at the butt crack of dawn."

Amusement dances in his eyes as he lifts a spoonful of cereal to his mouth and chews it.

I've known Hayes since grade school. He and River were never best friends, but they played on a lot of the same teams.

Unsure how to talk my way out of this situation, I press my lips together and remain silent.

"I'm curious. Does Mav know whose sister you are?" There's a pause before he answers his own question. "I can't imagine that he would have hooked up with you if he had."

"And it needs to stay that way," I growl.

When a slow smile tips the corners of his lips, the muscles in my abdomen spasm.

The urge to flee takes hold, and I swing around, needing to get the hell out of here.

As I pull the door open and step into the early morning sunlight, he calls out, "Be sure to tell your brother I said hello."

I snort.

Yeah, that's not going to happen.

Ever.

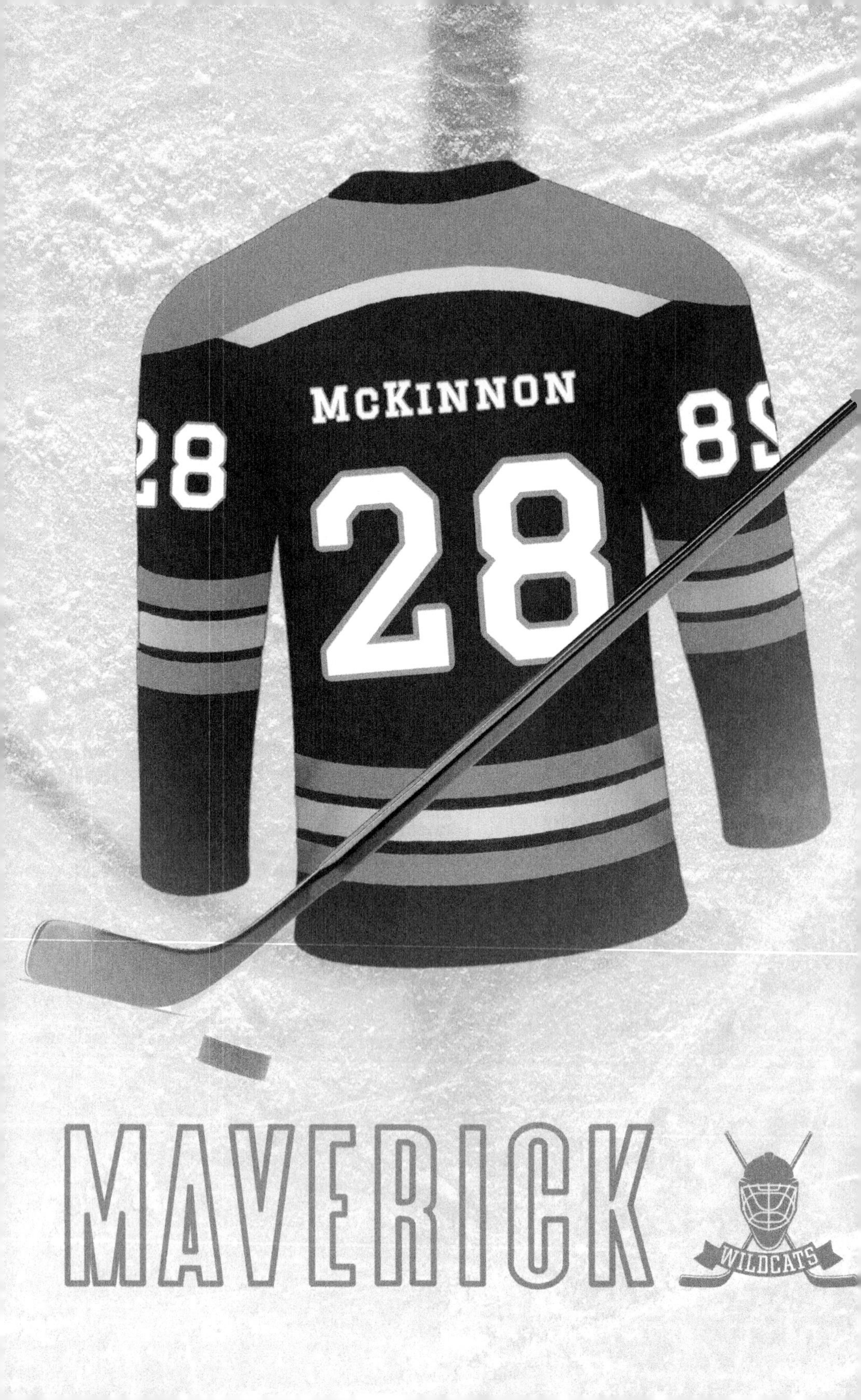
McKINNON
28
MAVERICK
WILDCATS

10

A raised voice from somewhere in the house jolts me from a sound sleep.

Damn, I haven't slept that well since—

That's the moment everything from last night slams into me with the force of a two by four.

The blonde from the game I couldn't stop staring at.

The very same one who ended up warming my bed last night.

My cock stirs at the idea of sinking inside her sweet heat again.

Fuck, but she'd been good.

And tight.

So damn tight.

The way her pussy had clenched around my dick had been nothing short of amazing.

No…it was better than that.

And I know the perfect way to start my day…

My morning wood is alive and well as I turn over.

Only to find the mattress empty.

With a frown, my fingers drift over the sheets. They're cool to the touch, which probably means she hasn't just stepped out to use the bathroom.

Well, hell.

My boner deflates.

Under normal circumstances, it's a relief when a one-night stand shows herself to the door the morning after.

This time, however?

I'm left feeling irritated.

Maybe even a little hurt.

Which doesn't make a damn bit of sense.

I roll from the bed and grab a T-shirt from the dresser before rummaging through another drawer for underwear and hauling them up my legs. Once I've found a pair of sweatpants, I head downstairs. It's not like I think she'll be lingering, but...

I want to make sure.

My heart sinks when I find the living room empty.

Maybe that's not altogether true. A couple of the younger players are sacked out on the couch.

Gross.

God only knows what fluids are embedded in the material.

My heart picks up tempo when noise emanates from the kitchen. I beeline into the room and find Hayes chomping on a bowl of cereal.

No sunshine in sight.

Fuck. I don't even know her name. There's no way to find her.

Disappointment bubbles up inside me.

I drag a hand through my hair as he watches me with a cocked brow.

"You, ah, didn't happen to see anyone take off this morning, did you?"

"Nope." He stuffs an overflowing spoonful of cereal into his piehole. Deflated by his response, I swing around to head back upstairs.

"Unless you're talking about the hot blonde who took off like she was escaping from a creeper in a white van. Because, yeah, her I did see."

When I narrow my eyes, his smile widens and his shoulders shake with silent laughter.

Why does everyone around here think they're such funny fuckers?

"Did she say anything?" I wince as the question shoots from my mouth. The last thing I want is to look desperate. Especially in front of Hayes. He'll only rub the circumstances in my face.

With glee.

"Yeah, actually, she did." He strokes his chin, all the while giving me a thoughtful expression. "I think it was something along the lines of how size really does matter."

In response, I give him the finger before stalking out of the kitchen. His laughter follows me up the staircase and down the second-floor hallway until I slam the door shut. Once I reach the bed, I sink to the mattress.

Had I been thinking with the right head, I would have refused to fuck her until she gave me her name. I should have tortured her body until she told me every fucking detail of her life.

What pisses me off even more is that I actually give a damn.

For fuck's sake, it was a one-night stand.

I've had plenty of them.

Once I sign my contract and play professionally, I'll be drowning in groupies. I won't even remember this girl. Or how perfect her pussy was. Or how much I enjoyed running my hands over her delectable little body.

Fuck.

Fuck.

Fuck.

Maybe what I need to do is sleep off the weird feelings that are swirling around inside me like a snow globe.

Clearly, I'm exhausted.

What other explanation is there for the thoughts that are filling my brain?

As I toss back the covers, something sparkly snags my eye, and I reach down to pick up the fine silver necklace that glints in the bright morning sunlight before holding it up in front of me.

There's a delicate W pendant attached to it. Vaguely, do I recall it dangling around her neck.

W?

I frown.

Is it possible that her name starts with a W?

Wendy?

Nah.

She didn't strike me as a Wendy.

Or a Winnie.

Or even a Winter.

I stare at it for a few more seconds before securing it around my own neck. It must have hung loosely on her, because it fits me perfectly.

Looks like I have a souvenir from our night together.

I recline against the pillows and stack my hands behind my head before staring up at the ceiling.

A slow smile tips the corners of my lips.

I guess if my little ray of sunshine wants her necklace back, she'll have to come and get it.

POCKETFUL OF SUNSHINE

WILLOW & MAVERICK

01:10 04:10

WILLOW

LEUKEMIA

11

I push through the glass doors into the Mexican restaurant and scan the colorful space. The place is packed and bursting with music and noise. Although, I've been here enough times to know this would be the case.

It's Tuesday.

Taco Tuesday, to be precise.

And the place?

Taco Loco.

When I announced last year that I would be transferring colleges, my brother flipped his lid. He couldn't understand why I needed breathing room.

Let's just say that the way he introduced me to his teammates the other night hadn't been the first time.

Or even the dozenth.

Getting together once a week for lunch was part of the agreement to soften the blow so he wouldn't grumble too much.

Unfortunately, it hasn't stopped him from complaining about the distance.

Or meant that he doesn't know what's going on in my life every second of the day.

"Hey, Willow," Lola, a waitress at the restaurant, greets from near the hostess stand.

My smile brightens when I spot her. "Hi! How are you doing? I haven't seen you around campus much this semester."

She blows out a breath before glancing around the crowded dining area. "I've picked up more hours here, and midterms have been brutal."

I nod in understanding. Balancing a job and school can be difficult. "Same. You must be excited to graduate this spring. I'm so envious. I still have another year to go."

Excitement sparks in her eyes. "Trust me, I'm counting down the days."

"I bet."

"Could use a little help here," another raven-haired waitress mutters as she speeds past with an overflowing tray of tacos and chips.

"And that would be my cue to get back to work." She cranes her neck and points to a table situated in the back. "Big bro is already here and waiting."

I roll my eyes. "He's only older by a handful of minutes."

Her expression lightens. "Still makes him older."

"Now you sound like my parents."

With a laugh, she takes off, stopping at a table crowded with a bunch of guys. From about a dozen feet away, her boyfriend, Asher Stevens, cranes his neck as he watches her. I'm sure if any of the patrons looked sideways at Lola, he'd be over there in a flash.

I met Lola in the fall through Elle Kendricks, who I got to know in a math class. We became fast friends and she introduced me to some of the girls she hangs out with.

From what I've seen, Asher treats Lola like a queen.

What's funny is that there are so many stories that circulate at Western about him being a major player on campus, and yet, I've never seen him look at another girl.

As far as he's concerned, there's no one else but Lola.

I wave to Asher and realize he's here with a bunch of his teammates and their girlfriends. Elle pops to her feet and waves with a big smile. She's the sweetest.

Her boyfriend, Carson Roberts, is such a hottie. I get a little tongue tied around him. He and Elle's brother were besties. She'd had a massive crush on Carson while growing up and he... Well, he tried his damnedest to convince her that he only saw her as a younger sister in need of protecting.

Ha!

The way he looks at her is far from sisterly.

Honestly, it's kind of feral.

Sometimes I really don't understand how guys think.

As soon as I'm within striking distance, Elle throws her arms around my neck and hugs me tight. "I haven't seen you in a few weeks. You were supposed to text me so we could make plans and get together."

"Sorry. Classes have been busy."

She rolls her eyes. "Classes-smasses."

I laugh. "Yeah, well, they're kind of important. Not all of us are going to end up on Broadway in a few years."

She grins. "From your lips to God's ears."

My attention gets drawn to the people crowded around the table. "Looks like you're getting your taco Tuesday on."

"Yup." She flicks a look toward the back of the restaurant. "I saw River walk in a few minutes ago."

"You know the drill—weekly lunch date." I jerk my thumb in his direction. "I should probably get moving or he'll come find me."

"Okay, but let's figure out a time for us to get together soon, all right? I really miss seeing your face."

With a nod, I give her another quick hug before navigating a path to my brother and dropping down across from him.

"Hi."

He sets his phone on the table and meets my gaze. "Hey. I saw you talking with Elle on your way over."

I glance at her again. Her boyfriend has her wrapped up in his brawny arms. "Yeah, we were making plans to get together."

He shoots a quick look over his shoulder at the crowded table. "Hot girl."

"Remember when I tried to set you up with her? You said you weren't interested. Now it's too late."

He shrugs. "A girlfriend is the last thing I need right now. I've got too much going on with school and hockey."

I cock a brow because even though that's true, my guess is that he's still hung up on Sabrina. Whenever I bring up the subject, his expression turns stony and he shuts down the convo. There hasn't been anyone serious since.

I pick up my glass of water and take a sip.

"Why'd you decide to bale Saturday night? One minute you were there and the next you were gone."

My hand freezes midway back to the table. Deflecting the question, I say, "There didn't seem to be much point in staying. Plus, you were busy sucking that girl's face."

He rolls his eyes. "Please."

Before he can fire off any more questions, Lola stops by. "I suppose you two want the usual?"

"Sounds good," River says with a lazy grin.

"Yes, please," I add.

"You still with your boyfriend?" he asks.

"Yup." She gives him a sweet smile before pointing to Asher. "I'll be sure to tell him you said hello."

River glances at the muscular football player who looks like he could bench press a small vehicle with ease. When the other guy glares, River lifts his hand in a wave.

A chuckle escapes from Lola as she disappears through the crowd.

"Umm, excuse me... What happened to you not wanting a girlfriend?"

He flashes a cocky smile. "Who knows? Maybe the right one could persuade me."

That's doubtful.

"I'm beginning to think you're the one who'll have to do the persuading."

"That's not very nice."

I jerk my shoulders. "Maybe not, but it's the truth."

"Funny...you sound just like Mom."

Eyes flaring wide, I stab a finger in his direction. "You take that back."

"I'll be sure to tell her you said that."

"Better not, or this will be the last lunch we have together."

When his lips tremble and his shoulders shake, mine do the same. This is the way it always is between us. We're the best of friends. Even when we're bickering. Our bond is one that can never be broken.

Less than ten minutes later, our taco platters arrive and we dig in. River eats with gusto. Kind of like he spent a month on that reality show *Survivor* and was finally voted off the island. I take my time, knowing that whatever I don't finish, which will be most of it, my brother will end up devouring. I can't think of one time when we walked out with a doggie bag.

Once I tap out, he spears his fork at my plate. "Are you done with that?"

"Yup." I slide the platter filled with rice, beans, and chicken-stuffed tacos his way before picking up my glass of water. A few drops dribble from the corner of my mouth onto my V-neck shirt.

With a smirk, River shakes his blond head. "Seriously, sis. I can't take you anywhere."

When I blot at the thin material with the napkin, his brow furrows.

"Where's your necklace?"

I gulp as my fingers sweep against my collarbone. I feel naked without the silver chain and the little pendant resting against my skin.

I drop my gaze and continue blotting. There's no way I can lie to my brother while holding his steady stare. He'll see the fib written across my face within seconds of it leaving my lips. "I took it off before showering this morning and must have forgotten to put it back on."

There's a second or two of silence that has my heart exploding into double time.

"I didn't think you ever took it off."

With a forced smile, I attempt to keep the panic from invading my voice. "I usually don't. As soon as I get home, I'll put it back on."

His brow remains creased as his tone dips. "I gave it to you right after you were diagnosed."

A thick lump of emotion swells in my throat, making it impossible to breathe. "I remember."

When a faraway look clouds his blue eyes, I realize that he's mentally tripping down that painful path again. I was diagnosed at age sixteen with Acute Lymphoblastic Leukemia, and sometimes I think it was harder on my family than it was on me. Or maybe it just felt that way because I was forced to put on a brave face in front of them so they wouldn't worry more than necessary.

Most nights, River would crawl into my bed. Sometimes, when he thought I was sleeping, his breathing would grow choppy. It would be impossible not to remember the sound of him trying to choke back his sobs.

We're twins.

There's never been a time when I haven't been finely attuned to both his thoughts and feelings. More often than not, I experience them as if they were my own.

And vice versa.

It's the reason I can never stay angry with him for long. I might not like what he's doing, but I understand the reason for it and that his response comes from a loving place.

He doesn't want me to get hurt.

I just wish he'd recognize when he's the one who's causing me pain.

"You know that I'm fine, right?" I murmur, wanting to draw his attention away from the past. "I've been in remission for two years."

He blinks and refocuses on me as his expression remains somber. "I still don't understand why you felt the need to transfer schools. I liked you being close."

I bite back the frustrated sigh that sits perched on the tip of my tongue. "Because it was time for me to spread my wings and be more independent."

"And you couldn't do that at East Town?"

With his constant hovering?

"We both know the answer to that."

Our gazes stay locked as a silent dialogue takes place between us. It's one of the benefits to being a twin. We don't need to say a word to communicate our thoughts and feelings. When we were kids, it used to get us into trouble.

"Fine," he grumbles. "We'll drop the topic." Then he tacks on, "For now."

I glance at my watch. "You should probably finish up. My shift at the tutor lab starts in twenty minutes."

As he picks up his fork, preparing to dig in, voices drift on the air and my skin prickles with awareness. I glance toward the entrance of the restaurant as the energy shifts and a bunch of hockey players walk in, jostling one another.

My belly spasms as a fresh burst of nerves explodes within me.

Maverick McKinnon.

A smile lights up his handsome face as he laughs with one of his teammates. The way his lips curve and the flash of white teeth hits me like a punch to the gut. Memories from the night we spent together roll through my brain like a slow-motion picture show.

The way he ran his strong hands over my body...

He hadn't been hesitant or careful.

After slipping into the townhouse I share with Holland the next morning, I'd shed my clothing for a quick shower. Right before I'd stepped into the enclosed space, I'd caught a glimpse of myself in the mirror. There'd been hickies and handprints all over my breasts and inner thighs.

It had been shocking.

But deliciously so.

Maverick had played my body like a fine instrument, making it come alive.

Even though it's only been a handful of days since we slept together, I've relived the memory at least a thousand times.

When he glances around the restaurant, I squeak and duck my head.

Shit. I really hope he didn't see me.

"Willow?" River frowns. "Are you all right?"

I flick a quick look at my brother as he shovels another forkful of rice and beans into his mouth. "I, um...don't feel well." I force a wince. "The tacos are hitting me hard."

"Really?" His brows pinch. "We come here all the time and you've never had a problem before."

"Yeah, I'm not sure what the issue is. My belly feels like it's in shambles."

He holds up a hand. "TMI."

"Would you mind grabbing the check and paying this time? Holland dropped me off, so I'll need a ride back to campus." I chance another peek at the hot hockey player. I'm certainly not the only girl eye fucking him. He draws female attention like bees to honey. "I'll wait in the SUV for you, okay?"

"Sure. No problem. Give me a few minutes."

As soon as Maverick and his group are shown to a table, I dip my head and race for the exit. On the way out, my gaze collides with Hayes's. That's all it takes for a wide smile to light up his face as he shakes his head in amusement. When he points to Maverick, whose back is turned to him, and widens his eyes, looking like he's going to tap him on the shoulder, I scowl and give him the finger.

That only makes him laugh harder.

One of these days, I'm going to strangle that guy.

It's a relief when I shove through the glass door and into the chilled afternoon air.

The only problem?

My brother is still inside.

With my one-night stand.

MAVERICK

12

My senses heighten as I do a double take and slowly scan the restaurant. For just a second or two, I could have sworn I caught sight of the hot blonde from the other night.

As I study each face in the crowd, none are hers.

I'd recognize her heart-shaped face, pouty pink lips, bright blue eyes and golden hair anywhere.

My hand drifts to the delicate silver chain that hangs around my neck.

This isn't the first time my mind has conjured her up and played tricks on me. It's happened more than once on campus. From the corner of my eye, I'll catch a flash of long blonde hair. When I pause to study my surroundings, there's no one in sight.

Of course there isn't.

She doesn't attend Western.

She's an East Town student. At least, that's my assumption.

Other than what she likes in bed, I know nothing about her.

As loathe as I am to admit it—even privately to myself—that's become a major issue.

All these sightings are starting to drive me a little crazy.

More than anything, I wish she'd turned out to be a forgettable lay.

Unfortunately, nothing could be further from the truth.

"Hey, man, it's good to see you again. Twice in one week. How lucky is that?"

Knocked from the tangle of my thoughts, I lock gazes with River Thompson.

Great.

Just the asshole I didn't want to see.

From what I understand, Hayes and River went to high school together and played on a couple of the same travel hockey teams while growing up.

They're still friendly.

We're not.

And never will be.

I open my mouth to unload when a glint of silver at the base of his throat snags my attention. My gaze zeroes in on the chain hanging around his neck, and I swallow down the sharp words.

What the fuck?

It looks suspiciously similar to the one that was left behind in my bed.

Instead of a W, there's an R pendant hanging from the necklace.

Was the jewelry a gift from him?

If that's the case, then the little ray of sunshine I slept with can't be one of his bunnies.

It's so damn tempting to pull out the necklace with the W pendant from beneath my T-shirt and show it off.

Can you imagine the look on his face if he discovered that I fucked his girl—a few times?

It would be the sweet justice he deserves.

Or maybe I should share how responsive she'd been in my arms.

Even remembering the way she'd come undone has me dragging a hand through my hair and swearing under my breath.

His narrowed gaze stays fastened to mine as he shifts, straightening to his full height. "What'd you say, McKinnon?"

A silent war erupts in my head. As much as I want to throw her in his face and gloat, I keep it to myself.

For the time being.

I lift my chin. "I asked where your girlfriend was." The question is out of my mouth before I can think better of it.

His expression turns stony as his phone buzzes with an incoming message. "None of your damn business."

He glances at his cell before his thumbs fly across the screen.

Is that her?

Is she texting him?

I've never wanted to wrestle someone's phone away from them more than I do at this moment.

What the hell is happening to me?

I almost shake my head to loosen those disturbing thoughts.

From the corner of my eye, Hayes's shoulders shake as tears gather in his eyes. He's practically dying over there.

I turn toward my teammate with an arched brow. "Do you have something to add to the convo?"

The sound of his laughter grates against my nerves.

It's only when I continue to glare that my teammate clears his throat. "Nope. I'm just watching the show and waiting for everyone to get caught up to speed."

River's phone dings for a second time and then a third in quick succession.

I grind my molars in silent aggravation. I just want to rip the device away and—

That thought is enough to stop me in my tracks.

Jealousy.

That's the emotion attempting to eat me alive.

It's not something I've ever experienced before.

Not even with Sabrina.

I liked the girl, but we were young and it was never that deep. What really pissed me off was that she dumped my ass for River fucking Thompson.

For some reason, this feels different.

And I have no idea why.

It doesn't make a damn bit of sense.

I don't even know her name. I only know what she sounds like when her pussy clenches around my cock and she's making those sexy purring noises deep in her throat.

Those thoughts are enough to have my junk stirring to life. And that should definitely not be happening when River and I are seconds away from coming to blows.

Anytime I even think about the blonde, this is the direction my thoughts trip down.

I draw a deep, cleansing breath into my lungs and attempt to wrangle all of these out-of-control emotions back under submission again.

River shoots a frown at Hayes. "Get up to speed with what?"

My teammate sends an innocent look my way. "Nothing. Just making small talk. Right, Mav?"

I grunt in answer.

When I remain silent, River glances at his phone for the umpteenth time. "As much fun as this has been, I need to take off. My sister's outside waiting for me."

"Oh?" Hayes turns gleeful at that bit of news. "Be sure to give her a big hello from me. It's been way too long since we've seen one another."

"Yeah, sure."

With one final glare in my direction, River takes off, disappearing through the front entrance.

"That was a fun surprise. Who knew there'd be dinner and a show?"

"Shut the hell up, Van Doren," I grumble, staring at the doors River just shoved through.

For reasons I can't explain, it's tempting to follow him out to the parking lot. Even stranger than that, I actually consider the merits of it for a second or two before shooting down the idea.

The last thing I need is to get into another fight with the guy.

But still...

I can't shake the weird feeling that's fallen over me.

As Hayes settles at the table, I blurt, "Do you have any idea who his girlfriend is?"

I hold my breath, hating that I even asked the question.

But I need to know.

His expression turns cagey as he shakes his head. "Sorry, dude. Not a clue."

As everything deflates inside me, I do the only thing I can and attempt to move the fuck on with my life.

It's easier said than done.

POCKETFUL OF SUNSHINE
WILLOW & MAVERICK
01:10
04:10
WILLOW
LEUKEMIA
SURVIVOR

13

My palms dampen with nerves as my gaze stays trained on the entrance of Taco Loco. When there's still no sign of my brother, I fire off another text, trying to hasten him along. It's been more than ten minutes since I sprinted from the restaurant like my ass was on fire. River should have been right behind me.

How long does it take to pay the check?

My mind spirals, imagining the worst-case scenario.

I really hope he and Maverick aren't getting into it. Those two can't be within ten feet of each other without coming to blows.

If Maverick thinks I'm with River, he might decide to throw it in my brother's face.

A little payback for past transgressions.

As far as I know, that's all Saturday night was to him—Maverick taking something that belonged to River.

A pit settles at the bottom of my belly. I really hope that wasn't the case. It would really suck if the best sex of my life turns out to be nothing more than a revenge plot.

A way to lash out at my brother.

I shift on the leather seat of River's SUV and stare out the passenger side window, silently willing my twin to walk out. The tacos I'd eaten for lunch threaten to make an unexpected appearance.

Just as I open the home screen of my phone to fire off yet another text, River shoves through the glass doors and stalks toward the vehicle.

My lungs empty of air until little spots dance across my vision.

His expression is grim as he slides into the driver's seat of his Chevy Blazer and stabs the ignition. Anger vibrates off him in suffocating waves. Any moment, he's going to blow a gasket.

I'm terrified to ask what happened, because it's apparent from his stony expression and demeanor that something transpired.

The only one capable of setting River off like this is Maverick McKinnon.

Oh god.

I never should have gone home with him.

What the hell had I been thinking?

If I could go back in time and—

I gulp as my brain somersaults.

Would I make different choices?

It's surprising to realize that I wouldn't change one single second that transpired between us. He's the only man to make me feel alive. Like I could soar above the earth untethered. Before him, I had no idea that kind of pleasure existed. And for all I know, it's not something I'll ever experience again.

My heart clenches at the depressing possibility.

So, no, I wouldn't change a single second.

No matter the fallout.

It's only when my fingers drift to where my necklace should be that I realize they're shaking.

Before I can work up the nerve to ask what happened in the restaurant, my twin's stormy gaze settles on mine. "Did you know that Maverick McKinnon was in there?"

My teeth scrape against my lower lip.

It's so tempting to lie.

But I'm already keeping too many secrets from my brother.

I'm loathe to heap any more onto the pile.

"Um...yeah, I caught sight of him on the way out."

The muscle in his clenched jaw tics a mad rhythm. "I really fucking hate that guy." His gaze sears into mine. "You know that?"

"You've mentioned it a time or two." It takes effort to swallow past the lump that has formed in my throat, and even more to keep the thin waver from invading my voice. "Did you two have another run-in?"

"Yup." A smirk lifts the corners of his lips. "Told him that it was great to see him twice in one week."

I groan. "So you're the one who instigated it?"

His brows slam together as his expression contorts. "After the fight he started during the game? You bet your ass I did. The guy is a total dick. He deserves to have the loss shoved in his face. He thinks he's so fucking special."

I release the painful breath clogging my lungs. "Maybe he's the one who has something to be angry about. Have you forgotten you stole his girlfriend in high school?"

River's upper lip curls as he glares. "Exactly whose side are you on?" There's a beat of uncomfortable silence before his tone turns suspicious. "Why are you defending him all of a sudden?"

My eyes widen as I shake my head. Fear slides through me and I gulp. "That's not what I'm doing."

"Yeah, you are." He reverses the SUV and nearly gives me whiplash.

My mouth dries. "I'm just stating the obvious. He's the one who has something to be angry about. Maybe at some point, you need to sit down and hash it out instead of constantly getting into fights on the ice."

That suggestion is met with a scowl. "What happened with Sabrina is ancient history."

"Clearly, it's not. It continues to rear its ugly head every chance it gets."

"We're not even together anymore," he mutters, some of his previous anger draining away.

When everything first went down, I thought River stole Sabrina as a way to mess with Maverick, but they were together for over a year before breaking up and going their separate ways in college.

My brother hasn't been the same since then.

I can admit it, even if he won't.

"Have you tried reaching out to her?"

His lips flatten as he gives his head a slight shake.

Even though Sabrina and I still follow each other on social media, we haven't spoken in years. I've seen pics of her with a few guys, but there doesn't seem to be anyone serious in her life.

"Maybe it's time for you to—"

"I don't want to talk about Sabrina." There's a brief pause. "Or Maverick McKinnon. Sabrina is part of my past, and nothing is going to change that."

Even though it'll fall on deaf ears, I can't resist adding, "It doesn't have to be that way."

"Yeah, it does. End of story."

When my fingers brush across my collarbone for a second time and come away empty, I realize that I need to get my necklace back.

The question is how.

MAVERICK

14

Sweat drips down the back of my neck as I shove into the locker room and throw my stick in the holder near the door. Even though practice ended a few minutes ago, I'm still breathing hard.

It only takes one glance around to realize that I'm not the only one. Coach has been skating our asses off since the loss on Saturday night.

Hey, losses happen.

No one likes it.

But when it's against our biggest conference rival?

That's when it becomes unacceptable.

We've just given our opponents for the next scheduled game a massive mental boost.

I unsnap the chin strap and yank the helmet off my head before tossing it into my locker and dropping down to the bench to unlace my skates.

Ryder huffs out a tired breath and takes a seat next to me.

As far back as I can remember, we've played for the same team. First, house teams, then when we were older, travel teams. I always played up with the older kids, so we were together. The only exception is when Ryder graduated from high school and started college.

I've never admitted this to anyone, but my senior season in high school sucked because Ryder wasn't there skating beside me. When I was on the ice, it felt like a vital part of me was missing. We've been teammates for so long that I know the moves he's going to make before they happen.

Maybe even before he realizes it.

There's comfort in being able to read someone so easily.

One glance and I understood how the play was going to unfold and where I fit into the schematic.

We were like a well-oiled machine.

Everything fell back into place once I graduated and started at Western the next fall. I'd assumed that we'd coast through the next three years before he signed his contract with Chicago.

"McKinnon, see me before you take off," Coach calls out, meeting my gaze as he crosses the locker room to his office.

"Fuck, you've done it now." Ryder chuckles from beside me.

I shoot him a dark look before glancing at the frosted glass door Coach disappeared through.

"Any idea what that's about?" Ryder asks as guys joke and strip off their gear around us before hopping in the showers.

"Nope."

All right, so maybe that's not altogether true.

I have the sneaking suspicion that this might have something to do with my shitty English grade.

He already ripped me a new one for getting into it with River after the game on Saturday. I can't imagine he's going to bring that up again.

Here's the thing about Coach—once we've discussed a topic, he expects you to take care of it and puts the issue to rest. He doesn't treat us like we're a bunch of toddlers in need of constant supervision.

It's one of the things I like about the guy.

When I sit and stare, lost in the whirl of my thoughts, Ryder bumps my shoulder. "You better get a move on. Don't want to keep Coach waiting."

A sigh escapes from me.

He's right about that.

Better to get it over with.

Ryder and our new coach haven't always seen eye to eye. It took a few months for their relationship to even out, but it's much better now. Any time a new coach comes in and shakes things up, there's bound to be growing pains.

Coach Philips had to break down Ryder to build him back up again so he could elevate his game. As much as I'm going to miss playing with him next year, I'm excited to see what he achieves. It wouldn't surprise me if he takes the league by storm.

He's that fucking good.

And I'll be stuck playing here for another year before moving on to the pros.

That is, if I can get this damn English grade up.

If not...

A shudder slides through me before I force the possibility from my head, unwilling to dwell on it.

Once I'm showered and changed, I rap my knuckles against the door and poke my head inside his office.

A flurry of nerves wings its way to life at the bottom of my belly. Getting summoned to the head coach's office is never good. If he wants to give you kudos, he does it in front of the team.

"You wanted to see me, Coach?"

With the remote in hand, he clicks off the game film he's watching and waves me in before pointing to the chair parked in front of the metal desk. There are papers scattered everywhere. He pulls off his Western Wildcats ball cap and plows his fingers through his blond hair.

"Take a seat, Maverick."

Well, hell.

That means I'm going to be here for a while.

I force myself farther inside the small space before dropping down onto the chair.

I just want to get this over with and move on with my life.

Coach steeples his fingers in front of him. "I spoke with Dr. Linstrom this afternoon."

Yep, hit the nail on the head.

English.

"Apparently, you didn't do so well on the last paper, and it's dropped your overall grade to a C minus in the class."

I shift as shame and embarrassment crash over me. English has always been a challenging subject. Anything with a lot of text to digest makes me feel like I'm drowning. It's the worst feeling in the world.

If I thought it would get better after high school, I was wrong.

There's even more reading in college.

More comprehending and synthesizing of information, all the while trying to make sense of it.

It's fucking exhausting.

If Coach is aware of my dyslexia diagnosis, he's never mentioned it. And that's exactly the way I want to keep it.

It's no one's business but my own.

When he stares at me expectantly, as if waiting for an explanation, I mumble, "I'm working on getting it up."

"You're right on the cusp. Anything lower and you'll be academically ineligible to play. I'd hate to see that happen with playoffs coming up."

Tension fills my muscles as his gaze stays pinned to mine. I get the feeling this conversation isn't going to end with a simple "work harder" speech the way I'd anticipated.

"Dr. Linstrom was kind enough to reach out to the tutoring center on campus and secure a student for you to meet with to help get this grade up. Your first session is scheduled for six sharp tomorrow after practice at the library."

That's definitely not what I wanted to hear.

He rips off a sheet of paper from a notebook before handing it over. I have no choice but to reach out and accept it. Everything sinks inside me like a heavy stone as the name and number blur before my eyes.

I really hate working with tutors.

And student ones are the fucking worst.

Like I need randoms all up in my business spreading gossip about me?

Fuck no.

Even if I don't disclose my learning disability, it doesn't take long before they figure out that there's something wrong. Their demeanor will change and they'll treat me like I'm in elementary school.

"Is that really necessary?" Heat stains my cheeks as I mumble the question. "I can do it on my own."

"Yeah, I think it is," he says with a heavy sigh. "As soon as you have a solid B in the course, you can drop the tutoring."

My mouth tumbles open and my eyes widen. "Seriously?"

Does he realize how impossible that is?

"It's important you get the support you need through the remainder of the season. I'm sure your tutor will be able to help with your other classes as well."

If given the choice, I would have preferred another ass reaming for picking a fight with River Thompson than this BS.

When I silently stew, he jerks a brow. "Any questions?"

I shake my head.

He pushes away from the desk. "Okay then. We're finished here."

I rise to my feet and head for the door, needing to get the hell out of his office. It feels like the walls are closing in on me.

As I cross the threshold, Coach says, "Maverick?"

I glance over my shoulder and meet his gaze. "Yeah?"

"I'll be keeping close tabs on all of your classes, but especially English."

My mouth turns cottony as I jerk my head into a nod.

Fan-fucking-tastic.

Even though it's tempting to slam the door on the way out, I fight the urge, taking care to close it gently.

It's a struggle.

As soon as the lock clicks into place, I glance at the paper.

My new tutor's name is Stacie.

Well, Stacie can go fuck herself.

I crumple the paper into a tight ball and shove it into my pocket before stalking back to my locker to pick up my duffle. Most of the guys have already taken off, which is for the best. I don't need those nosy bastards getting all up in my business. They're like a bunch of old ladies gossiping in a church parking lot after services.

My head is a mess as I leave the ice arena and stalk toward the lot on the other side of campus where I parked my truck this afternoon because I was running late for class.

English, to be exact.

It's become the fucking bane of my existence.

I can't help but think that none of this would be happening if my parents had allowed me to play juniors before entering the draft instead of forcing me to attend college. I'd already be playing professional hockey. In the grand scheme of things, this class is meaningless.

It's so damn frustrating.

Midway across campus, my phone rings. I slide the slim device from my pocket and glance at the screen before answering.

"Hey. What's up?"

"Not much," Dad says. "Just wanted to check in and see how practice went."

It's like the man has a sixth sense where his children are concerned. He's always able to detect when there's a disturbance in the force.

"It was fine. Coach came down on us like a hammer after the last loss."

"Can't blame him for that." Dad's deep voice simmers with humor.

I'm sure he's thinking about all the times his coaches busted his balls back in the day. It might not have been fun at the time, but they sure seem like fond memories now.

Who knows…maybe I'll look back and feel just as nostalgic.

Ha!

Doubtful.

"I spoke to Reed Philips earlier this afternoon."

My feet grind to a halt as surprise creeps into my voice. "You did?"

"Yup. I had a few things to discuss with him about Wolf and Ryder."

Dad reps both of my teammates through his sports management agency. He's negotiated their contracts with the franchises they'll be playing with next season.

There's a moment of silence before he clears his throat. "He did, however, mention your English grade."

Seriously?

It's gradually that I suck in a deep breath before releasing it back into the atmosphere as my gaze scans the surrounding area. At this time of the evening, campus isn't nearly as crowded. There are only a few pockets of students.

"I suppose he told you that I'll be working with a tutor," I grumble.

Just saying the words pisses me off all over again.

"He did. It certainly can't hurt."

I press my lips together in silent disagreement.

"Mav?"

I huff out a sigh. "Yeah?"

"It's not the worst thing in the world." There's a pause as his voice softens. "We both understand that."

He's talking about Mom's breast cancer diagnosis.

Nothing could be worse than that.

I don't even like to think about how terrible that year was. Every time I do, a pit the size of Texas takes up residence at the bottom of my belly. Even though I try not to dwell on it, in the back of my mind, I'm always concerned that the cancer will roar back with a vengeance, and she'll no longer be in remission.

Every time she gets a blood draw, I worry.

Every time she goes in for a mammogram, I hold my breath until the scans come back clean.

You know what I hate more than anything?

Fucking cancer.

And the way it blew our lives apart in the blink of an eye.

On the outside, everything might look like it's returned to normal, but that's not the case. Our family has been forever changed by this insidious disease.

"Yeah, I know," I mumble.

"I'm just asking that you keep it in perspective, all right? Control what you have the power to change."

His soft words leave me feeling like a sulky teenager.

From the corner of my eye, there's movement near one of the academic buildings and my head swivels in that direction. The fine hair at the nape of my neck prickles as I narrow my eyes, straining against the setting sun.

My heart leaps before slamming against my chest.

I blink and there's...

No one.

Whoever it was is now gone.

Or maybe I'm hallucinating.

For just a second I'd thought...

"Maverick? You still there, or have you chucked your phone into a snowbank?"

I snort out a laugh. "Totally chucked it."

"That's what I thought." His voice turns serious again. "You know I struggled with the same issues in school. It wasn't easy, but I did get through it. And you will too."

The tension filling my muscles drains. "So you keep saying."

"Just work as hard as you can. That's all Mom and I can ask of you."

"I'll try."

"We'll see you tomorrow for dinner?"

"Yup."

"Looking forward to it. Just remember that we love you and we're proud of all you've accomplished, Mav."

I drop my voice as warmth spreads through me. "Love you too, Dad."

With that, I end the call and slip the cell back into my pocket. Some of my previous irritation at the situation melts away, leaving me feeling resigned. Talking to my dad always helps me get my head on straight.

As I pick up my pace, my gaze slides to the building where I thought I saw her.

It's so tempting to look up River's socials, because I'm willing to bet that I'd find the hot blonde somewhere on there.

Maybe then I could figure out who she is.

As soon as the sneaky little idea pops into my brain, I quash it.

I've never looked up a chick on social media.

It seems stalkerish.

And that's the last thing I am.

Girls have always chased after me.

Not the other way around.

The cell burns a hole in my pocket as I hit the parking lot and click the locks on my truck.

No way in hell am I breaking down and doing it.

I shove the thought from my head and yank the door handle before sliding behind the wheel. One press of the ignition and the vehicle roars to life. Instead of hauling ass out of the parking lot, I sit and stew as an internal struggle takes place in my brain.

What I need to do is forget all about that chick.

Not make things worse by finding out who she is.

And where I can find her.

I mean... I *do* have her necklace, though.

She probably wants it back.

My hand rises to touch the tiny W pendant that hangs from the delicate silver chain.

So, maybe I should—you know—return it.

And the only way I can do that is—

Before I can finish the thought, I'm sliding my cell from my pocket and opening the home screen. I bring up Insta and type in River's name. A tiny icon of him on the ice pops up, along with a few other people with similar names.

Just as I'm about to hit the icon, my thumbs pause, hovering over the screen.

Am I seriously going through another dude's socials to find some girl who snuck out of my bed after we slept together?

Am I?

Fuck it.

Apparently I am.

I tap his name and wait for his profile to load. Information and images in a grid pattern populate the screen. My gaze slides over the photos until it lands on one with her in it. My heart stutters before slamming against my ribcage as I stare at them. Their arms are wrapped around each other's shoulders and they're both grinning at the camera.

That's all it takes for jealousy to explode within me.

All I have to do is tap the photo, and she'd probably be tagged in it.

That's the reason I did this, right?

To figure out who she is so I can track her ass down.

Fuck.

Fuck.

Fuck.

If this photo is anything to go on, the place I'll find her is warming River Thompson's bed.

I hit the line at the bottom of the screen and swipe my thumb upward until the images dancing before my eyes disappear and I'm back to the home screen.

Irritated with myself, I toss the phone onto the passenger seat and shift into drive before squealing out of the parking lot.

POCKETFUL OF SUNSHINE
01:10
WILLOW & MAVERICK
04:10
WILLOW
LEUKEMIA
SURVIVOR

15

"Are you sure this is a good idea?" Holland asks from beside me as she studies the blue Victorian set away from the road.

My teeth scrape across my lower lip as I carefully turn the question over in my head. "Nope. Not at all."

She snorts. "Just what I love—a well-concocted plan that has little chance of succeeding."

A fresh burst of nerves prickles at the bottom of my belly as my fingers drift along my collarbone. "I need my necklace back."

"Here's an idea you might not have explored—just ask him for it."

I rip my gaze away from the house long enough to meet her serious one. "He can't figure out who I am. And I can't take the chance that River will find out what happened between us either." I press my lips together and nod, as if trying to persuade myself this is the only path forward.

Because, apparently, I haven't convinced Holland of it. Her dubious expression tells me everything I need to know. She's never been one to sugarcoat anything. And with the way she grew up, I can understand the reason for it.

"This is the way it has to be."

"If you say so..." Doubt creeps into her tone as her voice trails off.

I straighten my shoulders. "I do."

If only I felt nearly as confident as I sound.

This is me taking a page from the fake-it-until-you-make-it book.

I just hope it doesn't blow up in my face, because that, unfortunately, seems like a distinct possibility.

"Fine. Let's go over the plan one more time."

I suck in an unsteady breath before gradually releasing it back into the atmosphere and attempting to calm the tension that vibrates inside me like a live wire. "As soon as Maverick leaves, I'll go to the front door and knock. Hopefully, someone I don't know will answer. I'll tell them that I left something in Mav's room last weekend. Then I'll hightail it up there and search it."

"And if no one's home?"

"If the front door is unlocked, I slip inside, haul ass to his room, and hope it's there."

"And I'll wait here, wishing I had some popcorn while you try not to get caught."

I turn and glare. "I could really use your support and good vibes."

Her lips crook. "This is me giving you my full support."

"I know, that's what's scary."

She points toward the house. "Looks like the canary has just flown the coop."

My head whips toward the front of the Victorian just in time to see Maverick stroll out with one of his teammates. It's tempting to press closer to the windshield for a better view. Instead, I hunker down, hoping he doesn't turn and spot me.

Even though Holland's rattle trap of a vehicle is parked a few doors down the street, I still feel exposed.

"Chickens," I mutter.

"Huh?"

"I don't think canaries live in coops. Pretty sure it's chickens."

She snorts. "Well, that changes everything."

I shift on the seat. "Is there any chance you'll reconsider doing this for me?"

Her eyes widen as she gives her head a vehement shake. "Fuck no!"

"We saw Bridger leave ten minutes before Maverick. There's no chance you'll run into him."

"I don't care. I refuse to breathe the same air as that dick." Her tone softens. "As much as I love you, you're on your own with this one."

"Fine," I grumble.

In silence, we watch as Maverick and his friend slide into a black pickup truck and take off.

"It's now or never," Holland says. "You've got this."

"I really hope so."

"Just pretend you're a dumb bunny looking to get laid. I'm sure there's a revolving door of them."

I frown at the idea of that being the case.

Although, Holland is more than likely spot-on in her assessment. Groupies probably crawl out of the woodwork to sleep with Maverick McKinnon. After the night I spent with him, I can totally understand the reason for that.

When a kernel of jealousy blooms to life inside me, I stomp it out.

We had one night together.

He's probably forgotten all about it by now.

"Get a move on, girl."

I meet Holland's steady gaze. "Wish me luck."

"You don't need luck." She points toward the house. "Now go."

I suck in a deep breath before jerking the handle and jumping from the car.

The passenger side window disappears between us. "How cool would it have been if you'd ducked and rolled?"

Before I can respond, she hums the *Mission: Impossible* theme music as she moves her shoulders from side to side. A reluctant smile simmers at the corners of my lips as I swing away and jog to the concrete walkway and then up the rickety front porch stairs. A tremor slides through me as memories of the way he'd slipped his arm around my waist and held me close tumble through my brain.

Once at the door, I peek inside the beveled windows, looking for signs of life.

There are none.

I throw a cautious glance over my shoulder and meet Holland's eyes. She gives me a thumbs up sign in response.

Just like she said—it's now or never.

My fingers wrap around the handle before twisting the knob and shoving the thick wood open. Air gets clogged in my throat as I peer inside and pause to listen. The only thing I'm able to hear is the hammering of my own heart as it echoes in my ears.

I throw another watchful look over my shoulder before slipping inside the entryway. My gaze slides over the interior. It looks different with the bright sunlight pouring in through the windows than it did in the darkness. Or even when I'd snuck out the next morning. I'd been much too intent on escaping to soak in my surroundings.

It reminds me of the house that River shares with a bunch of teammates near East Town University. There's a masculine presence that lacks any female touches or homeyness.

Just as I take the staircase to the second floor, a deep voice says, "So, is this going to become a regular occurrence? You sneaking in and out of our house?"

For the second time within a week, I yelp and swing around, only to find Hayes leaning against the wall outside the living room.

He grins, taking in the startled expression that must be plastered across my face.

"Funny, you just missed Maverick." With a tilt of his head, he crosses his brawny arms against his chest. "I could give him a call if you'd like. I'm sure he'd love to see you again."

"That's not necessary. The only reason I stopped by is because I, um, left something behind the other day."

"Night."

My brow furrows. "What?"

His smile widens. "What I think you meant to say is that you left something behind the other night." There's a pause. "When you came home with Maverick." My cheeks heat. "And then stayed until the wee hours of the morning."

"Thanks for the recap."

"No problem. I'm here to help."

"That's doubtful."

"No, really. I'm curious as to what you left behind. Is it a pair of panties? Maybe a bra?"

"Of course not." I straighten to my full height and point to the second floor. He's wasted enough of my time. "I'm going to take a look." Without waiting for a response, I rush up the staircase.

"Just let me know if you'd like some assistance," he calls after me, voice brimming with humor.

"No thanks," I mumble beneath my breath. "I'm good."

It takes a few moments to find his room. I open one door and peek inside before realizing that it's not the right one. Once I find his private space, I slip inside and shut the door before leaning against it.

My heart feels like it'll pound right out of my chest.

Only wanting to get this over with, I launch myself toward the bed. The sheets and comforter look like someone just rolled out of them. There's a maroon Western Wildcats hockey T-shirt crumpled near the end of the mattress. Unable to help myself, I pick up the cottony material and bring it to my nose before inhaling. My eyelids feather close as his masculine scent inundates my senses.

That's all it takes for memories to hit me like a freight train, knocking me off kilter and sending my pulse thrumming.

No guy should smell this amazing.

I really need to focus on the reason I've returned to the scene of the crime.

It's reluctantly that I drop the shirt and whip back the navy comforter, hoping that my necklace will be there.

Instead, I find the sheets empty.

Crap.

I pick up each pillow and glance beneath them.

Nada.

Then I look between the sheet and the comforter.

In desperation, I drop to my knees and peer under the bed. Swearing under my breath, I pull my phone from my pocket and turn on the flashlight to make sure I haven't overlooked it.

Other than a pair of shoes and a wadded-up piece of tissue, there's nothing.

Huffing out a breath, I blow a piece of hair from in front of my eyes as my brain cartwheels.

I really thought I'd find it here.

Is it possible that it fell off at the bar?

Or maybe the hockey arena?

Ugh.

I'll have to give both places a call.

As tempting as it is to tear the room apart, I need to get moving before my luck runs out. It's bad enough that I ran into Hayes.

Again.

I'm afraid he'll mention to Maverick that I dropped by.

Or River.

Just as I reach the door, ready to slip into the hallway, there's a loud slam from downstairs. A flurry of nerves explodes inside me and sweat springs to my palms as I press my ear against the thick wood, hoping it was Hayes taking off.

Dread pools in my belly when I hear a babble of male voices.

The distinct sound of feet pounding up the staircase has my eyes widening as I search the room, looking for a place to hide. With no other obvious options, I dive into the closet and bury myself at the back of it as the door flies open and Maverick bursts into the room.

Oh, shit.

Is he onto me?

Does he know I'm here?

Did Hayes tell him?

Air gets wedged in my lungs until I'm on the verge of passing out.

The closet door is open half a dozen inches. It's just enough for me to watch him pause near his desk before reaching down for something on the side of it.

Air leaks from my lungs as he swings around and moves back toward the hallway.

Before he can take another step, he pauses and searches the room with narrowed eyes. His brows pinch as he sniffs the air and makes a second visual sweep of the space before shaking his head.

I wince.

It never occurred to me not to wear perfume.

That was a rookie mistake.

I'd make a terrible spy.

Just when I expect him to leave, he swears under his breath and tosses whatever he'd picked up onto the bed.

Oh god...he knows I'm here. I'm about to be busted.

I'd squeeze my eyes tightly shut, but I can't stop staring at him.

My mouth tumbles open when he drags down the front of his gray sweatpants and boxers, allowing his cock to spring free.

My heart skips a painful beat as he palms the thick erection.

What the hell is happening here?

There's no way he's going to...to...

As soon as those thoughts circle through my brain, his grip tightens around the girth and he hisses out a sharp breath.

Holy crap, yes, he is.

He is most definitely going to—

The harsh sound that falls from his lips is all it takes to have my panties flooding with arousal. From my position in the closet, I have the perfect view.

As he strokes his hard length, his eyelids flutter closed and his head tips back, revealing the thickly corded muscles of his throat.

My mouth turns cottony as my clit throbs with awareness.

I don't realize that my hand has slipped beneath the band of my leggings and panties until my fingertips brush across the top of my slit and a gasp escapes from me.

That first slide feels so damn good.

Although not nearly as amazing as when he was the one playing with my body.

I clap my other hand over my mouth as fear slices through me.

It's a relief when he continues jacking himself off. I feel like a total deviant as my fingers rub soft circles across that tiny bundle of nerves.

"Yo, Mav! Let's get a move on it!" a voice from downstairs calls.

His dark lashes flutter as his expression twists as if in pain.

"I'll be there in a minute!" he grits from between clenched teeth.

Another groan escapes from him as he tightens his hold, pumping his cock even faster than before. My fingers move at the same speed as my gaze stays glued to the hand job he's giving himself.

"Fuck," he growls as pearly fluid erupts from the tip of his cock and lands on the T-shirt crumpled on his bed.

I press my hand tighter against my mouth as my own orgasm streaks through me and my inner muscles spasm.

His rigid stance loosens as he continues to pump his thick length until it softens before my very eyes. A musky scent hangs in the air as my muscles go limp and I slump against the far wall of the closet. My heart beats erratically as my breath comes out in harsh pants.

When he's finished, he tucks his cock back inside his sweats before plowing his other hand through his hair. Only then do I notice the slight flush staining his cheekbones.

My guess is that mine are tinged a similar shade.

A few seconds later, he disappears through the door.

Holy crap, that was a close one.

Everything that just happened somersaults through my brain.

It's the sound of the front door slamming that jerks me from my daze, and I force myself to climb out of the closet. As I make my way to my feet, my gaze settles to the bed and the shirt.

I can't help but step closer to get a better look at what he left behind.

As embarrassed as I am to have witnessed such a private moment, it's hands down one of the sexiest things I've ever seen.

I almost shake my head.

When the hell did I become such a perv?

Even though I should get the hell out of here, I can't stop staring at the maroon shirt. The one I'd pressed to my nose and inhaled not more than ten minutes ago. The very same one he just ejaculated all over.

The pearly fluid almost glows against the dark color. Just like in the closet when I'd slipped my fingers down the front of my leggings to touch myself, it's not a conscious decision to reach out and run them through his jizz. My heart pounds when I find it still warm, fresh from his body. I don't give it a second thought as I scoop up a dollop and lift it to my lips. My tongue darts out to lick my fingertips. As soon as I do, his scent envelopes me as his salty taste explodes in my mouth.

I can't resist taking another swipe.

Heat explodes inside my core as a fresh burst of arousal dampens my already wet panties.

It's so damn tempting to take the shirt with me as a little souvenir of what just happened. Instead, I swing toward the door and slip from the room before hauling ass down the stairs to the first floor.

"Find what you were looking for?"

I pause on the last step and meet Hayes's amused expression. "No."

Heat floods my cheeks as I force myself to maintain eye contact.

"Hmm. Maybe we should check lost and found before you take off. Never know what goodies you'll come across."

My gaze drops to the small brown box in his hands.

Is this guy serious?

They just throw the random stuff girls leave behind into a cardboard box, not really caring if it ever gets reclaimed?

He pulls out a tiny scrap of black material that I assume is a thong. "Would this happen to be yours?" With a squint, his gaze runs over the length of me. "It's probably the right size."

My face scrunches before I can think better of it. "Ewww."

"Hey, don't yuck someone else's yum."

I don't bother with a response as I hurry down the last step and head for the door. I'm sure Holland is wondering what happened to me.

"Just out of curiosity, do you know what you're doing?"

All his previous humor has fled. The seriousness shining in his eyes is far more disconcerting than the thong dangling from his finger.

"No, not at all."

"Well, good luck with that. We both know that River will shit a brick if he finds out you've been banging his archnemesis."

Ugh.

He's not wrong.

With nothing left to say to that bit of truth, I slip out the door.

MCKINNON 28

MAVERICK
WILDCATS

16

As soon as I slide into the back seat of Ryder's truck, he squeals away from the curb and does a U-turn in the middle of the street.

His gaze flickers to mine in the rearview mirror. "Find what you needed?"

"Yup." I don't mention the familiar floral scent tinging the air in my room. I can't be certain, but it smelled like the same one that clung to the blonde from Saturday night.

Unfortunately, as soon as I'd caught a whiff, it sent my senses into overdrive and my cock had stiffened right up.

And since I didn't want to sport a hard-on for the rest of the evening, I'd gotten myself off in record speed.

This is definitely getting out of hand.

Pun intended.

I stare out the passenger side window and watch the landscape roll by as we head home for dinner with my parents.

I really need to move on from this girl. Scenting her perfume in my space and catching glimpses of her all over campus is really starting to fuck with my head. My fingers brush over the necklace that hangs around my neck. I'd thought I lost it the other day and panicked, tearing my room apart.

Turns out I'd left it in the bathroom before hitting the shower.

It's only after I fastened it around my neck that everything settled within me.

Juliette twists toward the back seat. "Have you talked with Mom lately?"

My eyes slice from the landscape to my sister. Her brow is furrowed. "A couple days ago, why?" I hate the suspicious tone that enters my voice.

It's like I'm always waiting for the other shoe to drop.

It's exhausting.

"She went for a checkup yesterday."

Her words are like a gut punch.

"No, she never mentioned it," I mumble, fingers drifting to the necklace before tightening around the silver W pendant that hangs from it. For some odd reason, it makes the tension attempting to flood my system dissipate. Maybe not completely, but enough to stop my brain from spiraling with fear.

"I'm sure she'll mention it at dinner."

I can't help but notice the way Ryder wraps his hand around my sister's fingers before giving them a gentle squeeze. She glances at him, and some of the concern marring her expression melts away.

It only makes me feel lonelier.

Isolated.

With an irritated huff, I close my eyes and allow my head to fall back against the seat. I just want to forget about the crap that's been swirling around inside my brain like a chaotic storm.

The constant concern I have that Mom is one step away from a relapse.

If that happens, it's doubtful we'll come out of another battle unscathed.

Then there's my changing relationship with Ryder.

And my English grade that's now in the shitter, jeopardizing whether I get ice time, which in turn could affect my future.

Last but not least, there's the elusive girl who continues to haunt my thoughts like a specter.

The very same one who belongs to River fucking Thompson.

POCKETFUL OF SUNSHINE
01:10
WILLOW & MAVERICK
04:10
WILLOW
LEUKEMIA

17

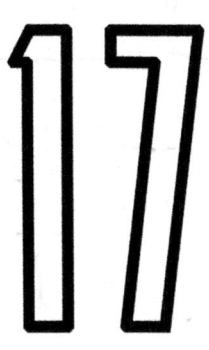

"Good job, Eric. I think you're really starting to understand the concepts. Same time next week?"

"Thanks. But that's only because you're amazing at analyzing text and explaining it in a way that makes sense. Dr. Moore could take a few pointers from you."

Heat floods my cheeks as I tuck an errant lock of hair behind my ear. "Yeah...you probably shouldn't tell him that. I doubt it would end well for either of us."

With a snort, he flashes a grin. "It can be our little secret." With his books held tightly against his chest, he sidles closer. "Um, I was wondering—"

Stacie pokes her head into the room where we've been working. "Hey, Willow. Are you busy?"

Eric shoots her a frown.

"Nope. We were just finishing up. Right, Eric?"

His shoulders sink. "Yeah. We're done here." He takes a step toward Stacie, one of the other students who works at the tutoring center, before shooting me another look. "See you next week, Willow."

I lift my hand in a wave. "Bye."

Stacie smirks as he slides past. We both wait a beat or two until the outside door closes with a resounding thud.

"One of these days, you're going to have to rip the Band-Aid off and admit that you're not interested."

A sigh escapes from me as I massage my temples. "I know."

"It's been a month and he still hasn't lost interest. And didn't he show up to your session last week with your favorite iced coffee?"

"Yeah. The weird thing is that I don't even remember mentioning how much I love iced mochas." The edges of my lips wilt. "It would be so much easier if he found someone else. That's going to be such an awkward convo."

A chuckle escapes from her. "Boo hoo. Let me get out my tiny violin. Someone has a crush on Willow."

More heat rushes to my cheeks as I clear my throat, only wanting to change the subject. "Did you need me for something, or were you just trying to help me out?"

"Both." She flashes a grin. "Aren't I a good friend? One you wouldn't mind doing a favor for?"

Uh-oh.

With raised brows, I wait expectantly.

She glances at the pink sports watch wrapped around her left wrist. "I'm supposed to meet a student at the library and didn't realize I double booked myself. Any chance you can fill in?"

Eric was supposed to be my last student for the day. I was really looking forward to heading home and chilling out with Holland. She mentioned something about watching a new movie that just came out. After the week I've had, that sounds like heaven.

When I hesitate, Stacie holds her clasped hands out in front of her. "Please? You do this for me and I'll meet with Eric next week and let it slip that you have a new boyfriend."

A gurgle of laughter escapes from me.

Stacie knows exactly how to sway me.

"Deal."

"You're the best!" She rushes forward and throws her arms around me before squeezing tight. "Dr. Linstrom called personally to make sure someone could meet right away with this student, so it must be important."

"Do you have a name?"

"Ummm...let me find it and get back to you." There's a pause. "If I remember correctly, I'm supposed to meet this kid on the third floor near the periodicals." Her brows scrunch. "I think he's a football player. Maybe soccer. Or lacrosse. You know…" She rolls her wide hazel eyes. "Another jock who's barely passing by the skin of their teeth and needs to stay eligible."

"What time is the session?"

She winces. "Will you kill me if I say six?"

I glance at my phone. That's in ten minutes. "I better get moving if I'm going to make it to the library on time."

"You're seriously the best!"

I wave off the compliment. Over the last semester, Stacie has become a good friend and I don't mind helping her out. "No worries. I'll see you tomorrow."

"Definitely."

With that, I gather up my books and shove them into my backpack. What I like best about this job is that when it's slow, I'm able to get my own work done. It's like getting paid to study.

Double win.

Right before pushing through the door, I call out, "If you find his name, text me!"

"Will do. I know it's here somewhere."

I love Stacie to death, but organizational skills are not exactly her strong suit.

The cool evening breeze slaps at my cheeks as I push through the glass doors. Darkness has already settled over campus. The walkways are lit with bright light, lending a modicum of safety. I burrow into my jacket and pick up my pace, hustling to the library. When I'm halfway there, my phone buzzes with an incoming text. I slip it from my pocket, hoping that it's Stacie.

Instead, it's Mom.

Hi sweetie! Haven't heard from you in a day or so. Give me a call. I worry about you.

I huff out a breath, wishing she would give me a little bit of space.

Instead of responding, I slip the phone in my jacket as my mind circles back to the issue at hand. The only thing I can do is hope that the place we're supposed to meet won't be crowded, and it'll be obvious who the jock I'm tutoring is.

As I enter the sprawling brick building, I give it one more shot and hit her number. Instead of picking up, it goes straight to voicemail.

Well, I tried.

There's nothing more I can do.

With a resigned sigh, I take the stairs to the third floor. My feet slow as I reach the landing and survey the area. There aren't many people here this evening. It's one of the reasons we use it to meet with students. Two girls and a guy are parked in the corner with their books spread out around them. To the left is a couple with their laptops opened. A lone girl is hunkered down in the corner.

Hmmm.

Maybe this guy flaked and I'll get my movie night after all.

I scan the desks that dot the space amid rows of bookshelves.

If this joker thinks I'm going to lie and report back that he showed up for his tutoring session when he decided to blow it off instead, he couldn't be more wrong.

Unfortunately, it happens all too often. Some of these athletes don't care about their education.

It's a real shame.

Especially when they've been given free rides.

Instead of taking full advantage of it, they squander the opportunity. There are so many people who can't afford an education and would kill for a full scholarship to a prestigious university like Western.

Just as I'm about to text Stacie again, movement from the other side of the large space catches my attention and I freeze. That's all it takes for a shot of electricity to sizzle through my veins.

No.

It can't be him.

My pulse thrums as I take a hasty step in retreat, hoping to slip away before he notices.

That's the exact moment he glances up and our gazes collide.

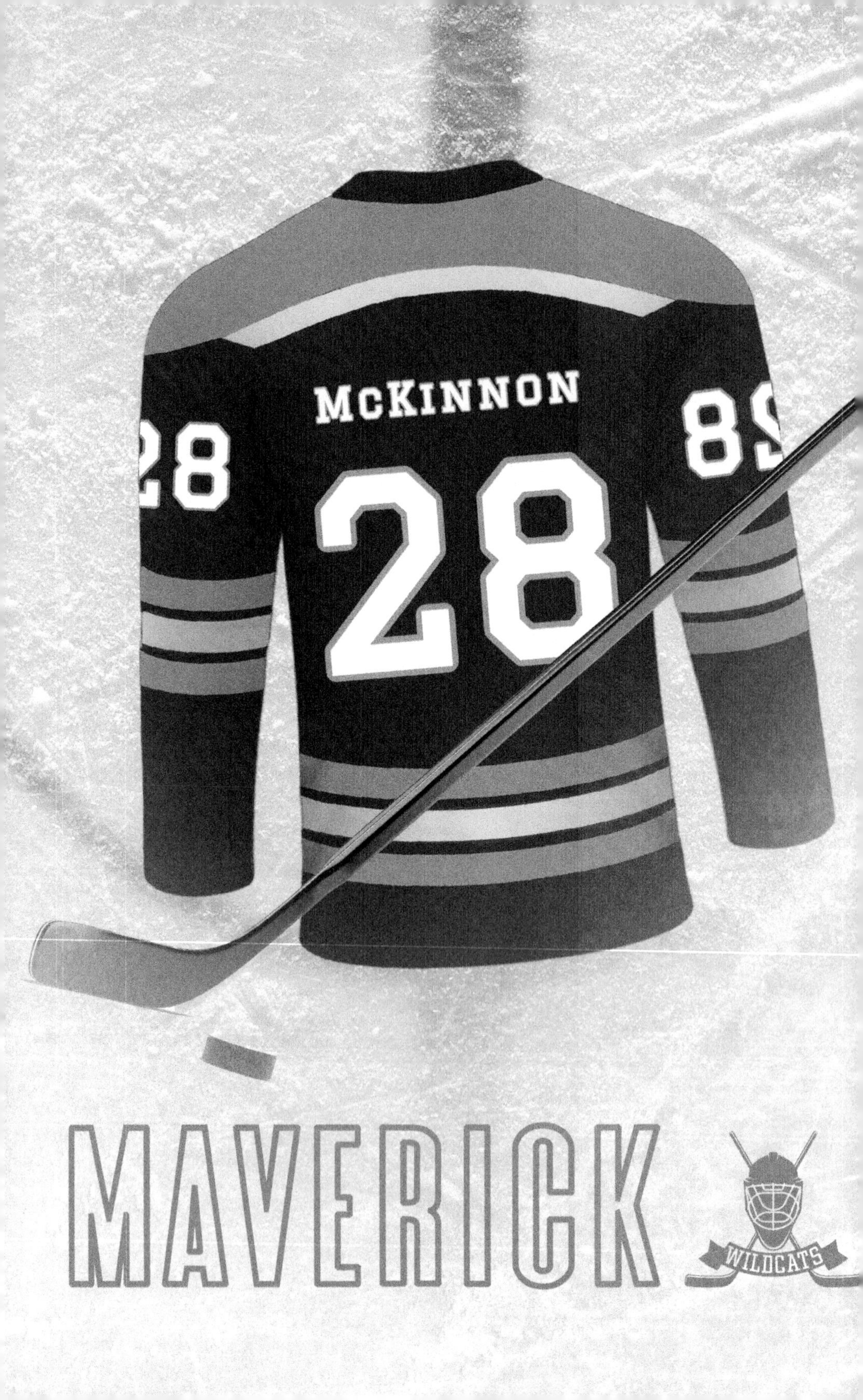
McKINNON
28
28
MAVERICK
WILDCATS

18

I blink as tension fills every line of my body.
There's no way this is happening.
It has to be a figment of my imagination.

Just like all the other times I'd caught sight of her on campus or at Taco Loco. Or when I thought I caught a whiff of her perfume in my room days later.

It's almost enough to make me wonder if I'm losing my damn mind.

When she doesn't move a muscle, I narrow my eyes. There's no way that the girl who snuck out of my bed last weekend is standing on the third floor of the library.

Her wide blue eyes stay locked on mine as shock colors her expression.

Something at the back of my brain prods me into movement, and I shoot to my feet. Fear flashes across her face as she swings away and races down the staircase.

"Fuck." I grab my backpack and take off after her.

As I hit the staircase, I catch a flash of long blonde hair from below and hurry my steps, only wanting to catch up to her.

A potent concoction of anxiety and frustration swirls through me.

"Hey!" I raise my voice, even though I know it won't do a damn bit of good. "Wait up!"

By the time I reach the lobby, there's no sign of her.

My heartbeat thunders as I plow a rough hand through my hair and stare out the glass doors, searching the darkness.

A couple holding hands walks inside the library.

"Did you happen to see a blonde girl leave the building? I think she was wearing a black jacket." The question is out of my mouth before I can stop it.

They glance at each other before shaking their heads.

"No, sorry."

Before I can question them further, they disappear up the staircase.

It's like she vanished into thin air.

Again.

Maybe I really am having a mental breakdown. It's true, I've been under a lot of stress lately. Dad has mentioned in the past that I could talk to someone if I ever started to feel overwhelmed.

It might just be time to take him up on the offer.

For a handful of minutes, I contemplate heading outside to search the surrounding area just to be sure. Although, by now, she's probably long gone.

If she was ever here in the first place.

Fuck...it's official.

I've lost it.

Plus, how can I do that when I'm supposed to meet with the tutor my professor set up? School and hockey need to be my priority. I can't keep obsessing about this girl.

It's surprising that I've already given the situation this much mental energy.

You know what?

I'm tapping out.

It ends here and now.

I swing around, ready to head back to the third floor, when I find her standing about fifteen feet away. My steps stutter to a stop as air gets clogged in my lungs, making it impossible to breathe.

My gaze rakes over her, trying to memorize every little detail.

She's even more beautiful than I remember.

I flex my hands. It's so damn tempting to pounce, but I'm afraid if I move one muscle, she'll disappear.

Just like a mirage.

Time stands still as we soak in the sight of one another.

The spell is only broken when she says, "You have something that belongs to me, and I need it back."

POCKETFUL OF SUNSHINE
WILLOW & MAVERICK
01:10
04:10
WILLOW
LEUKEMIA
SURVIVOR

19

With a tilt of his head, he takes a tentative step in my direction.

It's tempting to take one in retreat.

The last thing I want is for him to get too close. I'm terrified of what will happen if he lays his hands on me. I've been thinking nonstop about the night we spent together and how good he made me feel.

If only it were possible to evict Maverick McKinnon from my brain.

Every nerve ending goes on high alert as he bridges the space between us. "I assume you're talking about your necklace."

Relief rushes through me. "Yes."

"If you want it, you'll have to come back to my place and get it."

My mouth turns parched as I gulp at the idea of being alone with him. It takes effort to push the words out. "I can't do that."

He jerks his shoulders, as if my decision doesn't affect him one way or the other. I'd almost think it was true except for the intensity that blazes from his eyes and the cautious way he continues to inch closer.

Almost as if he's trying to approach a skittish animal.

"Then it's not that important or you don't want it badly enough."

My gaze stays fastened to his as I draw my lower lip between my teeth and chew the plump flesh, indecision warring inside my head.

"You're wrong about that. It means everything to me and I need it back."

"If that's the case, then the choice is a simple one." There's a beat of silence. "Don't you think?"

Even though I don't want to take my eyes off him for a second, it's impossible to think straight when I'm staring at him. It's like gazing directly at the sun.

It's hazardous to your health.

He's just...

Too much.

Too everything.

His masculine presence is overpowering in every sense of the word.

I've never met anyone like Maverick.

I force my gaze to his. Even though it feels like a mistake, the question is out of my mouth before I can think better of it. "Do you promise to give it back if I come with you?"

I don't realize how rigid his muscles had become until they loosen and his lips lift into some semblance of a smile. The feral look glowing in his eyes is enough to send a fresh burst of nerves scampering across my skin.

"You have my word."

Don't do it.

Don't spend any more time alone with him.

I shut down the little voice in my head. If this is the only way to get my necklace back, what choice is there?

The silver chain and pendant are too important to let go of.

"Fine."

Instead of closing the distance between us, he shoves open the heavy glass door. "After you."

Heat emanates from him in heavy, suffocating waves as I slip past, trying not to touch him. The woodsy scent of his cologne wraps sly fingers around me, cocooning me in memories of the night we spent together and how easy it was for him to make my body sing.

When I stumble, his arm snakes around my waist and he tugs me close to his muscular body.

His warm breath ghosts against my ear. "Are you all right?"

"I'm fine. Thanks."

I chance a peek at Maverick, only to find him watching me.

Why does this man affect me like no other?

I rack my brain but can't come up with an answer that makes sense.

I just know that he does.

It's an undeniable truth.

"Is your car on campus?" he asks, knocking me from my thoughts.

"Um, yeah."

"Where are you parked?"

I point to the lot closest to the library. It's centrally located and always easy to get to.

"What a coincidence. So am I." He continues to steer me along the path. "It's the Bronco, right?"

"Yeah." I'm surprised he remembered.

As we arrive at the small SUV, I click the key fob as he reaches around my body to open the door.

Before I can slide inside the safety of the vehicle, he holds out his palm. "Give me your phone."

I frown. "Excuse me?"

"I'm going to input the address."

My brows pinch. "That's not necessary. I'll just follow you."

With a smirk, he shakes his head before crowding my personal space until it becomes necessary to crane my neck in order to hold his mahogany-colored eyes.

"Do you really think I'm going to take the chance and let you get away now that I've finally found you again?"

My belly somersaults.

When he continues to stare, waiting patiently, I slip my hand into my jacket pocket and pull out my cell before opening the home screen. It's only when he swipes it from my palm that I realize I'm trembling.

And it's not just my hands.

My entire body is shaking.

He sets my nerves on edge, all the while ripping away the hazy film that has blanketed my life since I was sixteen.

When there's a distant chime, I realize that he texted himself my number.

His focus stays riveted to my phone as he taps away. When he's satisfied, the cell is passed back with the Maps app open on the screen.

"All set." He nods toward a truck parked a few rows over before his gaze refastens on mine. "I'll be right behind you."

My pulse thrums an erratic beat as I slip inside the Bronco. He closes the door before jogging to his truck and starting it up. I do the same and pull out of the parking lot with Maverick tailing me. It doesn't take more than five minutes to reach his house. I probably should have told him that I didn't need directions.

The second I turn off the ignition, the driver's side door is popped open and he's assisting me to the sidewalk. With his muscular arm wrapped around me, there's no escaping him.

Part of me wonders if I even want to.

I've never felt more conflicted.

In silence, he steers me toward the front porch and up the rickety stairs before shoving open the front door. Barely do I catch a glimpse of the people sitting around the living room, playing video games. A few call out greetings, but he ignores them, hustling me up the staircase to his room.

Once I'm over the threshold, he closes the door and leans against it. He doesn't say a word as his gaze stays pinned to mine. Only now do I realize that he's been keeping himself firmly under control this entire time.

That's no longer the case. The thin veneer has been torn away.

A potent concoction of nerves and excitement bursts at the bottom of my belly as I rip my attention away from him, needing to get all the emotions careening out of control back under submission.

All it takes is one fleeting glance at the queen-sized bed for memories to press in at the edges, threatening to suffocate the life out of me.

Am I the last girl who's been there?

Or have others already taken my place?

The thought sickens me. It's enough to have bile rising in my throat.

And it shouldn't.

Our worlds were never supposed to collide again. It doesn't matter if I haven't been able to banish him from my thoughts.

"I'm curious... Does River know I fucked you?" The question comes out sounding as if his voice has been scraped from the bottom of the ocean.

Air leaks from my lungs as my wide gaze slices to his and fear scampers down my spine.

When I remain silent, he growls, "Does he?"

The thought of my brother finding out about what happened between us makes me sick to my stomach.

He would be furious.

I have to moisten my lips before forcing out the response. "Of course not."

His eyes narrow. "Do you plan on telling him?"

Is he really asking this?

"Well, sunshine? I need to know."

I clear my throat and force out the words that have become lodged there. "Why would I do that? We slept together one time. It's over, and we've both moved on with our lives."

A muscle in his jaw tics as one sculpted brow rises. "Is that all it was to you? A fuck in the sheets?"

No.

But to admit that to him would be dangerous.

It would only send us tripping down a path neither of us wants.

My attention slices to the door he's leaning against. It's so tempting to race past and escape his suffocating presence.

"You're not really thinking of running away from me, are you?"

I straighten my shoulders and focus on the reason I've returned to the scene of the crime. "I'd like my necklace."

His inscrutable expression never falters. "Yeah, sure. It's the only reason you came here, right?"

He shoves away from the door before his fingers grip the hem of his sweatshirt. I blink when he draws the thick cotton up his torso and over his head, leaving him in a navy Wildcats T-shirt.

My mouth dries. "What are you doing?"

"Getting your necklace."

Before I can ask anything else, he strips off the snug material that fits him like a glove, leaving him bare chested.

My gaze licks over sculpted abdominals and chiseled pecs that stand out in stark relief. And his biceps...

Holy hell.

Even his muscles have muscles.

Hands down, he's the most beautiful man I've ever laid eyes on. Not that it's saying much, but still...

I have no idea how much time ticks by as I drink in his male beauty. He's like a work of art that needs to be silently appreciated. My panties dampen just looking at him.

It takes a herculean effort to mentally shake myself from the stupor that's fallen over me and refocus my attention. "My, um...necklace... Where is it?"

His hand rises to his throat to touch the pendant that hangs from the silver chain resting against his sun-kissed collarbone.

My eyes widen. Barely am I able to push out the question, "You've been wearing it this entire time?"

His shoulders lift in a nonchalant gesture that belies the tension straining his muscles, looking for an escape. "I wanted to keep it safe."

When I remain silent, processing the response, the corners of his lips quirk. "Well, what are you waiting for, sunshine? If you want it so badly, all you need to do is come and get it."

I suck in a sharp breath.

He doesn't make any effort to unclasp it or hand it over.

He simply stands there, as if daring me to make the first move.

When he raises a brow in silent challenge, I force my feet into motion. Every step has my heartbeat ratcheting up, galloping beneath my breast until it reverberates throughout my body and in my ears.

This is a bad idea.

Then again, Maverick McKinnon has bad idea stamped all over him.

And yet, that knowledge isn't enough to stop me.

To stop whatever's about to happen from unfolding.

I'm not sure if there's anything capable of dousing the spark that's flared to life.

Satisfaction leaps in his eyes as I tentatively close the distance that separates us. Red lights blare in my head, making me question my decisions, and I grind to a quick halt.

What am I doing?

I'm tap dancing on a dangerous line.

When I remain still—at a crossroads—he whispers, "Come on, sunshine. Just a few more steps."

My gaze drops from his to the necklace draped around his neck.

I'm so close.

And then I can walk away.

Unscathed.

I can leave Maverick McKinnon where he belongs.

Safely tucked away in my memories.

I force myself to eat up the remaining distance. Air gets clogged in my lungs as my shaking palms settle on the broad expanse of his chest. His muscles bunch and tighten, straining beneath the flesh. All the warring thoughts within my brain go silent as my senses are bombarded by him.

The heat of his skin.

The woodsy scent of his cologne that cocoons me in familiarity.

The steady tempo of his heart beating beneath my fingertips.

The harsh breath that belies the calm expression on his face.

I want to soak in this moment so I don't forget a single second of it.

When my palms slide toward the necklace, his larger hands settle over them, drawing them upward until they're tangled around his neck and my body is flush against his.

Our gazes stay fastened.

I couldn't look away even if I wanted to.

"We shouldn't do this," I whisper, trying one last time to stop this from happening.

Even to my own ears, the protest is weak.

"Do you love him?"

"Of course." The truthful response is out of my mouth before I can think better of it.

Fury flashes in his eyes as his voice dips, sounding as if it's been roughed up by sandpaper.

"I've never been one to fuck other dudes' girlfriends." Just as relief rushes from my lungs, he tacks on, "But I'm going to make an exception in this case."

I don't realize that he's walked us toward the bed until the backs of my thighs hit the edge of the mattress and I tumble onto it. My brain spins out of control as he follows me down, his larger body caging me in.

"Tell me you don't want this to happen."

My tongue darts out to moisten my lips.

One word has the power to stop this in its tracks.

Except, when I open my mouth, not a single sound escapes.

I'm slammed with the realization that I can't give him a response.

Because when it comes down to it, I want this.

I want Maverick to run his hands and lips over me like he did the night we spent together. More than anything, I want him to make my body come alive so I can forget the reason this can never be more than a few stolen hours.

When I remain silent, satisfaction dances in his eyes right before his lips crash onto mine.

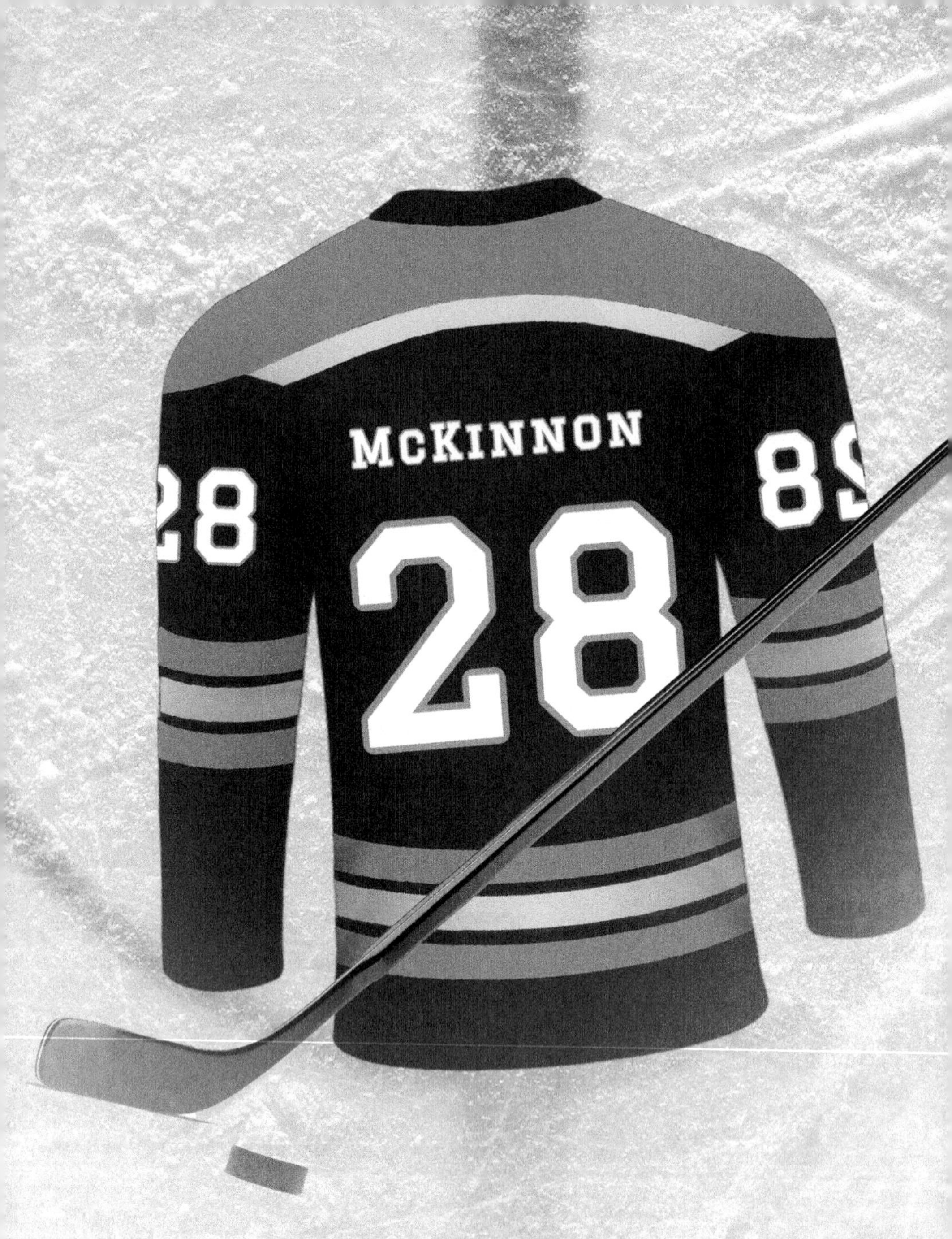

MAVERICK

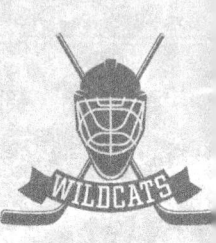

20

How is it possible that her mouth tastes just as sweet as I remember?

Actually, that's a lie.

It somehow tastes even sweeter.

I was really hoping that it wouldn't.

That I'd overembellished it in my memories.

What I want most of all is to fuck this girl out of my system once and for all so I stop thinking about her every waking second of the day. Along with the not-so-waking ones.

I don't want to catch glimpses of her around every corner on campus. Or smell her delicate floral scent when I step into my room.

I want to banish her from my thoughts and memories.

She shouldn't mean a damn thing to me. And yet, the harder I try to convince myself of that, the more I realize just how much of a lie it is and the tightly clenched jaws it has me in.

At some point, I need to face facts.

Because the scary truth—the one I've tried desperately to pretend doesn't exist—is that I'm obsessed with this girl.

And I still don't know what her name is.

The other thing I'm aware of?

That she belongs to River fucking Thompson.

Even the thought of him touching her the way I do, making her scream out her orgasm, makes me want to lose my shit.

Those thoughts are all it takes for my kiss to turn harsh and demanding. Maybe what I'm really trying to do is punish her for sneaking into my thoughts and setting up residence.

I'm beginning to wonder if there's anything I can do to evict her from my brain.

Or wipe her from my memories.

My tongue tangles with hers as our teeth scrape. If I'd thought she would shrink away from my silent demands, that doesn't happen. When a throaty moan tries to escape from her, I swallow it down, taking it deep inside me where it'll never see the light of day.

Somewhere in the back of my brain, I realize that I'm being too rough, but I can't seem to help myself.

When I grow lightheaded from lack of oxygen, I pull away with a growl and nip the point of her chin. Instead of pushing me away, she surprises me by bearing the delicate flesh of her throat in silent offering. I didn't think there was anything that could soothe the beast fighting to break free and escape its confines, but that does the trick.

I suck a deep breath into my lungs in order to calm the chaos that rages beneath my skin. Any moment, I'll burst from it. My touch gentles as I slide down the slender column, kissing and licking my way to the zipper of her jacket.

Fuck.

I didn't realize she was still wearing it.

All of this needs to go.

Now.

I rear back, attacking the layers of clothing that keep her hidden away from me.

Once she's divested of the jacket, I drag her sweater up her torso and over her head before tossing it to the carpet.

My gaze drops to her breasts. The lacy material does nothing to shield them from view. Or maybe the point is to showcase way more than it conceals.

As much as I love it, I fucking hate the idea of her wearing the pretty little garment for anyone other than me.

Instead of dwelling on that thought, I shove it from my brain and lower my face to the valley of her cleavage. I press my lips against the soft flesh between her breasts before nipping at one of the stiffened peaks poking through the sheer material. I make sure to give the same attention to the other side.

The need to see her bare-chested pounds through me like a steady drumbeat until it's all I can think about. I slip my hands around her ribcage and unhook the clasp. As soon as the stretchy material springs free, I pluck the straps from her arms, drawing away the bra.

It meets the same fate as the jacket and sweater.

Her breasts are gorgeous, with tiny blush-colored nipples that are too tempting to ignore. I'm salivating for another taste.

I press the outer sides of each one together before drawing one stiff bud between my lips. Her spine arches off the mattress as I take her deep into my mouth.

"Please," she gasps, fingers tangling in my hair, as if to hold me in place.

Doesn't she realize that it's unnecessary?

There's nowhere else I'd rather be than right here with her.

I release the puckered tip with a soft pop. "Please what? What do you want, sunshine? I'm going to need you to spell it out for me."

A frustrated explosion of sound escapes from her.

I nip at the other hard peak with sharp teeth. "Not good enough."

"I want you to touch me," she says on a gasp.

My tongue darts out to swirl around the areola. "Isn't that what I'm doing? Touching you?"

"Not like that."

"Then how? Tell me."

"I want you to suck on my breasts."

Color stains her cheeks. It's the most adorable thing ever.

"Like this?" I circle my tongue around the little bud before drawing it deep into my mouth.

Another choked response escapes from her as her fingers tighten, the nails scraping against my scalp.

The pain of it grounds me in the moment unfolding between us, and I wouldn't have it any other way.

She's the only thing I'm cognizant of.

All I want to do is give her more pleasure than she knows what to do with.

I want her addicted to my hands, mouth, and cock.

More than anything, I want to make sure that I'm as stuck in her brain as she is in mine.

Is that even possible?

I have no idea.

Once I release her nipple, I lift my head to meet her dazed eyes. They're heavy lidded. She looks blitzed out of her mind. Pride swells within me that I'm the one who put that expression on her face.

"Is that what you needed, sunshine?"

She blinks away the mental fog until her gaze can once again focus on mine. "Yes."

"Do you want more of what only I can give you?"

"I do."

"Then say it."

When her lips press together, I nip the tip of her breast.

She squeaks as the response trembles on her lips. "I want what only you can give me."

I rise, hovering over her until my mouth can ghost across her plush one. Back and forth I strum, barely making contact. When she attempts to close the distance between us, I retreat, not allowing it. That's all it takes for a frustrated groan to break free from her.

I can't help but smirk. "So fucking greedy, aren't you?"

"Not usually."

That admittance calms everything that rages dangerously inside me.

"But you're greedy for me...aren't you, sunshine?"

This time, coercion isn't necessary.

"I am."

"Good answer." My mouth crashes onto hers.

I want to blot out thoughts of all the other guys who've come before me.

When I'm done with her, I'll be the only man who matters.

And that includes River fucking Thompson.

My tongue strokes across the velvety softness of her own.

It wouldn't take much for me to drown within her sweetness.

It takes effort to rip myself away. "You're still wearing entirely too much clothing."

That being said, I crawl down her lithe form, licking and kissing as I go.

Fuck, but she's sweet all over.

Every damn inch of her is sugary goodness.

When I reach the waistband of her dark-wash denim, I pop open the button and drag down the zipper. The grind of metal along with the harshness of her breath is all that can be heard in the silence of the room.

The effect I have on her is music to my ears.

As soon as the turquoise fabric of her panties peeks through the opening, I yank the thick material down her slender hips and thighs before tossing them over my shoulder. I sit back and allow my gaze to lick over her nearly-naked form.

Have I ever seen anyone as gorgeous as this girl?

With her long golden hair spread out around her, it almost glows against the navy comforter she's sprawled out on.

Her nipples are rosy and hard from being played with.

My fingers slip beneath the elastic band that encircles her waist. It's the final scrap of material that bars me from seeing all of her.

As soon as that thought pops into my brain, I draw the silky fabric down her long, lean legs until she's completely bared to my sight.

Fuck.

Fuck.

Fuck.

I'm just as entranced by her now as I was the first time.

I force out a gradual breath, only wanting to slow everything down and take my time.

"Spread your legs, sunshine," I rasp. "I want to see all of you."

For a heartbeat, then two, she holds my gaze before sliding her knees upward and allowing them to fall open. Her delicate lips part, allowing me to glimpse her little pink pussy.

Heaven.

That's the only thought filling my head.

My mouth waters for a taste of her honey.

I slide my hands beneath her ass cheeks to lift her pelvis. My tongue swipes from the bottom of her slit to the top where her clit is buried. I circle the tip around the tiny bundle of nerves before drawing it into my mouth and sucking.

The tortured whimper that escapes from her is music to my ears. I want her cries to make a sweet symphony that stretches on for hours.

I continue lapping at her shuddering softness until she's writhing beneath me.

The more I lick, the creamier she becomes. The taste of her arousal is more delicious than anything I've ever had on my lips.

How the fuck will I ever get enough of her?

Slender fingers tunnel through my hair, locking me in place as I eat her soft flesh.

Before I can even think about making her beg for her orgasm, she cries out, "Please, please, please."

That's all I need to hear.

I stab my tongue deep inside her before pressing my thumb against her clit and rubbing soft circles at the same time. It's more than enough to send her careening over the edge and into oblivion.

Her muscles tighten as she moans out her orgasm. Her pussy spasms the entire time. Not once do I let up on my gentle assault. I don't stop dipping my tongue inside her heat as I stroke her clit. It's only when her body loses its rigidity that I press a kiss against her slit, licking up the honey before straightening to my full height. I pop the button on my jeans before dragging down the zipper. My cock is painfully hard as it throbs with a life of its own.

If I'm not careful, I'll come in my boxers.

When was the last time that happened?

High school?

The more I stare at her slim body, the harder I get.

I kick off my shoes along with the denim before shoving my underwear down my hips and thighs until I'm just as naked as she is. I take a step toward her before remembering that we need protection. With a quick pivot, I round the bed and yank open the nightstand drawer before pulling out a small foil package. I tear it open before returning to the end of the bed.

Instead of remaining sprawled out, she's pulled herself up to a lounging position, resting on her elbows and watching me with eyelids at half-mast. Her legs are still spread wide, allowing me a glimpse of heaven. Unlike before, her pussy is swollen and drenched from my attention.

Another shot of arousal slams into me.

My fingers shake as I prepare to slide the latex over my erection.

"Wait."

My brows draw together as she scoots to the edge of the bed. Her gaze stays pinned to my boner before she flicks her eyes upward to meet mine.

"Can I do it?"

I shake my head, only wanting to slide the rubber into place and sink into her tight heat.

It's all I've been able to think about.

"You don't have to."

Her luminous blue eyes plead with mine. "I want to."

How the hell am I supposed to say no to the beseeching expression on her face?

She's like a damn angel that fell from heaven right into my bed.

I want to tie her up and keep her there forever.

That thought is jarring enough to have everything going silent inside me.

I have no idea where that even came from.

It's so primitive and dark.

Her attention settles on my erection as it bobs inches from her mouth. Before I can say anything else, her tongue darts out to swipe over the tip.

My eyes nearly roll to the back of my head.

Holy hell.

"Mmmm...delicious."

I'm not proud of the garbled sound that escapes from me.

Her wide blue eyes fasten on mine as she draws me inside the warmth of her mouth. It's slowly that she slides up and down the length.

A groan rumbles up from my chest as she sucks the tip, swirling her tongue around it before taking me deep inside. It doesn't take long before I'm nudging the back of her throat and the muscles are constricting around me.

Fuck.

I've had my fair share of blowjobs over the years, but nothing has ever felt as good as this.

It's so damn tempting to tip my head back and close my eyes. All I want to do is immerse myself in the pleasure that threatens to swallow me whole, but there's no way I can look away from the sight before me. The way she holds my gaze while taking my length inside her hot little mouth is nothing short of pure nirvana.

The way she looks sucking my cock is a mental snapshot I won't ever forget.

It'll be one I take out and relive a thousand times over.

Just as my balls tighten, she pops my cock free from her mouth. Her tongue slides along my length to the base before retracing her path to the tip. She plucks the condom from my fingers as she draws the head into her mouth again. I grit my teeth, trying to hold back as she releases me for a second time before slipping the thin latex over my erection and drawing it down carefully so it doesn't tear.

When I'm fully covered, she smirks before scooting back on the mattress and reclining against it again. Another growl vibrates from my chest and a wave of need crashes over me when she spreads her legs wide.

Fuck, this girl...

Actually, that's exactly what I'm going to do.

Pent-up need crashes through me as I crawl onto the bed.

Unable to resist teasing her in the same manner she did me, I tongue her pussy until she's the one breathing hard and squirming. She might have just come, but I'll be damned if I don't wring at least one more from her body.

Maybe two.

When her muscles tighten, I know she's close.

Which is good.

After that blowjob, there's no way in hell I'll last long.

Maybe a dozen strokes or so.

What I refuse to do is come before she does.

With a final kiss, I crawl up her body until the head of my cock is nestled against her entrance. Even through the latex, I feel the way her drenched heat surrounds me.

I bite my lower lip in an effort to maintain some semblance of control and not drive inside her softness.

All I want to do is fuck her into oblivion.

Even that might not be enough.

I've been dreaming about this moment since I got my first taste of her.

Thank fuck it isn't my last.

My muscles turn whipcord tight as I hold myself steadily above her. "Now that you've had that sweet little pussy licked and eaten, are you ready to get fucked?"

In answer, she raises her ass off the mattress, trying to impale herself on my cock.

Every instinct within screams at me to take her, to mark her as my own.

Instead, I lock my jaw and mutter through gritted teeth, "I could have sworn that we had a convo about how you need to use your words."

A whine escapes from her as she wiggles against me, trying to draw me into her tight heat. I don't think I've ever been more at war with myself than I am at this moment.

"Please, I want you to fuck me." Her voice dips, trembling with the need I've stoked to life inside her. "Isn't that what you want? To hear me beg?"

Those pretty words go straight to my head.

The other head.

"Hell yeah. You want my hard dick deep inside your cunt the same way I was down your throat? Then beg for it."

Her eyes widen before her tongue darts out to moisten her lips. I can't resist teasing her entrance, dipping inside an inch or so, only to withdraw, leaving her frustrated and achy.

Her pupils dilate as I continue to torment her. "Please give me your cock."

When her eyelids feather closed, I snap, "Eyes on me. I want to see every expression that flashes in those gorgeous blue depths. Now, try again."

"Please fuck me with your big dick." She gulps before admitting, "I need it."

The way her cheeks flush as I force the dirty words from her mouth turns me on more than anything. I could come in this condom without even being inside her.

As much as I'm tormenting her, it doesn't escape me that I'm doing the same damn thing to myself.

And I love every second of it.

"Tell me how much you need to be fucked."

When I pull away, leaving her bereft, she widens her legs before arching, attempting to close the distance between us.

My eyes narrow. "Watch it, sunshine. Or I'll slap that little pussy for trying to lure me back inside."

The way she thrusts out her lower lip in a pout is adorable. It's tempting to nip at the plump flesh. I'm even more compelled to plunge inside her before I totally lose my mind.

I'm tap dancing on the precipice.

"I want you to fuck me. Just you. *Only you.* I loved having your cock in my mouth and sucking it. The saltiness that leaked from you drove me crazy and made me so horny. Hornier than I've ever been.

Please, I need more. I need you to fill my pussy to the very brim until I can't think about anything other than the way you fuck me."

Possessiveness rushes through my blood as the beast clawing beneath my skin, searching for a way out, manages to tear his way free. With a roar, every tightly held constraint falls away as I drive inside her shuddering softness.

She screams as I bury myself deep inside her body until there's no way to tell where I end and she begins.

Just like she begged me so prettily to do.

For a second or two, I don't move a single muscle.

I simply soak in the way her body wraps around my thick length. When I finally find the strength to pull out, teasing her entrance with the tip, her pussy contracts, drawing me back inside.

Did I really think I could go twelve strokes before losing it?

Ha!

I'll be lucky if I make it half a dozen.

It'll be humiliating if I can't even last that long.

Her pussy feels too damn good.

She feels too damn good.

Everything about this girl does.

Even though I try to fight through it, my balls tighten as I stare into her eyes. Our bodies fit together perfectly, rocking against each other as if we were made for one another.

I can't get that thought out of my head as I continue to fuck her, attempting to force another orgasm from her body.

A muttered prayer of thanks leaves my lips when she moans and her inner muscles spasm. As much as I want to hold out, that's impossible. I do the only thing I can and follow her over the edge and into oblivion. The way her pussy milks my cock, strangling it, has me seeing stars. They dance across my vision. If I weren't having the best damn come of my life, I'd be concerned that I was in the middle of a medical emergency.

It's almost painful.

I ride the wave as long as possible until we're both exhausted from the enormity of what transpired. And then I do the only thing I can and bury my face against the delicate hollow of her throat, inhaling a breath of her sweet floral scent before holding it captive deep in my lungs.

If I thought I wanted her before, it's nothing compared to the need that careens through my veins now, destroying everything in its path as it demands that I lock her down and make her mine.

POCKETFUL OF SUNSHINE
01:10
WILLOW & MAVERICK
04:10
WILLOW
LEUKEMIA
SURVIVOR

21

A gasp escapes from me when he rolls to the side and takes me with him so I end up sprawled across his chest. I squeeze my eyes tightly closed, unwilling to allow reality to intrude just yet.

What just happened between us was...

Perfect.

So perfect that moisture pricks the backs of my eyes.

What I don't want is for him to catch a glimpse of the emotion I'm struggling with.

The gift he just gave me is exactly what I've been searching for all these years. A man who isn't going to treat me like I'm fragile and need to be handled with the utmost of care.

I'm knocked from those thoughts when his arms tighten, pressing me closer to his chest.

His voice is a deep rumble. "Are you going to tell me your name, or should I just keep calling you sunshine?"

It's almost agonizing, the way air leaks from my lungs.

If I were smart, I'd untangle myself from him before slipping from the bed. Then I'd make a promise to do a better job of steering clear of Maverick McKinnon in the future.

But...

How can I do that when he's the only one capable of making my body soar?

His muscles fill with tension. "Is there a reason you won't tell me?"

My heartrate kicks up tempo, beating faster. I nibble my lower lip before reluctantly admitting, "Willow."

"Willow," he murmurs, as if tasting my name on his lips.

That's all it takes for a shudder to slide through me.

His fingers slip beneath my chin to lift it until there's no other choice but to meet the steeliness of his mahogany-colored eyes. "Break up with him, Willow."

When I remain silent, his voice dips, turning harsher. "Did you hear me, sunshine? I want you to break up with him."

"I heard you."

Tension vibrates off him in heavy waves. "Then give me an answer."

I force myself to stay strong. "I can't do that."

A growl escapes him as he flips me onto my back and cages me in with his strength until he's all I'm cognizant of. Before I can draw in a deep, cleansing breath, his lips slam into mine. His tongue plunges inside me the same way his cock had driven into my body a handful of minutes ago.

And then I'm lost in a sea of sensation.

In the taste of him.

The possessiveness of his touch.

Just when it feels like I'm drowning, he breaks off contact and rips himself away. It doesn't escape me that our breathing has turned labored.

Anger sparks in his dark depths as he narrows his eyes. "Does *he* make you feel anything close to this?" There's a pause. "Has *anyone* ever played with your body the way I do?"

I press my lips together and shake my head. This, at least, I can answer with absolute honesty. "No."

"The fucker disrespected you by making out with another girl in front of your damn face." His upper lip curls in disdain. "How can you want to be with someone like that?"

His question churns through my brain. The situation is so much more complicated than he understands. I'm afraid to tell him the truth. Afraid that it'll destroy and taint everything that's happened between us.

When I remain silent, he growls, "You deserve so much better. If he doesn't realize how special you are, then fuck him. I would treat you like a queen." There's a pause as his deep voice dips, flooding with unspent emotion. "Give me a chance to prove it. Just one. That's all I need."

My heart twists beneath my breast. It's so much more agonizing than I could have imagined. "Maverick…"

He shakes his head before nipping at my lower lip and drawing it inside his mouth. Our gazes remain locked in silent battle.

It's only when he releases the plump flesh already swollen from his previous kisses that he demands, "Break up with him."

"It would be for the best if we didn't see one another again."

There isn't a single drop of humor in the laughter that escapes from him. "It's much too late for that, sunshine. Your fate was sealed the moment I caught sight of you on the other side of the plexiglass. It's just that neither of us realized it in the moment."

He's wrong.

The second our gazes collided, I felt the shift in energy. Almost like an impending storm was about to wreak havoc in my life.

And I wasn't wrong.

In a blink, my world was forever altered. Never to be the same again.

But…

If he discovers the truth, everything will change. We're nothing more than a sandcastle. All it'll take is one strong wave to crash onto the shore and destroy everything we've built.

I can't help but try to sway his decision one more time. "We can still walk away from this," I whisper.

The steely look returns to his eyes. "How's that possible when you're my tutor?" He cocks his head. "We're going to be spending a lot of time together this semester. Coach promised that you'd be able to help with all my classes if that's what I needed." His eyes glint. "And I do. I need it. I need *you*."

My heart lurches. "I'll find someone else. Stacie is the tutor you were originally scheduled to work with." Even though I hate the idea, I force myself to say, "She's great. If you gave her a chance, you'd really like her."

His gaze bores into mine as he shakes his head. "Forget it. You're the only one I'll work with."

"But—"

Dismissing me, he slips from the bed and straightens to his full height before stretching lean muscles.

Even though I should look away, I can't. He's beautifully built. All that tightly harnessed power humming beneath the surface, ready to be unleashed.

I can't imagine what it would be like to have that kind of strength.

He probably never catches so much as a cold, while I've spent the previous four years being coddled as if I'm weak.

Sickly.

Maverick is the first person to come along and not treat me like one germ will be enough to take me down.

And I love it.

I've relished the time we've spent together.

But there's a reason for that.

And it's because he doesn't know the truth.

There's so much I've refused to share.

Everything would change between us if he knew. I wish he would accept that the decision I'm trying to make is the best one for both of us.

Unable to sit still for another moment, I throw off the covers and force myself from the bed. "I should go."

He glances over his shoulder with narrowed eyes to meet my gaze. "Are you running back to him now?"

I hate that he thinks I'm happy to bounce between two men. "No. I just need a little time to think."

He pivots, eating up the space between us with a few strides until he's standing directly in front of me. Until I have to tilt my chin to hold his steady gaze. In silence, he unclasps the necklace before carefully placing it around my neck and fastening it so the delicate chain once again hangs there. He toys with the W pendant for a second or so before his fingers drift upward along the curve of my jaw. Only then does he tighten his grip so I can't break free.

"Now that I've found you, I'm not about to let you go, sunshine. If you don't show up at the library at six sharp on Wednesday, I'll rip this damn campus apart to find you."

My heartbeat stutters before slamming into overdrive. "Is that a threat?"

His lips lift into a wry grin as he brushes them across mine for a soft kiss. "No, baby. It's a promise. And if there's anything I pride myself on, it's being a man of my word."

POCKETFUL OF SUNSHINE
WILLOW & MAVERICK
01:10   04:10

WILLOW

LEUKEMIA

22

I push through the glass doors of the Union and into the warmth of the building. My scarf is wrapped around my neck to keep out the biting wind that whips through campus. The temperatures this week have been below average, and I can feel it in my bones. Spring break will be coming up soon, and I'm jealous of everyone who has plans to travel to tropical destinations for some R and R.

I could definitely use a little vitamin D right about now.

The chatter of voices fills my ears as I glance around the crowded space for Elle.

After running into her at Taco Loco, we made plans to meet for lunch and catch up. Even though we just met in the fall, she's turned out to be a good friend.

She's always bubbly and positive.

I caught her in Western's production of *Heathers* last semester, and she was phenomenal. Her dream is to star on Broadway. With her talent, there's no way it won't come true.

When I don't immediately catch sight of her dark head, I consider shooting her a text. It's altogether possible she's not here yet. Just as I reach into my jacket pocket, I see her waving from a corner near a long stretch of floor-to-ceiling windows.

My lips lift into a smile as I wave back and navigate my way through the lunch rush. The Union is always packed this time of the day. There are so many different restaurants to choose from. The options are practically limitless.

The moment I'm within striking distance, Elle tugs me into her arms and gives me a quick hug. "I've missed you, girl. We definitely need to do this more often."

"Maybe if someone wasn't so busy with another production and her hunky boyfriend, we could do that."

The grin that lights up her face makes her appear even more beautiful than she already is. With her coffee-colored eyes and long straight hair that matches in shade, Elle Kendricks is absolutely gorgeous.

A few guys stare as she beams at me.

"Please."

I unzip my jacket and loosen my scarf as we settle at the table. The bright sunlight that pours in through the eastern facing windows feels amazing. Even though it's cold outside, there's not a single cloud marring the cornflower blue sky.

She slides half a sandwich and a bowl of soup in my direction. "I arrived a few minutes early and bought lunch. I hope you like tomato bisque."

"It's perfect. Thanks."

Elle unwraps her turkey and swiss before taking a bite. "I'm starving."

I nod in agreement and do the same.

While we eat, she tells me all about the new campus production she has a part in. Even though Elle is only a sophomore, she's been given a larger role in the spring play. This time they're performing *The Wolves*, a story about a high school soccer team.

"So, what about you?" she asks. "Anything going on? Have you been out with anyone interesting lately?"

I glance away, unsure if I should mention my one-night stand that's turned into a two-night stand. It's not like we went out on a real date or anything like that.

When I remain silent, her brows shoot up. "I know that look. Spill."

I nibble my lower lip as indecision spirals through me.

Elle narrows her eyes. "If you don't tell me right this minute, I'll call in reinforcements. Holland will tell me, for sure. And if she doesn't know, she can help drag all the juicy details out of you."

"All right, all right. Sheesh." With a grimace, I roll my eyes. "I'm sorry I ever introduced the two of you. Every time I turn around, you two are plotting against me."

She flashes a devilish smile. "Just remember that it's all done out of love."

I snort. "Oh, is that what you tell yourself to sleep better at night?"

There's not an ounce of remorse in her expression. "I sleep just fine, if you must know." There's a beat of silence. "Now, tell me."

Ugh.

I wasn't planning to share the details with anyone until I get a better handle on the situation.

And just how I'm going to untangle myself from it.

A little pang of sadness fills me at the idea of never seeing Maverick again or feeling the way his strong hands stroke over me, leaving a trail of delicious sensation in their wake.

"You've left me with no choice. I'm pulling out my phone and calling—"

"Fine... I'll spill." I scoot my chair closer to the table and tuck a stray lock of hair behind my ear before dropping my voice. "I, um, hooked up with someone. Twice."

Her jaw drops and her eyes widen until they look like they're on the verge of falling out of her head and rolling around on the table that sits between us. "Shut up. You're lying."

Heat blooms in my cheeks. I wish I could be more blasé about the encounter, but that's just not me.

And Elle gets that.

She was a virgin before getting together with her boyfriend, who also happens to be her older brother's best friend.

"Like I'd lie about something like that."

She presses against the edge of the table, attempting to bridge some of the distance between us. "Now I really need all the details."

With a jerk of my shoulders, I glance around, hoping that no one is eavesdropping. "It was just a guy I met at a bar."

"Umm...excuse me? Since when do you hang out at bars?"

"I was out celebrating with River after a game."

It's almost comical the way her brows skyrocket into her hairline. "And River let you go home with some dude? Color me stunned. Seriously."

"He doesn't know."

"Well, that makes way more sense. Doesn't he normally run off any guy who tries to shoot his shot with you?"

"Yup," I say with a sigh before waving a hand. "It's one of the reasons I'm here at Western."

She takes a sip of her bottled water. "Then I should thank him. Otherwise, we would've never met."

Some of the tension filling me drains away. "I suppose not. Although, it's doubtful he'd appreciate it."

"So, when are you going to see this mystery man again? Were numbers exchanged?"

"I just saw him yesterday." Even thinking about the way he laid his hands on me is enough to have sparks of arousal detonating in the pit of my belly.

"Any chance this will turn into something more than casual?"

I shake my head.

Sadness chases away any of the desire that had bloomed to life inside me. "I don't think so." The next words tumble from my mouth before I can stop them. "River would definitely have a problem with him."

"Let's be real here, River would have a problem with anyone you dated. That's just facts."

The girl isn't wrong.

"You know that I went through something similar with Brayden? He lost his shit when he found out that Carson and I were sneaking around behind his back. It caused a lot of problems in our relationship. And theirs."

When she ends her story at that point, I say, "You realize that what you're saying doesn't make any of this better, right?"

The edges of her lips quirk. "What has helped is time. He needed to wrap his brain around the fact that I was a grown woman who was more than capable of making her own decisions. And mistakes. River needs to do the same."

"You're right. It's just not an easy conversation to have. He's my twin and super protective."

Any humor brimming in her expression or voice falls away. "After Dad died, Brayden felt like he needed to step up and into that role. It was only after he found out about Carson that we got into a massive fight and stopped talking for a bit. That's when he finally agreed to back off. Sooner or later, River's going to have to accept that you have your own life to live. And that you won't be doing it in a convent."

"He'd be thrilled if I did," I reluctantly admit.

"That's too bad. He needs to get with the program."

Every time I try to tell him that, he refuses to listen. I can't imagine anything I say having a big enough effect to change his behavior.

My shoulders wilt as those thoughts buzz around in my brain. "Like I said before, I'm not sure if it'll go anywhere with this guy."

She waggles her brows. "Well, I certainly hope you enjoy finding out."

"Hey, Elle!" a curvy girl with bouncy brown hair calls out with a wave as she makes her way in our direction. The girl she's with has long, straight hair that's the color of mahogany.

"Hi, Brooke!" Elle glances at the other girl before smiling at her. "Juliette! I haven't seen you for a while." Elle turns to me before making introductions. "This is Willow. She transferred to Western last fall. Willow, this is Brooke and Juliette."

"Hi, it's really nice to meet you." My gaze bounces between the two.

They both seem friendly and approachable.

Although, if they're close with Elle, I can't imagine anything else being true. She surrounds herself with good people.

My gaze resettles on Juliette.

There's something strangely familiar about her. I don't know if I've seen her around campus or if we've had a class together. Is it possible that she's popped into the tutoring center for help?

The little tickle at the back of my brain refuses to be dismissed.

With a tilt of my head, my eyes stay locked on Juliette. "You look really familiar. Have we met before? Maybe had a class together?"

Brooke pats her friend on the shoulder. "Unless you're pre-med, probably not. Little miss smarty pants here is heavy on the sciences, which is exactly why you won't see her around at a lot of the parties."

Guess I can cross tutoring center off the list.

She could probably work there if she had the time.

I can't help but chuckle. "Then, no. We definitely don't have any classes together. I'm in the education program."

Emotion flashes across Juliette's face as she nods. "I thought about teaching as well, but then decided in high school that pre-med was a better fit."

That's all it takes for my mind to tumble back to all the doctors and nurses who helped take care of me. They all have a special place in my heart. Without them and the marvels of medicine, I might not be here right now. I give credit to anyone who wants to pursue a career in the medical field.

"Juliette's boyfriend plays hockey for the Wildcats," Elle adds when silence descends.

Grateful for the change in topic, I say, "My brother plays for the East Town Rattlers."

"We just played that team the other week!"

I nod and say lightly, "Yeah, I was there. It was a hard-fought game." The last thing I want to do is rub the loss in their faces.

"Juliette's brother also plays for the Wildcats," Elle adds conversationally. "His name is Maverick." There's a pause. "Maverick McKinnon. Maybe you've heard of him?"

My eyes widen, and for a heartbeat, it feels like the air gets knocked from my lungs. "Yeah. I think so."

Juliette shrugs. "My brother was pretty upset after that game. Actually, the entire team was. They took the loss hard."

Apprehension skates down my spine.

She leans closer before lowering her voice. "There's a player on that team that he's always had issues with. It goes back to high school when the guy stole his girlfriend. Even after all these years, it still gets chippy when they play each other."

"Oh, ummm..." I shift on the chair, only wanting to shut down this conversation.

With a tilt of her head, interest ignites in her dark eyes. "I'm curious as to who—"

Before she can finish the rest of the sentence, I grab my phone and glance at the screen. A second later, I jerk to my feet. "Shoot. I have a meeting at one. I need to get moving or I'll be late." My gaze flicks to Elle, whose brows are pinched together.

"Really? I thought you were free for the afternoon."

I shake my head as my heart pounds a painful staccato. "Yeah, I thought so too. I can't believe I forgot about the appointment I set up with my advisor to discuss my summer class load."

"Bummer."

I gather up my bag before forcing a smile to my lips. "Brooke and Juliette, it was really nice to meet both of you."

"You too," they say in unison.

"Maybe we can all get together another time. You can meet some of our other friends. I bet you'd like them," Juliette adds.

The sincerity etched across her face has guilt blooming within me.

As much as I'd enjoy getting to know these girls better, that's not going to happen.

With a quick wave, I rush from the table.

It's only when I've put some distance between myself and Maverick's sister that a relieved breath escapes from me.

McKINNON

28

MAVERICK

WILDCATS

23

Impatience simmers beneath my skin as I shove through the locker room doors and toss my stick into the holder before unsnapping the chin strap and yanking the helmet off my head.

Instead of being focused on hockey the way I should be—the way I always have been—I'm more interested in hustling my ass to the library. I'm worried that Willow will attempt to hide from me.

From *this*.

Whatever the hell *this* happens to be.

At the moment, I'm none too sure.

I just know that what I feel for her is different.

It's...more.

The thing that drives me crazy is that this isn't one sided. I know damn well she feels it too. For some reason, she's dead set on fighting this.

On fighting *me*.

And that, I won't allow.

Ten minutes later, I'm showered and dressed, ready to take off.

Ready to get my hands on her. It's only been a few days since I've touched her, and already I'm going through withdrawals.

I flex my fingers to keep everything loose.

A pit has taken up residence at the bottom of my belly. As much as I've been thinking about Willow, I can't stop thoughts of River from invading my brain too

Did she run back to him after we had sex?

Even the thought of that makes me want to plow my fist through something.

Preferably River Thompson's face.

There's no way that douchebag deserves her.

He doesn't even deserve to look in her direction.

Remembering how he'd allowed another girl to maul him in front of her...

It pisses me the fuck off.

She's better than that.

Deserves better than that.

After Sabrina, I didn't bother with relationships. They seemed like more work than they were worth. Especially once I hit college. Division I hockey is no joke. It's more like a full-time job. Add school to that, and it doesn't leave much time for anything else. My only interest in the fairer sex was to release a little steam.

And for the last three years, that's worked well.

There are plenty of groupies on this campus that are happy to have no-strings-attached sex on the regular.

Or blow me.

They never meant anything.

And they sure as shit didn't rent space in my head.

All I can say is that Willow is different.

She's so fucking perfect.

And if River doesn't realize it, he doesn't deserve her in his life.

If I have any say in the matter, he won't.

Willow might not realize it yet, but she belongs to me.

Those thoughts only make me more anxious to see her. I grab my backpack from my locker and swing toward the door.

"Hey, where are you off to?"

I glance at Ryder as he drags a T-shirt over his head.

Things are still...weird between us.

What I don't know is if he's aware of it.

I've considered broaching the subject. But the possibility of coming off like a whiny bitch is what continues to hold me back.

When I remain silent, lost in the tangle of my thoughts, he pops a brow. "Mav?"

I hitch the backpack higher on my shoulder. "The library."

He laces up his shoes. "Maybe I'll come with you. I have a test to cram for, and Jules is out with Carina."

With a frown, I digest that tidbit.

So if Juliette's busy, he can make time for me?

I try to squash the irritation before it has the chance to multiply.

I can't help but snap, "Sorry, already meeting up with someone. Maybe another time."

"Oh? Anyone I know?"

"Nope."

"Huh." Oblivious to my curt tone, a gleam enters his eyes.

"See you back at the house," I mutter, swinging around and stalking to the metal door before he can investigate the situation any further.

It's a relief when I shove into the arena. The icy air stings my lungs as I draw it into my body. Strange as it sounds, it never fails to calm everything that vibrates within me. Ice rinks have always been like a second home to me. Some of my most cherished memories are of watching Dad play hockey or him teaching me how to skate.

When I'm looking for peace, this is the place where I've always found it. There's something about the serenity of it.

Like when Mom was diagnosed with cancer and the chemo left her feeling like shit.

I shake off those painful memories as I shove through the doors and hit the sidewalk.

They're not ones I like to dwell on.

There's nothing worse than wondering if the most important person in your life will be around in six months.

Or a year from now.

Actually, that's not true. The worst thing is coming to the realization that there's not a damn thing you can do about it, that the situation is completely out of your hands.

That's when feelings of helplessness and fear make sucking a full breath into your lungs impossible.

There aren't many things that scare the shit out of me.

Losing someone I love is one of them.

I don't ever want to be put through that kind of hell again.

The relief that rushes through me is palpable when the library comes into view and thoughts of Willow shove cancer from my brain. I slip inside the sprawling brick building before hustling up the staircase to the third floor. As I crest the landing, my gaze coasts over the area, searching for her blonde head.

Part of me wonders if she'll ditch me and I'll have to track her ass down.

At least this time, I'll have more to go on. If that means knocking on River Thompson's door and demanding to see her, that's exactly what I'll do.

Everything loosens inside me when I spot her tucked against the far wall. Her head is angled downward and there's a pair of black glasses perched on the bridge of her nose. The punch of arousal is like a straight shot to my dick.

And here I didn't think it was possible for her to look any sexier.

I was wrong.

Her long hair has been pulled into a messy bun at the top of her head. From this angle, I'm able to glimpse the graceful line of her neck. The sweatshirt she's wearing showcases the delicate curve where it meets her shoulder. All I want to do is kiss my way down the long column of bared flesh.

It's only been a couple days since I've seen her, but it feels more like years. I'm so damn hungry for the sight of her.

The taste of her.

There were a handful of times when I picked up my phone and considered shooting her a text.

In the end, I deleted the messages.

I'm trying to dial it down and not come on too strong.

It's taking every ounce of willpower to hold myself back and not pounce on her.

When I have myself under control again, I close the distance between us before dropping down beside her.

"Hello, sunshine."

Before she can respond to the greeting, I wrap my fingers around the side of her chair and drag it closer. Her eyes widen a second or two before my lips crash onto hers.

Maybe I told myself that I needed to play this cool, but I'm unable to do it.

This girl makes me lose all control.

It's as exhilarating as it is frightening.

When a gasp escapes her, my tongue slips inside the warmth of her mouth. Sweetness blooms to life inside me before rushing through my veins.

There's something addictive about her. It's like I can't keep my hands or lips off this girl.

It's only when someone in the vicinity clears their throat and grumbles about how inappropriate PDA in the library is that her palms flatten against my chest and she gently pushes me away.

That doesn't stop my body from straining toward hers.

Already, her cheeks are stained pink and she's breathless.

I love that I'm the one who does this to her.

As unaffected as she tries to pretend she is, her body gives her away every single time.

More than anything, I want to unravel her and figure out who she is. What makes her tick. Her likes and dislikes.

And not just in the bedroom.

Already, I'm learning those preferences.

My gaze flicks back to hers when she clears her throat. "If I'm going to tutor you, we should probably keep our relationship professional."

A burst of laughter escapes from me. "Professional? Are you being serious?"

Her brows slide together as uncertainty flickers in her eyes. "Yeah."

"Sorry. It's much too late for that. There's nothing professional about our relationship. And FYI—there never will be." I lean closer before whispering, "Now that I've tasted how sweet your pussy is, it's all I can think about."

A dull flush crawls up her cheeks. "Maverick..."

I pop a brow. "Yeah?"

"You shouldn't say things like that."

"Why? It's the truth. One taste of your honey and I was addicted."

I stroke my fingers across her cheek and then her lower lip.

Fuck, but I'm so tempted to nip at her mouth, because I know exactly how much it'll turn her on.

Her pupils will dilate until the black swallows up the bright blue.

There's nothing sexier than Willow when she's aroused.

What I need to do is break down all her defenses until she finally accepts that this one-night stand has turned into something more. Something neither of us saw coming.

When she studies me in silence for a long moment, I wonder if she'll argue.

Here's the thing—she can fight this as much as she wants. It won't change the outcome.

And we sure as hell aren't going to maintain a professional relationship in the interim.

She clears her throat. "So, from what I understand, you need help with English?"

The change in conversation has me releasing the air wedged in my lungs. Until now, I hadn't realized that I'd been holding it captive.

"Yup. I've been working on a paper."

Some of the tension wafting off her dissolves. She seems more comfortable now that talk has turned to school.

As long as she understands that I'll be stealing kisses while we work, we'll be just fine.

"Can I see it?"

I unzip my backpack and pull out my laptop before firing it up. That ordinary act is enough to have dread rushing through my veins. As much as I don't want to show her, that's the reason we're here.

The one way I forced her into spending time with me.

Now I actually have to go through with it.

Fuck.

Maybe this wasn't such a hot idea after all.

Willow seems like a smart girl. It won't take long for her to arrive at the conclusion that I'm either stupid, don't try, or have a disability.

And then she'll see me in a different light.

Or worse, feel sorry for me.

My leg bounces with the nerves that have burst to life within me.

Pity is the last thing I want from her.

I chew my lower lip as I pull up the document and stare at it. Even now, the letters swim before my eyes.

I fucking hate this.

I blink in hopes that the words will make sense.

Frustration spirals through me when it doesn't happen, and I shove the computer toward her.

I should have agreed to work with a different tutor. Maybe I could have said that the only way I'd do it is if she agreed to let me take her out. This was short sighted on my part. But I was afraid she'd disappear again.

Or try to hold me at a distance.

The girl didn't even want to give me her name.

When her glasses slip down the bridge of her nose, she pushes them back in place.

That really shouldn't be so alluring. For the first time in my life, I get the whole sexy librarian thing.

It takes effort to bite back the groan that rises in my throat.

Because trust me, there was nothing hot about our school librarian. She was somewhere in her seventies and would threaten to take a chunk out of you if you returned a book late or—God forbid—damaged one of them. The one time I returned a late paperback, she snatched it from my hands before baring her dentures. As I hightailed it from the library, I'm pretty sure she cradled it in her arms and referred to it as her precious.

So…yeah.

I nibble my lower lip as Willow pulls the laptop toward her and focuses on the screen. I'm watching so closely that I see the exact moment her brow furrows.

That's all it takes for my muscles to lock as I prepare myself for a barrage of questions and comments. Ones that will ultimately leave me feeling like a dumbass.

And that's the last kind of guy she's going to want to fuck.

The longer she remains silent, pressing the down arrow and scrolling through the second half of the paper, the more tension gathers in my shoulder blades as my foot thumps a steady rhythm.

I really fucking hate writing.

And reading.

It's so damn difficult.

Torturous.

How anyone finds pleasure in the activity is beyond me.

The computer helps. Spellcheck and other grammar tools are a lifesaver.

It sucked when I was in elementary school and everything had to be handwritten. Most of my teachers couldn't make heads or tails out of my penmanship.

And spelling?

Forget about it.

I can't spell to save my life.

Even if I memorized the word, the letters don't always come out looking like they should.

I steal another glance at her.

Yep, definite mistake.

There's only one way this is going to end.

And that's badly.

POCKETFUL OF SUNSHINE

WILLOW & MAVERICK

01:10   04:10

WILLOW

LEUKEMIA

24

My thoughts churn as I digest the final paragraph of Maverick's paper. The topic focuses on whether college athletes should be paid. Despite the punctuation and grammatical errors, it's both interesting and informative. There are some paragraphs that are short and abrasively to the point. They need to be expanded with more supporting examples and evidence to back up the ideas. Then there are others that seem to ramble and meander before finally coming to a close. It's almost like he forgot the main point he was trying to get across to the reader. Better organization of his thoughts would also help.

Those are all correctable problems we can work on.

What struck me most is that reading Maverick's paper reminded me of all the times I helped my brother with his homework in high school. There are the same patterns of errors with punctuation, grammar, and organization that lead me to believe Maverick might have the same issue.

Dyslexia.

I'm certainly not an expert, and I could be wrong.

That's what I'm most afraid of.

As I gather my thoughts, I peek at the hockey player, only to find him watching me intently.

The easy confidence of before is notably absent from his expression. In its place is a look of tension.

It only reinforces my hunch.

If he's anything like River, it's a sensitive topic.

My brother struggled all through elementary school before finally being diagnosed in fourth grade. By then, the damage had been done and he hated school. He was often made to feel like he wasn't as smart as his peers. When he would get frustrated, he'd end up acting out and causing problems for his teachers. Or he'd get into fights with other students.

There were times when I wondered if River would have the grades to get into college. He worked with a tutor all through high school and managed to turn things around for himself.

I'm proud of him for that.

His path to playing hockey at East Town wasn't easy.

How ironic is it that the more I get to know Maverick, the more I realize how much he and River have in common. If they weren't constantly pitted against one another, they could have been friends.

It's not always easy to find people who have walked a similar path and understand the challenges you've faced.

"Is it total trash? Just don't tell me that I have to start from scratch, because this paper is due in two days and there's no way in hell I'll be able to get it done."

I force a smile, wanting to alleviate the strain woven through his deep voice. Before I realize it, my hand drifts to his bare arm where he's shoved up the sleeves of his sweatshirt.

His attention drops to the place where we're now connected.

Heat stings my cheeks when I realize what I've done.

Which is kind of comical, because we've been far more intimate than me touching his arm in a public space and offering support. Although, this is the first time I've initiated physical contact.

The moment I try to remove my fingers, his other hand settles over mine, locking it in place.

My gaze collides with his before becoming ensnared in his dark depths. That's all it takes for my mouth to turn bone dry, making speech impossible.

"I like when you touch me."

The gravel in his voice settles at the bottom of my belly like a heavy stone.

Truth be told, I like touching him too, but I'm not about to admit that. I get the feeling if I give him an inch, he'll take a mile.

"You don't have to redo it. There's a lot here for us to work with," I reassure.

His muscles gradually loosen and his brows rise. "You think so?"

A mixture of hope and surprise rings throughout those three little words.

My lips lift into more of a smile as his fingers stay locked around mine. "Yeah. We just need to give it a little more organization, add a few more supporting statements, and clean up some of the grammar and sentence structure. It'll take some work, but it's much easier than starting over. And two days is plenty of time to make adjustments."

"That doesn't sound so bad," he says with a nod.

"I promise it won't be. Here's the caveat—I'm more than willing to point out areas that can be improved and give suggestions, but I'm not going to rewrite the paper for you." I don't necessarily want to bring up his possible disability, but it would help to know exactly what I'm dealing with. "I spent a lot of time in high school helping my brother with his homework." I force out the rest. "Your paper reminds me of his."

He stills as his grip tightens around mine. "Oh?"

"He has dyslexia and really struggled with it. Especially before he was diagnosed..." Unsure what else to say, my voice trails off.

I know I've hit the mark when color seeps into his cheeks and he glances away.

My heart twists as I scoot closer. "I'm not trying to embarrass you. It's just...it'll be easier for us to work together if I understand what the issue is."

His gaze settles on mine as he releases a pent-up breath. "Yeah, I have dyslexia. My parents realized what was going on right away because my dad also has it. So, I had early intervention."

"I'm sure that helped. My parents were reluctant to believe that there was anything wrong with my brother."

Some of his embarrassment fades. "You never mentioned having a sibling. Is he older?"

I chew my lower lip and nod. "Yeah."

Technically.

By four minutes.

"Does he attend Western?"

"No." I clear my throat, no longer wanting to discuss my family. I'm afraid he'll put two and two together and figure out that River isn't my boyfriend.

But my brother instead.

And then all hell will break loose.

It would be so much easier if I didn't feel anything for Maverick. If I didn't like the way it feels when he lays his hands on me. Or enjoy the time we spend together.

But that's not the case.

It takes effort to banish that thought.

"What about you?"

As soon as the question leaves my lips, I realize that I met his sister the other day at lunch. It's tempting to admit the truth, but I hold it back.

"Just a sister. She's older by a year and also attends Western. She's pre-med."

"That's really impressive."

His lips curve as he nods. "Juliette is really smart. She's the one who helped me in school when I needed it. Even when I came here, she made time to work with me, but the more challenging her classes have become, the less she's been able to do that." He jerks his shoulders and stares at the computer screen. "Plus, she'll graduate this spring and won't be around much longer, so I need to figure it out on my own."

It's obvious from the pride that fills his tone that he doesn't resent her for not struggling with the same academic challenges.

"Sounds like you two are really close."

"We are." For a long moment, he's silent before admitting in a softer voice, "Our family was always tight, but after Mom was diagnosed with breast cancer, we became even more so. It's the reason Juliette decided to become a doctor."

A thick lump swells in my throat at what he's just revealed. The emotion that had flashed in Juliette's eyes when she'd told me about her career choice now makes more sense. "That must have been difficult."

I know exactly how much a loved one's diagnosis can affect their family members. It's like a windshield getting hit with a rock and the cracks in the glass spidering outward, touching everyone. Even distantly.

Emotion flashes across his face. "It sucked. I've never felt so powerless in my life."

"I can imagine."

"There were times when she was so weak and sick from the chemo, all I could do was sit by her side and keep her company so she wasn't alone. Nothing I did took away her pain or lessened it. The worst was watching as she lost weight and then her hair. At one point, she was a much thinner, paler shadow of her former self. And I lived in constant fear that she'd be taken from us."

My heart contracts at his rough words. It's so tempting to gather him up into my arms and hold him tight.

"I'm sure it meant a lot to her that you were there, offering support and cheering her on. When someone is battling an illness, having that love can be a source of real strength. It gives you something to fight for during those days when you're so tired and sick that you just want to give up."

His gaze sharpens on me as he nods. "Yeah, that's exactly what she said. Sounds like you've been through a similar situation."

I glance away as everything he confided swirls through my brain. "Unfortunately, I think most people have been touched by cancer in some way."

Air deflates from his body as his shoulders collapse. "You're right about that. Cancer fucking sucks."

I squeeze his hand again, only wanting to pull him back to the present and out of the painful memories. "Is she all right?"

"Yeah. She's been in remission for a couple of years now. Although, every time she goes in for bloodwork or a checkup, I worry that something will pop up and it'll send our family tumbling down the rabbit hole again. When she was first diagnosed, I did a ton of research so I could understand what was happening and how bad it was. I was afraid that my parents weren't being truthful about the prognosis because they didn't want us to stress. What I know is that if it comes back for a second time, it'll be more aggressive."

Goose bumps break out across my skin. Even though they don't mention it, I'm all too aware that my family worries about the same thing.

It only makes me realize that River and Maverick have even more in common.

Although, it's doubtful either of them would appreciate me pointing out the similarities.

"I know it's easier said than done, but you can't live your life waiting for the other shoe to drop or worrying about things that might never come to pass." The words burst out of my mouth before I can stop them. "None of us are guaranteed anything in this world. I don't know your mom, but I doubt she'd want you to live in constant fear for what the future will bring."

It's certainly not what I want for the people in my life.

"And she doesn't want to be constantly reminded of her sickness and what will happen if it returns."

There's nothing worse than your family staring at you like you have an expiration date tattooed across your forehead. Almost as if they're already mourning your loss.

His brows knit as he digests my outburst. "I get what you're saying. It's just..." His tongue darts out to moisten his lips as his steady gaze searches mine. "Hard to make peace with the fact that one of the most important people in your life could be taken from you at any time."

"I know. But what's the alternative?" There's a beat of silence. "To hold yourself back from caring or loving anyone? To isolate yourself so you never have to feel pain? It's part of the human condition. No one goes through it without experiencing both love and loss. It's just not possible. Maybe you don't realize it, but there's freedom in accepting and embracing that during our lifetime, you'll have to get through it."

"I guess I'm still trying to work through everything in my head." His attention drops to where our hands are still clasped. "I'm not there yet."

My muscles soften at the heartfelt conversation we're having in the middle of the library.

It's not something I would have expected.

At every turn, Maverick continues to surprise me.

His gaze lifts to mine again. "Thank you."

"For what?"

"I don't know," he mutters with a shrug. "Letting me unload. Other than talking to my sister, it's not something I usually do." His lips quirk as some of the heaviness fades from his expression. "Shocker...it actually feels good."

My heart swells with so much emotion that there's a possibility it'll burst. He has no idea just how intimately acquainted I am with what he's been through. It's so tempting to share my experiences with him, but I'm afraid that Maverick would look at me differently.

Treat me differently.

And that's the last thing I want.

Before I can refocus our conversation and suggest that we get back to work, he pops to his feet and pulls me up with him.

My eyes widen at the sudden movement. "Where are we going?"

"You'll see."

With his fingers locked around my wrist, he drags me through the stacks until we're buried in a distant corner, away from prying eyes.

When he grinds to a halt, I stumble into his bigger body. His hands wrap around my upper arms before he forces me backward until my spine hits the shelving unit.

"Maverick?" I squeak.

"I'm taking your advice and living in the moment."

Before I can come up with a response, his mouth crashes onto mine and his tongue sweeps over the seam of my lips. As soon as I open, he slips inside to tangle with my own. And then I'm lost. My palms settle on the steely strength of his chest. Instead of pushing him away, I drag him closer until my arms can twine around his neck.

A groan rumbles up from him. The deep vibration of it is enough to flood my panties with heat.

He pulls away enough to mutter, "You have no idea how much I've wanted to do that. It's all I've thought about these past few days."

And then his lips are colliding with mine again, and he's dragging me down to the bottom of the ocean where sucking in a full breath becomes impossible. I don't realize that his hand has slipped down the front of my leggings and panties until he slides a finger deep inside my pussy.

When a gasp escapes from me, he swallows it up.

It's leisurely that he pumps his finger a few times. The thick slide of it feels amazing. It's enough to make me forget that we're in the middle of the library and anyone could walk past and catch a glimpse of what we're doing.

When I whimper, he nips my lower lip before asking, "Feel good, sunshine?"

The more he plays with my body, the less I care about what's going on around me.

The stroke of his tongue matches the pace of his finger. There's something so delicious about the way he takes me from zero to one hundred in the blink of an eye. It doesn't take long before my body is straining for more and I'm dancing precariously close to the edge, waiting to be nudged over the precipice.

"Your pussy is so damn creamy," he groans, all the while continuing to torment me. "I haven't been able to stop thinking about how good you taste."

That husky admittance is all it takes to send me tumbling over the cliff. The orgasm that slams into me is enough to steal my breath away.

"That's it. Ride my hand. Show me exactly how much you like the way I play with you."

Stars explode behind my eyelids as I grind my pelvis against him. There's so much sensation rushing through my veins. It almost becomes too much for the confines of my skin.

By the time the last shockwave zips through me, my knees weaken. If he weren't holding me pressed against the bookshelves, I'd slide to the floor in a puddle.

Maverick brushes another kiss against my lips as his finger glides in and out of my over-sensitized body.

"You're gorgeous when you fall apart."

His eyes darken with hunger as he pulls out before rubbing soft circles against my clit and slipping free of my leggings. His gaze stays pinned to mine as he brings his finger to his mouth and sucks the digit between his lips.

I didn't think it was possible for his eyes to become any more heated.

The sparks that fly from them nearly singe me alive. Even though he just made me come, already need is brewing to life inside me.

"Just as delicious as I remember."

When I remain silent, unable to wrap my brain around an appropriate response, there's a flash of white teeth as he grins.

"I think we've studied enough for one night. Let's get out of here."

MAVERICK

McKINNON 28

Wildcats

25

I sneak another peek at Willow as we drive. It's been a long time since there's been a girl I was interested in sitting beside me in my truck.

There's a slight furrow to her brow as she stares out the windshield. I get the feeling she's lost in the thorny tangle of her thoughts. When I mentioned grabbing something to eat, reluctance had flashed across her face, and I knew her mind had circled back to River.

It had taken every ounce of self-control not to ask if she'd broken up with him yet. I'm trying to take this slow and give her time to make a decision. There's no damn way he'd treat her the way I would. She already admitted that no one else has ever made her feel the way I do.

Shouldn't that be enough?

Instead, I'd tangled my fingers with hers and pressed sweet kisses against her lips. What I've learned is that I can bend her to my will if I distract her with my mouth.

And hands.

And cock.

I'm not above doing any of those things to get what I want.

Which is her.

I just need to be patient.

My mind trips back to the library and everything I'd divulged. I never expected that opening up and sharing my fears about Mom would be so easy. The words had tumbled off my tongue before I could stop them. We might not know each other well, but I feel like I could share my deepest darkest secrets with her.

Stranger than that, I trust her to keep my confidence.

And I don't have any reason to believe that. Especially when she's with the one guy I can't fucking stand.

But I do.

The knowledge is innate.

There are times in life when you meet someone that you instantly click with. Someone you feel like you've known forever, even though that's not the case.

It's a rare occurrence.

Like a shooting star.

That's exactly what it feels like with Willow.

I'm afraid that if I loosen my grip, I'll lose it.

I'll lose *her*.

The more time we spend together, the more wrapped up in her I get.

I'm afraid of what will happen if she decides not to end it with River.

That thought is enough to have my fingers tightening around the steering wheel until the knuckles turn bone white.

It takes effort to loosen them.

I flick another glance in her direction. What I've discovered from the little time we've spent together is that she's not very adept at hiding her feelings. Every thought is written across her expressive features for all to see.

It's just one of the things I like about her.

Her kindness is the other. It hadn't been easy to divulge my diagnosis, but when I did, she treated it as if it were normal.

As if *I* were normal.

Until that moment, I hadn't realized that it was a burden I carried with me. Like it was a dirty secret, even though no one in my family had ever made me feel that way.

Sharing it with Willow had somehow lightened the load.

I steal another glance at her. The way she avoids my gaze, all the while pinning her lower lip with her teeth, is just more evidence that she's conflicted about the situation.

It's not like either of us saw this coming.

Sure, maybe the first night I took her home it was to strike out at River. But that had only been a small part of it.

More like the cherry on top of a decadent sundae.

The real reason is that I wanted her.

Had to have her.

I consider broaching the subject as I turn into the parking lot of Harvey's Eats and Treats.

Maybe that's exactly what I need to do.

Put it all on the table and tell her how I feel.

"Is this where we're eating?" she asks, gaze sliding to me for the first time.

"Yeah. Have you been here before?"

She shakes her head. "Looks cute, though. Kind of like one of those diners you'd see in the movies."

"A few of my teammates were talking about it, and I thought we could check it out." I pull into a space and cut the engine. "You good with that?"

"Yeah."

We exit the truck and meet near the tailgate. I don't think twice about slipping my fingers around hers and tugging her closer. When we reach the glass door to the restaurant, I pull it open and usher her over the threshold. A little bell chimes as we step inside.

It's like tumbling back in time.

The floor is made up of black and white checkered tiles while the ceiling is covered with shiny silver tin. Framed photographs of old Hollywood stars decorate the walls along with Coca-Cola memorabilia. Booths and tables dot the brightly lit space. The former are upholstered in red vinyl with gleaming white linoleum tops. Music from decades ago pours through the speakers from a jukebox at the far end of the restaurant.

The joint has a cool vibe.

Just as a waitress snags my attention, someone calls out from one of the tables, "Hey, Mav! Over here."

I turn and scan the area, only to find Wolf and Colby along with their girlfriends.

I mean their wives.

I raise a hand to Wolf in greeting. I've always liked him. Even when he was moody and mostly kept to himself. Now that he's with Fallyn, he's opened up and seems happier. More content. Hell, every now and then, the guy actually cracks a smile.

"Pull up a chair," Colby adds. "We just got here ten minutes ago."

I glance at Willow with a raised brow, hoping she's cool spending a little time with my teammates. "Is that okay?"

Uncertainty flashes across her face as she takes in the couples before her lips lift into a hesitant smile. "Sure."

I grab two chairs from a nearby table before making introductions. Both Fallyn and Britt are friendly and welcoming. I could kiss them for doing their best to make Willow feel comfortable. They include her in the conversation, trying to get to know her. It doesn't take long before Willow is laughing and chattering as if she's known them for years.

Honestly, it's nice to take a moment and simply watch her. The way her shoulders loosen and her eyes brighten. The throaty chuckle that falls from her lips feels like a warm blanket I want to cocoon myself in.

It's strange to realize that I could spend the entire night doing exactly that.

The spell woven around me is only broken when Colby nudges my shoulder with his own. It takes effort to tear my attention away from Willow.

When our gazes finally collide, he gives me a knowing look before saying under his breath, "Looks like another Wildcat has bitten the dust."

WILLOW

POCKETFUL OF SUNSHINE
WILLOW & MAVERICK
01:10 — 04:10

LEUKEMIA

26

Both Fallyn and Britt hug me goodbye as if we're long-lost friends instead of just meeting for the first time a couple of hours ago. The three of us part ways outside the diner, with the promise of getting together without the guys, before Maverick hustles me into the front seat of his truck.

As we drive back to campus, he says, "You seemed to really hit it off with Britt and Fallyn."

"I did." I shift on my seat before admitting, "I'm still getting to know people at Western, so thanks for introducing us. They seem really great."

I spent all junior year of high school and then part of my senior year in and out of the hospital. After a while, a lot of my friends moved on with their lives. They were busy going to parties on Friday nights, football games, dates with boys, or hanging out at the mall.

Activities I couldn't take part in.

Holland is the only one who stayed steadfast by my side. Anytime I ended up in the hospital, she'd show up with games to play and books to read. When I was home and well enough to have company, we'd watch movies and eat buttery popcorn. When that wasn't possible, we'd watch something together over FaceTime. Holland has a real weakness for horror movies. There was tons of shrieking and laughing at the jump scares.

She will always be my ride or die.

"The whole group they hang with is cool." The casual look he flicks in my direction belies the intensity brewing in his eyes. "Including my sister. You'll have to meet her some time. I think you two would like each other."

My teeth scrape across my lower lip. It's tempting to tell him that we've already met and that I do like her. She was so sweet and kind. "Sure."

"Sounds like you've already made plans to get together with them."

I nod as my fingers twist in my lap. Whatever this is with Maverick feels so much more serious than before I met up with him at the library. We've hit the gas pedal and are now rocketing through hyperspace. "Maybe early next week."

"I don't think anyone mentioned it, but around the locker room, they're known as the girlfriends."

The girlfriends?

That's kind of funny.

Before I can comment, a smile simmers across his lips and he adds, "Correction, Fallyn and Britt are known as the wives."

My brows shoot up. "Excuse me?"

"From what I understand, Wolf and Fallyn were close childhood friends. Something happened when they were teenagers that ripped them apart, and he's been secretly pining for her ever since. Once they got together, he decided to lock her down for good. Last month, we all flew to Vegas for their wedding, and while we were there, Colby and Britt tied the knot as well." His gaze flicks my way. "Maybe I'm just clueless, but I didn't even know they were going out. It all happened so fast. So, yeah...those two are the wives, and then Carina, Viola, Stella, and my sister Juliette are the girlfriends."

I turn toward him, needing to clarify what I remember being mentioned at the lunch with Elle. "So, your sister is dating one of your teammates?"

Now that's interesting.

River would flip the fuck out if I mentioned any interest in one of his friends.

Then again, he'd lose his shit if I got serious with anyone. His overprotectiveness knows no bounds.

Some of Maverick's previous mirth drains away as sadness flickers in his eyes. "Yeah. Juliette is dating Ryder."

"So…are you two just teammates or actually friends?"

"We've been neighbors since kindergarten and always played on the same travel teams. We all grew up together."

I study him in the darkness. "Did their relationship take you by surprise?"

"Do you want an honest answer?"

"Of course."

"It did. In hindsight, I realize there's always been something brewing beneath the surface." He jerks his shoulders. "Maybe I just didn't want to acknowledge it."

His response circles through my brain as I try to put myself in his shoes. "Is it weird between the two of you?"

His brows pinch, as if giving the question serious consideration. "Yeah, it is. We used to spend a ton of time hanging out, and now that they're an item, that's no longer the case. If Ryder has down time, they spend it together. It's like they're attached at the hip." There's a pause before he adds, "When it came to the two of us, Juliette was always the odd man out. Not in a bad way or anything. We had our inside jokes and stories, and now it's them who have that. Sometimes, they'll just look at each other and smile or laugh, and I'll stare at them, feeling like I've missed something." He chances a look at me. "She gained a boyfriend, but it feels like I've lost my friend. Kind of sucks."

I can't help but reach out and squeeze his thigh. "I'm sorry. Have you considered talking to him about it?"

The horror that flashes across his face as he shoots another look in my direction is enough to make me laugh. "Fuck no. Are you kidding me?"

"I'm really not. Ryder probably doesn't have any idea that you're hurt or miss your friendship."

"Do you have any idea what a wuss that would make me look like?"

A sigh escapes from me. "You realize that it's perfectly normal to discuss your feelings, right?"

"Maybe for chicks it is, but not for a guy."

I shake my head, feeling even worse for him. "That's not true at all. Men have feelings just like women, and it's okay to express them. In fact, it's necessary. Healthy. There's so much strength in being able to do that," I say lightly.

His lips press together, and I can almost see him turning over my words. "I'll think about it," he finally concedes.

"Good."

As we reach the edge of campus, he throws out the invite. "Come home with me?"

I really shouldn't.

The more time I spend with Maverick, the more layers I peel back. There's an unexpected depth buried beneath the surface that continues to draw me in.

"Sunshine?"

For better or worse, the endearment is enough to send the last of my walls crumbling.

"Okay."

McKINNON
28
89
28

MAVERICK WILDCATS

27

Hayes flicks a look our way as I walk through the front door of the hockey house with one arm thrown around Willow's slender shoulders. All I want to do is keep her anchored to my side for safekeeping.

More than that, I want to know she's mine.

I've never wanted to belong to someone else, but with her, I do.

I want her to claim me.

The thought should knock me back a step and have me reevaluating everything. Instead, something inside me settles. It's like the tumblers of a safe finally falling into place.

I'm still mentally tripping about all the things I've shared with her this evening. When we're together, everything I normally keep tightly contained or try to ignore pours out of me. I have no idea why I'm so comfortable in her presence. She manages to smooth out all my rough edges.

She really is like pure sunshine in a bottle.

And when I'm with her, I feel the warmth of it radiating on my face. I just want to bask in her light.

I give Hayes a quick chin lift in greeting. He returns the gesture before his gaze slices to Willow. His brows pinch as his easy-going expression turns inscrutable.

The tension that fills the atmosphere is almost enough to give me pause.

Willow doesn't make eye contact with him. Instead, her attention remains focused on the staircase.

A minute or so later we're in my room and I'm locking the door behind us, shuttering away the rest of the world.

But still...the weird energy downstairs circles through my brain.

"Do you know Hayes?" The question is out of my mouth before I can rein it back in.

She glances away before her gaze resettles on mine again and she straightens her shoulders. "We attended the same high school."

My brows shoot up at that bit of information. "Huh. I didn't know that."

She shrugs. "We were never close."

A strange silence descends as she unzips her black jacket. I consider asking a few more questions, wanting to lay the matter to rest, but I'm more interested in getting my hands on her.

Within seconds, my arms slip around her body and my lips are descending. There's something about the feel of her that quiets all the static in my brain, making it impossible to think about anything but her.

Instead of making me work for it, she opens so that my tongue can slip inside her warmth to tangle with her own.

The first taste is dizzying and hits me like a freight train.

The need to touch her bare flesh spirals through me. I can't stand the layer of clothing that separates us and keeps me from her.

I shove the jacket off her shoulders. That's all it takes for the heavy material to drop to the floor at our feet. Her sweatshirt is the next item to be removed. We only break away long enough for me to whip the soft fabric over her head. Already, her blue eyes are dazed and lips swollen from my kisses.

Everything inside me swells.

I fucking love that I'm the one who put that expression on her gorgeous face.

It's one that says she needs a good fucking.

By me.

Only me.

Unable to resist, my hands cup the softness of her breasts through the silky material of her bra. It doesn't take long for her nipples to stiffen. I tweak the hard little buds until a moan slips free from her lips.

"Do you like that, baby?" I know she does. Every reaction I'm able to tease from her tells me so.

But I want her to acknowledge it.

"Yes."

When I tweak them again in tandem, her pupils dilate in response.

"Do you enjoy the way I bring your body to life?"

Her tongue darts out to moisten her lips. "You know I do. No one's ever touched me like this."

It wouldn't matter if they had, but it fucking gets me off to hear her admit that I'm the only one who's figured out the way she likes her body played with. What turns her on and makes her pussy sob uncontrollably. All I want to do is please this woman and give her everything she craves.

When it comes down to it, I want her addicted to my touch.

I want her in as deep as I am, with no way to get free.

I don't even want her thinking about it.

The need to see her golden strands all long and loose thrums through me. It's carefully that I pull the tie from her hair until the thick mass tumbles around her shoulders and down her back.

Only then do my fingers slip around her ribcage to unclasp the clasp of her bra. A few seconds of fumbling has it snapping apart. The thin straps slide down her arms until the sheer cups fall away from her breasts.

A groan works its way up my throat. "Fuck, but you're beautiful."

Unable to resist, I play with the stiff peaks before drawing one inside my mouth and then the other.

When another whimper escapes from her, I drop to my knees, dragging both the leggings and panties down her hips and thighs until the material puddles around her ankles. Her hands brace against my shoulders as she lifts one leg before doing the same with the other so I can strip the cotton away until she's totally bare.

Her palms drift to my cheeks as I stare up at her. With her long, golden hair floating around her shoulders, she looks like an angel dropped from heaven. I could stare at her like this for hours.

My hands slide around her slender hips before pulling her forward until I can bury my nose against the V between her legs and inhale a deep breath, drawing her sweetness into my lungs. I've had my fair share of pussy, but none of them have ever affected me like this.

The small taste I had at the library has only whetted my appetite for more.

I've never been so hungry for a woman.

I knead her ass cheeks with my palms, loving the feel of her firm flesh in my hands, as I inhale her sweet scent for a second time. Her fingers tunnel through my hair as my tongue delves between her thighs to lick her. I've barely touched this girl and she's already drenched.

She's so fucking needy.

Greedy.

And I love it.

Get off on it.

I continue eating at her, nibbling at her soft flesh along with her clit. The whimpers that I'm able to tease from her are music to my ears.

Only wanting to get closer, I lift one leg over my shoulder, opening her up wide so I can lick every fucking inch. The more I play with her, the more soaked she becomes.

I drag my tongue over her slit from the top of her mound to the bottom and then back up again before dipping inside. Her fingers tighten in my hair to the point of pain, but it's exactly what's needed to keep me grounded in this moment.

There's nowhere else I'd rather be than between her legs, giving her as much pleasure as possible. When her muscles tighten, I know she's close to finding her release. Instead of pushing her over the edge the way every instinct within me demands, I press a kiss against her swollen lips and rise to my feet.

A gasp escapes from her as her eyes widen. "I thought you were going to..."

Her words come out sounding garbled and breathless, desperation dripping from every syllable.

I smirk. "Oh, I know exactly what you thought, sunshine."

As soon as I lift her to my chest, her arms tangle around my neck and her legs lock around my waist.

When she grinds her pelvis against my sweatshirt as if her life depends on it, I growl, "You get yourself off before I have a chance to get inside you and I'm going to smack that delectable ass. Understand?"

A puff of frustration escapes from her.

There's something ridiculously sexy about how wound up she is.

Not to mention, she's completely naked while I'm fully clothed.

With our mouths fused, I lay her on the mattress before straightening to my full height. The way she wriggles around makes my cock unbearably hard. Any moment, I'll unload in my jeans.

And just like I refuse to allow her to come until I've teased and tortured her, I won't allow that to happen either.

I drag the sweatshirt and T-shirt over my head before tossing them to the floor. The thick denim is the next article of clothing that's removed in record speed, until I'm as naked as she is.

The way her heavy-lidded eyes roam over my chest and abdominals before settling on my dick feels more like a physical caress. One I'll never get enough of.

"Please." The word sounds as if it's been wrung from her body.

Instead of touching her, my hand drops to my erection until my fingers can tighten around the thick length before I slide it from the tip to the root and then back again.

"Please what?"

My gaze never relinquishes hers as I stroke my cock, tightening my grip until it turns painful. Moisture beads from the slit before dripping. I use my other hand to gather it on my fingertip before closing the distance between us and swiping it over her parted lips.

"Open for me."

When her pretty little mouth pops wide, I slide the finger inside. She doesn't need to be told to suck. She does it instinctively. My eyelids droop at the way she pulls on the digit. It's enough to have even more arousal leaking from my dick.

I could come from this alone.

Unable to stand another second of the sweet torment, I slip my finger free. I can't resist tweaking her nipples before giving the top of her pussy a sharp slap. It's not enough to cause pain. Just enough for pleasure to rush in and make her throb with awareness. Her pupils dilate as she squirms beneath my steady gaze. My hands tighten around her hips before I flip her over and drag her to the edge of the bed.

"On your knees, sunshine."

Satisfaction floods through me when she scrambles to do my bidding with her pert little ass facing me. My hand settles between her shoulder blades before pressing her front into the mattress. Her breath quickens as her head swivels until one cheek rests against the comforter.

My fingers stroke down the long line of her spine to the cleft between her heart-shaped ass.

"You look so fucking beautiful like this, just waiting for me to take you."

I press her legs farther apart until I'm able to glimpse every delicate inch.

Both her pussy and ass are on full display.

Open.

For me.

Pleasure swells within me as more wetness gathers on her pouty lips, making them shiny.

I stroke my hands over her ass cheeks, massaging away the tension that fills her muscles, keeping them—and her—pliable as my gaze zeros in on both of her pretty little holes.

I drag my thumb over the puckered muscle. "Has anyone ever touched you here?"

Her breath catches, and if I weren't so attuned to her every intake of air or shift of her body, I would have missed the whispered response.

"No."

I can't help but love that she's never allowed anyone else to play with her ass.

"Arch your back," I command.

The way she bows her spine, raising her ass higher in the air until even more of her is visible, is enough to make me come undone. I drop to my knees until I'm eye level with her backside.

This girl has no fucking clue how sexy she is.

"So damn beautiful," I groan, my teeth scraping across the rounded curve of her flesh.

My fingers dip inside her pussy before I pump them rhythmically. Only when they're completely coated in her cream do I carefully probe the tight ring.

A gasp slips free from her as her body turns rigid and she clenches against the foreign intrusion.

I pepper kisses against her delicate flesh. "Do you want me to stop?"

She sucks in a lungful of air before releasing it back into the atmosphere. "I...don't think so."

"As much as I'm dying to play with this perfect little ass, we don't have to take this any further."

"Just...go slow." There's a pause. "Please."

"I will, sunshine. Promise. All I want to do is give you as much pleasure as possible. If it's sometimes tinged with pain, I promise it'll be worth it."

When her muscles loosen, I press another kiss against her soaked lips, licking up her honey.

I don't think I'll ever be able to get enough of it.

There's something profound about the trust she's so willingly handed over to me. And I refuse to take it lightly.

I caress her rosebud, grazing the muscle as she continues to relax. When a moan falls from her lips, I take that as a sign to proceed. It's gently that I press the blunt tip of my finger into the warmth of her body.

The fact that she's allowing me to play with her so intimately turns my cock to stone.

It would be impossible not to feel the way she stretches to accommodate the width of my digit.

I keep my movements measured and shallow, wanting her to get used to the invasion.

When she squirms against me, I caress both cheeks before praising, "You're doing so good, baby. The burn from the stretch won't last long. It'll just take time for you to get used to me playing with your ass like this. The way your body has opened up to me is the most beautiful thing I've ever seen."

Every time I withdraw, a sigh of relief escapes from her. Instead of giving her time to catch her breath, I surge forward, conquering new territory with each movement. I pepper kisses across her skin before licking her pussy and dipping my tongue inside her soaked heat.

"Does it still hurt, or is your little ass getting used to me playing with it?"

"There's a bit of a sting, but..." Her voice trails off.

My movements still. If this kind of intimate play isn't something that turns her on, then I don't want to do it. I don't get off on dominating her, only showing her the pleasure her body is capable of.

The pleasure we're capable of creating together.

"Tell me, sunshine. You can be honest."

She squeezes her eyes tightly closed as color floods her cheeks. "I like the way you're touching me. Even though there's a little bit of pain, it still feels good."

I press another kiss against her flank. "I'm glad. All I want to do is make your body sing. If this doesn't do it for you, then we'll figure out what does."

"I don't want you to stop. At least, not yet."

"Okay." I nibble at her pussy, wanting to distract her as I withdraw before pressing forward, going deeper. Another moan breaks loose from her as I bury myself to the second knuckle.

I pull away just enough to inspect her backside.

"You're so tight," I growl. "The way that gorgeous ass swallows up my finger is so damn sexy."

I give her body time to adjust before fully retreating. Another sigh escapes from her right before my finger breaches the tight muscle for a second time and slides even deeper inside her body. With my other hand, I massage her cheeks, pulling and stretching them as I fall into a steady rhythm of surging forward and gaining new ground before retreating.

After a few minutes, she sinks into the pleasure as I continue the gentle onslaught. The muscles of her backside loosen the more I play with them, allowing me to slide in and out with more ease.

Her eyelids feather closed as a look of utter bliss replaces the conflicted expression. A soft moan escapes from her as she presses her ass against me.

"Feel better?"

"Yes." Surprise weaves its way through her voice.

Her body hums with pleasure as she meets each thrust.

"Good girl," I praise. "I bet it wouldn't take much to make you come like this. All I'd have to do is rub your clit while stroking my finger in and out of your tight little ass and you'd fall to pieces."

Her breath catches as another moan escapes from her.

I can't help but stop and admire how beautiful she looks with my palm flattened against the curve of her backside. "I wish you could see how perfect you look with my finger buried deep inside your ass. So fucking gorgeous."

For a long, silent minute, neither of us moves a muscle. It's as if time stops and we hang in suspension.

I love the way her body has stretched to accommodate me, and that I'm the only man who's claimed her like this.

The need to taste her thrums through me as I press a kiss against her drenched pussy. That's all it takes for another whimper to escape from her as my tongue slides between her lips.

"Delicious."

When she bows her spine in a silent request for more, I draw away, peppering her backside with butterfly-like kisses as my finger stays buried inside her. As tempting as it is to continue playing with her like this, I slip my finger from her ass before brushing my lips against the small of her back.

"Don't move a single muscle."

My cock feels like it's going to explode as I round the bed and yank open the drawer, grabbing the first condom my fingers encounter. Instead of taking my time with the wrapper, I tear into it with my teeth before sheathing my cock.

All I want to do is bury myself deep inside her body and drown in her soft heat.

I give her ass a gentle swat before positioning my cock at her entrance and sliding inside with one swift movement. The pleasure is so damn great. It's like a wave pummeling my senses. My eyelids feather closed as I bury myself to the hilt.

"Fuck, it's such a tight fit," I rasp. "Any moment, your pussy will strangle the life out of my dick. As much as I want to make this last, there's no way that's going to happen." I'm too torqued up.

My larger body presses against her smaller one as my hips piston. Our harsh breaths mingling together along with the slapping of skin are the only sounds that fill the room.

I gather up the thick strands of her hair and hold them tight until it becomes necessary for her to tilt her head. My balls draw up as the orgasm builds like an impending storm.

When I press the tip of my finger against her rosebud, she comes unhinged and shatters around me.

Thank fuck.

My movements turn frenzied as my head falls back and I find my own release.

There's nothing on the face of this earth that feels more amazing than our bodies being in perfect sync.

A guttural groan escapes from me as her inner muscles contract, milking every last drop until there's nothing left to give.

Until I'm completely drained.

I huff out a contented breath and collapse on top of her. My heart pounds as I squeeze my eyes tightly closed and soak in the utter perfection of this moment.

"Fuck," I mutter, slipping my finger from her ass as the last shudder squeezes my dick.

There's a blissed-out expression on her face as a tiny smile quirks the corners of her lips.

With my hand still locked around the length of her golden hair, I carefully turn her head until her neck is bared to me so my lips can graze the delicate hollow. I just want to stay fused like this forever.

When it's no longer possible to delay the inevitable, I slip from her body. As soon as I do, the loss of warmth slams into me with the force of a tidal wave.

Dropping to my haunches, I press a kiss against her pussy before straightening to my full height and sliding the condom off my softening cock. I tie the end and wrap it in a tissue before dropping it in the trash can.

I nab my boxers from the floor and haul them up my thighs. As the elastic band snaps against my waist, my fingers stroke over the curve of her ass.

How am I ever going to get enough of this girl?

She's become an addiction.

My gaze slices from her delectable backside, that's still in the air, to the dazed expression on her face. Any moment, she's going to pass out.

"I'll be right back."

A smile quirks my lips when she mumbles something unintelligible.

I slip from the room, careful to close the door behind me before stepping into the hallway and beelining to the bathroom I share with the guys who reside on the second floor. After taking care of business, I dampen a washcloth with warmed water and return to the room.

The sight of a naked Willow with her ass in the air, eyelids feathered closed, and golden hair spread out around her like a halo is enough to rob the air from my lungs.

This girl couldn't be more perfect if she tried.

It only makes it more imperative that I do whatever it takes to hold on to her. And if that means playing with her body and giving her as many orgasms as I can, I'll do it.

I need her to see that I'm the one she should be with.

Not River fucking Thompson.

It takes a handful of long-legged strides to eat up the distance between us. Her eyelids spring open as I press the warm cloth against her sensitive flesh. When she struggles, I place a hand against the small of her back to pin her in place.

"Let me clean you off, sunshine."

"I can do it myself," she says, embarrassment coloring her voice.

After the way she allowed me to play with her, this kind of intimacy shouldn't be a big deal. She needs to understand that I'm here to take care of her.

And her needs.

Even after I make her orgasm.

"I want to," I murmur. "So let me do it."

That's all it takes for the fight to drain from her as she allows me to wipe away her arousal. My gaze stays pinned to her pink little pussy, so swollen from our fucking.

Even though I've just spent myself, already need is stirring to life within me.

It's so damn tempting to lick up all that cream instead of wiping it away.

Once I finish, I place a kiss against her swollen lips before tossing the towel in the hamper next to the desk. Then I gather her up into my arms and slide beneath the covers. I align my chest to her spine so I can spoon her smaller body. Only then does a sense of rightness settle over me.

I can't remember the last time I felt this kind of overwhelming contentment.

I search my brain for an answer.

The question is out of my mouth before I can think it over. "Will you come to my game on Thursday?"

Her eyelids flutter open as I nip her earlobe with sharp teeth.

When silence stretches between us, I force myself to remain calm, even though I'm a chaotic mess inside. "Sunshine?"

"Yes," she whispers. "I'll come."

Relief rushes through me as I fall asleep with her wrapped up tight in my arms.

It's exactly where she belongs.

POCKETFUL OF SUNSHINE
WILLOW & MAVERICK
01:10
04:10
WILLOW
LEUKEMIA
SURVIVOR

28

"I'm sorry...let me get this straight. You're sleeping with Maverick McKinnon, and he still has no clue that your brother is none other than River Thompson." Holland's wide eyes stay locked on mine. "*And* he asked you to go watch him play tonight?"

I release a steady breath. "Is there a question in all that?"

"Yeah, I'm wondering where my best friend of thirteen years went." She stabs a finger in my direction. "Who exactly is this fun-loving ho in her place?"

The edges of my lips tremble as a snort escapes from me. "I promise that I'm the same person who moved in with you last fall."

She folds her arms across her ample chest. "Listen, girl, I'm all for you living your best life, you know that."

"Why do I sense a *but* coming?"

"Because you know me well."

I press my lips together and steel myself for the truth bomb she's about to drop.

Holland settles on the bed beside me before searching my eyes for a long, silent moment. Her voice dips, becoming huskier. "The last thing I want to see is this situation blow up in your face. Or you getting hurt. That's all."

My chest expands with love. No matter what, she always has my best interests at heart. I'm lucky that she took a liking to me in the second grade.

It's only because I trust her judgment implicitly that I realize she's spot-on regarding the situation with Maverick.

It has disaster written all over it.

In black Sharpie.

It's the reason my instincts were blaring at me from the very beginning to avoid him at all costs.

And I tried...

I really did.

But there's something about Maverick McKinnon that I find irresistible.

"You need to tell him the truth before you get in any deeper."

My shoulders collapse under the heavy weight of her words as guilt pricks at me.

Yeah... I think it might be a little too late for that.

Not only does he not know that River and I are related, but he has no idea that I was diagnosed with childhood leukemia. Most guys shy away when I share that info. The ones who don't turn tail and run, treat me as if I'm fragile.

Even though I think he'll be pissed when he finds out about the first issue, I've grown more concerned about the second one. Especially since his mother fought her own battle recently and he was so affected by it.

It wouldn't surprise me if our diagnoses and subsequent treatment overlapped.

Ugh.

The thought makes my belly pinch with nerves.

If he doesn't pull away and disappear from my life, I'm afraid he'll treat me differently.

After what I've experienced at his skilled hands, that would be a deal breaker for me.

My mind tumbles back to the way he fucked me the other day. I've never even fantasized about a man touching me in that way.

Playing with my body like that.

It was...delicious.

Even though it's been a few days, I haven't been able to stop thinking about it.

"Oh god…you've already fallen for him, haven't you?" Her voice is tinged with a blend of disbelief and sadness.

I blink out of the memories trying to take hold, and stare at my bestie with wide eyes. My inclination is to shake my head.

No way!

Of course I haven't!

But…

It's a jolt to realize that Holland is right.

I've fallen for Maverick.

Or maybe I'm in the process of it.

What I do know is that I've never met anyone like him before. The scariest part is that I'm not sure if I ever will again.

As much as I don't want to burst the little bubble I'm living in, I can't continue lying to him.

Well, I haven't exactly *lied*. Although, it's doubtful Maverick will see it that way once I come clean.

I cringe, realizing exactly what needs to happen. The sooner, the better. Only then will my conscience be cleared and we can hopefully move forward with our relationship.

"I'll tell him tonight," I whisper.

My belly dips at the idea of sitting down with him and admitting all the secrets I've been keeping.

Holland worries her lower lip as her brow furrows. "I know it's scary, but it's the right thing to do."

I draw in a lungful of fresh air and force myself to nod in agreement.

Deep down, I realize she's right, but that knowledge doesn't make it any easier.

Just as Holland opens her mouth to no doubt impart some wisdom, there's a knock on the front door of our townhouse.

With a frown, she peers into the short hallway on the other side of my threshold before popping to her feet. "I swear if those creepy religious dudes are back again, I'm going to totally lose it."

I didn't think it was possible for anything to lighten the solemn mood that's fallen over me, but that does the trick, and a snort breaks loose.

Without a backward glance, she stalks into the hallway before disappearing from sight. From within the townhouse, I cock my head, hoping to hear the tirade when she unloads on them.

The door opens and the muffle of voices barely reaches me.

As tempting as it is to follow her, I remain on my bed. It doesn't take long for my mind to tumble back to Maverick. My teeth scrape across my lower lip as I consider alternative solutions.

Other than disappearing from his life, there are none.

Plus, it's doubtful he'd allow it.

My shoulders wilt under the heaviness of that conversation. It's important that he hear the truth from me rather than someone else. Like Hayes. That'll only make the situation worse.

Then it'll look like I was deliberately keeping it from him.

Which...well...I was.

Ugh.

It's the light rap of knuckles against my open door that has me jerking out of those depressing thoughts. My gaze flies to the guy hovering over the threshold. I blink, wondering if I've somehow managed to conjure Maverick up from my thoughts.

Joy is the first emotion that rushes in. Every time I catch sight of him after we've spent time apart, I'm bowled over by how handsome he is.

The mahogany-colored eyes and nearly inky black hair. The chiseled cheek bones and ridiculously thick lashes. The light coat of stubble that dusts both chin and cheek.

I could stare at him for hours.

When I continue to silently soak in the sight of him, a lopsided smile curves his full lips before he jerks a thumb over his shoulder. "I hope it's all right that your roommate let me in."

It takes effort to shake off the haze attempting to cocoon its way around me before straightening as reality forces its way in.

"It's fine."

I hadn't considered bringing up the situation before his game tonight, but maybe that's exactly what needs to happen. Once the truth is revealed, he might not want me sitting in the stands and supporting him. Sadness blooms inside my chest before spreading outward, infecting my body like a virus, because it's a distinct possibility that can no longer be denied.

As I stare at him, mentally grappling for the right words, I wish I'd been honest from the beginning.

It's just that I'd wanted him to get to know *me*.

Willow Thompson.

Without my brother to cloud his judgment.

Or that I'd spent the last two years of high school sick, unsure if I'd live to celebrate my eighteenth birthday.

The uncertainty that flickers across his face melts my heart.

"I wanted to stop by and make sure you still planned to attend the game tonight."

I glance away as the truth sticks uncomfortably in my throat. "Oh, um...about that..."

When my voice trails off, he steps farther inside my space. He's so tall and broad in the shoulders that everything shrinks around him. The normally airy room now feels anything but.

He swallows up the distance with a handful of long-legged strides before dropping to his knees in front of me so that we're eye level. It's so tempting to reach out and sift my fingers through his thick hair.

Instead, I keep them locked on my lap.

His brows jerk together as he studies me. The intensity of his stare leaves me feeling unexpectedly vulnerable. It's as if he's capable of picking through all the private thoughts circling through my brain.

The ones I've been so careful to keep hidden away.

Disappointment floods his dark depths. "Did something come up?"

My fingers bite into my jean-clad thighs as I shake my head. "No, it's nothing like that."

The concern marring his expression dissolves as he flashes a relieved smile. One large hand rises to cup my face. "Good."

It takes effort to swallow down the anxiety that gnaws at my insides. "We should probably—"

Before I can force out the rest, my gaze dips to his other hand and I lose all train of thought.

How didn't I realize he was holding something when he walked in?

His voice dips, turning raspy. The confidence that normally brims in it falls away, making him sound younger. "I was hoping you'd wear my jersey tonight."

I can only gape at the orange and black fabric in his hand as my belly drops in free fall. It's like I'm sitting at the very tippy top of a roller coaster and I'm harnessed in the first car as it plunges to the earth.

When I remain silent, at a loss, he clears his throat. "Sunshine?"

My tongue darts out to lick my parched lips.

There's no way I should accept such a personal gift without revealing the truth.

"Please say something," he whispers, eyes pleading with mine.

My heart twists as I blurt, "I'd love to wear it, thank you."

As soon as I release the words into the atmosphere, I want to snatch them back.

All I've done is further complicate matters.

He sucks a breath into his lungs as a wide grin breaks out across his face and a relieved laugh bursts free. "I'm not gonna lie—you had me worried for a second or two. I thought I'd misread the situation."

Before I realize what's happening, he drags the thick material over my head and helps shove my arms through the large sleeves. A handful of seconds later, the hem settles around my waist.

His gaze roves over my chest and belly. "Fuck, sunshine. You look amazing." He slants a look upward until our eyes can collide. "Almost as good as you looked the other night stretched out naked in my bed."

Heat suffuses my cheeks as the memories once again push in at the edges before flooding my brain.

Another chuckle escapes from him, but this one is deep, husky, and knowing. The low scrape of it does funny things to my insides, making it impossible to hold on to rational thought.

His fingers drift across my cheek. "I'd strip you bare and take you right now if we had more time. But the one thing I refuse to do is rush when I'm making love to you. I enjoy drawing out your pleasure for as long as possible, until that sweet little pussy is sobbing for what only I can give you."

Out of everything he just confided, two words echo throughout my head.

"Making love?" I repeat, surprised by the description.

Is that really what he considers it to be?

Maverick gives me a lopsided smile before pressing a kiss against my lips. "That's what it was, don't you think?"

"Yeah," I admit. "I do."

There was such a sense of closeness between us that isn't easily found.

I'd laid myself bare and allowed him to touch me in ways I've never contemplated.

That kind of intense sexual exploration can only come from trust.

At least, the foundation of it.

"Then it would seem like we're both on the same page."

He straightens before pressing my back against the mattress and stretching out on top of me. His lips hover over mine as his tongue dances with my own, making me forget everything that needs to be cleared up between us.

Unable to help myself, my palms slip beneath the thick fabric of his sweatshirt until they're sliding over the warm flesh beneath.

"Are you sure there's not enough time?"

His lips quirk against mine as our breaths mingle. "Unfortunately, no." He peppers kisses against my mouth. "I promise that after the game, we'll have a repeat performance."

My belly swoops as he pulls away and rises to his feet. His dark depths are filled with so much hunger and heat that it's enough to scorch my skin and have me going up in flames.

It's reluctantly that he jerks his head toward the door. "I should get moving."

My confession slams back into me. "Can you give me a couple minutes? There's something I need to tell you."

He slips his hand into his pocket and pulls out his phone before glancing at the screen. "Sorry, sunshine, I can't. If I don't get to the arena pronto, Coach will rip me a new one. We'll talk afterward, all right?"

Unsure what else to do, I jerk my head into a tight nod. "Sure, that's fine."

He flashes another grin before bridging the distance between us and lifting me to my feet. His mouth crashes into mine right before he nips at my lower lip, tugging it with sharp teeth before finally releasing it with a soft pop.

Already, my mouth feels swollen from his kisses.

"That was for good luck." His gaze darkens as it drops to my lips. "Unlike the other game, I look forward to seeing you root for me in our section."

And then he's gone, disappearing into the hallway before I can gather my scattered thoughts.

Silence descends as regret blooms inside me.

A few minutes later, Holland pokes her head into the room.

Her narrowed gaze sweeps over my disheveled appearance. "I take it you didn't tell him?"

It's not a question.

We both know the answer.

My fingers rise to my lips. "I didn't get a chance."

"Looks like he gave you something to wear tonight."

I glance down at the Wildcats jersey with his name and number stamped across the fabric. That's all it takes for warmth to gather in my chest.

Other than my brother's, I've never worn another player's jersey.

Holland's eyes turn somber. "You have to tell him, Will. There's no way he won't discover the truth. And then..." Her voice trails off as she jerks her shoulders. "I'm afraid of what will happen when he does."

Everything inside me deflates like an overfilled balloon pricked by a pin.

"I'll confess everything tonight." I straighten my shoulders and attempt to put on a brave face. "And if he doesn't understand, then it's his loss."

Even as I force out the last part, I'm none too sure if I believe it.

I can only hope that Maverick proves me wrong.

POCKETFUL OF SUNSHINE

WILLOW & MAVERICK

01:10   04:10

WILLOW

LEUKEMIA SURVIVOR

29

Hours later, Holland and I push our way through the crowded arena. Some of the more devoted fanatics have painted their faces orange and black. Just like weeks ago, people are decked out in Wildcat gear and sporting their favorite player jerseys. It would be hard not to notice just how many girls are wearing the same one I am.

When jealousy tries to rear its ugly head, I stomp it out before it can take root.

It's not just university students who've shown up to support their hometown team. People come from all over the state to watch the Western Wildcats play. Especially now that we're deep in the season and the playoffs are right around the corner. They have an amazing record, and everyone wants to watch them win and be part of their story.

Cool air slaps at our cheeks as we step inside the arena. That's when the *Jaws* theme song erupts from my pocket. With a frown, I pull out my phone and stare at it. Mom's name flashes across the screen.

A smile trembles around the corners of my lips as I hold up the device and shake my head. "Really?"

Holland grins as her eyes dance with humor. "What? It's funny."

I arch a brow. "I doubt Mom would think so."

"Becks doesn't find much funny, now does she?"

True statement.

The woman needs a life.

Maybe then she would stop trying to commandeer mine.

When the phone continues to ring, Holland holds out her hand. "Please let me do the honors. Think of it as an early birthday present."

I twist away, giving her my back before answering the call and blurting, "Hi, Mom. Can't talk. We're at a game. Love you."

Then I disconnect before shoving the cell back into my pocket.

"You're going to catch hell for that," she sing-songs before adding, "You didn't even thank her for the care package that was dropped off yesterday. Please let her know that I enjoyed the homemade cookies."

With a snort, my gaze scans the raucous crowd as I search for our seats. "I'll be sure to do that."

It's strange to sit in the home team section and not with the visitors. This is the first time I've attended a Wildcat game with the sole purpose of supporting them and not East Town.

It shouldn't come as any surprise that the student section is packed. Holland glances at our tickets before pointing to the one filled with a sea of orange and black. "Looks like we're over there."

I loop my arm through hers and steer her through the mass of excited fans. It took a lot of cajoling to talk my bestie into attending the game. This is the last way she wants to spend her free time. And I can't blame her for that. There's one hockey player in particular she can't stand and does everything in her power to avoid.

Bridger Sanderson.

She's always been tight-lipped about what went down between them, but I have my theories.

So, I owe her big time for being supportive.

It takes another five minutes to make our way to our seats. Once we do, I unzip my jacket, revealing the jersey and the turtleneck beneath it. As we settle in, one of the girls in the row in front of us turns.

A smile lights up her pretty face when our gazes collide. "Willow?"

The dark-haired girl with a high ponytail next to her whips around as well.

Britt and Fallyn.

"Hi!" I say in surprise.

"I didn't know you'd be here!" Fallyn says, twisting more in her seat.

"Sorry, I must have forgotten to mention it."

Or, more accurately, I thought Maverick and I wouldn't be together.

Wanting to change the convo to safer terrain, I point to my friend. "This is my roommate, Holland."

Both girls wave after introductions have been made. Holland has never been good at letting new people into her life. The friends she has are ones she's known forever.

It's not easy to earn her trust.

I've seen a few try and ultimately give up because the walls she surrounds herself with aren't easily breached. Sadness pricks my heart. Holland is such an amazing person, and I wish more people were able to see that.

It takes a moment or two before I realize that Britt and Fallyn are here with a larger group as a few turn in our direction.

The recognition that slams into me is instantaneous.

Juliette McKinnon.

Her brows draw together before the lightbulb goes off in her head. "Willow, right?"

I nod. "Hi, Juliette. How are you doing?"

She twists in her hardback chair. "Good!" With a smile, she glances at her friends. "Small world. I didn't realize you knew Fallyn and Britt."

"Actually," Britt cuts in before I can respond, "we were grabbing something to eat at Harvey's when she walked in with *your brother*." The last part is emphasized with a cheeky grin and a waggle of her brows.

Fallyn cocks her head. "You wouldn't by any chance be wearing Mav's jersey?"

I stare at all three girls and find curiosity filling Juliette's eyes. That's all it takes for heat to slam into my cheeks as her gaze drops to the jersey I'm sporting. The front of it has the university emblem, but his name and number are stamped across the back.

"Ummm..." My voice trails off.

"I'll take that as a yes," Britt says with a smile.

Juliette leans closer. "Are you dating my brother?"

I'm thrown off by the genuine excitement that floods her voice.

"Well, I don't—"

"If they're not," Britt cuts in with a laugh, "he's doing his damnedest to persuade her to give it a shot."

"You should have seen the way he was watching her," Fallyn adds with a heartfelt sigh. "So adorable."

The blonde sitting next to Fallyn elbows her in the ribs. "Kind of like the way Wolf stares at you almost obsessively?"

Happiness dances in Fallyn's blue eyes. "I certainly hope so."

The blonde rolls hers before refocusing on me. "It's nice to meet you. I'm Carina." She points to Juliette. "I live with Jules."

"Willow." I bump my bestie's shoulder, who's silently taking all this in. "And this is Holland."

Carina stares at Holland for a handful of seconds before narrowing her eyes. "You look really familiar. I feel like we've met before. Are you in the dance program?"

Holland snorts. "Given that I have zero rhythm, that's a very hard no."

Carina's lips tremble at the blunt response. "Maybe a gen ed course, then? Or you've dated someone on the team?"

I wince when Holland's defenses go up and her expression turns guarded.

"Absolutely not. I enjoy being disease free."

A few of the girls stare at Holland with wide eyes before dissolving into laughter.

When I catch her gaze, she jerks her shoulders and scowls. She doesn't care how she comes across or if they like her.

That's the beauty of being Holland.

Luckily, they all laugh it off.

Especially Carina.

She flashes a bright smile at Holland. "I think you and I were meant to be friends. Can't say I didn't feel the same way before I started dating Ford."

Everyone's attention drifts to the ice as the team warms up. Mine fastens on Maverick. Even though they all look similar with their helmets, jerseys, and black pants, I know exactly which one he is.

I'm reminded of how impossible it was to take my eyes off him at the game a few weeks ago. My belly dips when his gaze locks on mine and he lifts a gloved hand to wave.

"So, let me get this straight—you're all dating hockey players?" Holland asks.

A petite blonde next to Britt shakes her head. "No way. My dad would stroke out if I brought home one of these guys."

"That's because he's the head coach with a strict no-fraternization rule in place," Britt adds.

"Makes perfect sense," Holland says. "Trust me, you're better off." As soon as that comment shoots out of her mouth, a dull blush crawls up her cheeks.

Carina waggles her brows and presses closer. "Ohhh, I sense a story. Did you get with one of these guys?"

With a shake of her head, Holland grumbles, "No comment."

"Damn. Whatever the story is, I'm willing to bet it's a juicy one."

Thick tension radiates from my friend. Her expression turns stony as her gaze is drawn back to the ice and the players who continue to stretch.

After one of the other girls brings up someone they're all acquainted with, they change the topic and chatter about that.

"If I didn't mention it before," Holland whispers as she leans closer, "you totally owe me for this."

"Whatever you want."

One side of her mouth quirks. "You're going to regret that."

"Probably. But I'm still glad you came with tonight. I need you here for moral support." My gaze flicks toward the row of girls seated in front of us. Every so often, they turn, including us in their conversation. "They seem really nice."

Holland mulls over the comment before grudgingly admitting, "Yeah, they do. Even if they are dating hockey players."

The girls might not realize it, but they've just earned Holland's rare stamp of approval.

McKINNON

28

MAVERICK

WILDCATS

30

As soon as I shove into the locker room, I toss my gloves and helmet into my locker and grab my phone, firing off a quick text to Willow.

Really loved seeing you in my jersey

Three little dots appear before her message pops up on the screen.

I'm certainly not the only girl who was wearing a Maverick McKinnon jersey tonight. You're incredibly popular with the female fans.

I only noticed you, sunshine. Plus, you're the only one who was wearing one from me.

I wait a second or two before firing off another text. The last thing I want is for her to have second thoughts and take off on me.

I saw you with my sister. Just stick with her and I'll find you once we're released, okay?

When she doesn't immediately respond, I tap out another message.

Sunshine? Don't make me hunt your ass down. You know I will.

Okay. I'll meet you in the lobby.

I can't help but grin, oblivious to all the commotion and the good-natured ribbing that unfolds around me.

Good girl. Then I tack on a winky face.

All I can think about is getting my hands on her and finishing what we started in her bedroom a couple hours ago.

On second thought, maybe we won't head to the bar at all. I'd much rather strip her bare and—

"What the hell are you grinning at? The expression on your ugly mug makes you look like a total psychopath," Hayes says, knocking me from all thoughts of Willow.

He raises a brow as I toss the cell back into my locker.

"Nothing," I say, shrugging off the comment.

If this guy thinks I'm about to hand over info about Willow, he couldn't be more wrong. Hayes is notorious for giving people shit.

When I sink to the bench to unlace my skates, he settles beside me. "Does it have anything to do with the hot blonde you've been screwing?"

My head snaps up and I bite out, "You know what her name is, and I haven't been *screwing* her."

His brows shoot up. "Huh. Interesting. If this isn't straight-up fucking, what is it?"

"None of your damn business. How about that?"

The whistle that escapes from him is long and low. "Damn, dude. Sounds like it could be serious. Can't say I was expecting that."

"Maybe it is."

"Have you met the fam yet?"

I jerk my shoulders, refusing to admit that I'm still trying to convince this girl to dump her boyfriend and give me a shot. "Nope."

He tosses his skates into his locker before stripping off his pads until he's down to his jock. "Maybe you should do that before you start making plans and thinking long term."

I blink, thrown off by the strange comment. Before I can ask what the hell he means, he takes off the cup and heads to the showers.

Not that I'll admit it to Hayes, but it's much too late to slow my roll with Willow. Even though she's still with River, long-term thoughts are already circling my brain. The more time we spend together, the more obsessed I find myself.

Everything about her drives me crazy and has me falling a little bit harder.

She's the first girl that I've actually wanted in my bed at night. I love spooning her smaller body and wrapping her up tight in my arms.

When it comes down to it, I just love being with her.

Even if that means we're at the library studying. She's so patient and caring. As much as I've always hated working with tutors, especially peer ones, Willow is different. She takes the time before we meet to organize what we're working on into small, digestible chucks. She suggested that I get a smartpen, which records lectures while taking notes and then syncs them together. I've always been resistant to using any kind of device or aid that will tip off the people around me that I have a learning disability.

I hate to admit how much it's helped.

She also encouraged me to ask for extra time on tests if I need it.

And my grades have improved because of her suggestions.

Just like hockey is my passion, teaching is hers.

I can just imagine her in a classroom with a bunch of kiddos hanging on her every word.

Is it weird that I can picture having one or two, maybe more with her?

I drag a hand through my sweat-soaked hair.

Clearly, I'm getting way ahead of myself.

This is the first time I've given my future outside of hockey serious consideration. The thoughts circling around in my head should freak the fuck out of me.

What does it mean that they don't?

All I want to do is lock her down tight and make her mine.

More than anything, I need to know she feels the same about our relationship. That this isn't all one sided. That what she has with me is different—*better*—than what she has with River.

Only then will I be able to ease up and loosen my grip. I hate feeling like she'll slip through my fingers any second.

The need to see her crashes over me like a tidal wave as I strip off the pads and head to the shower. Ten minutes later, I've dried off and am dressed in jeans and a sweatshirt. I plow my fingers through my hair, shoving the damp strands away from my face before slicking on some pit sauce.

Voilà—ready to go.

As I grab my duffle and head to the door, Ryder calls out, "You're not gonna wait for me?"

"I'll catch you out there," I throw over my shoulder.

I'm much too impatient to make sure Willow stuck around.

My earlier threat wasn't an idle one.

I'll hunt her ass down.

Before he can fire off anything else, I'm shoving through the thick metal door and into the corridor. My steps quicken as I turn the corner and find the lobby crammed with people. It's not uncommon for friends and family to stick around after games and wait for the players to get released from the locker room. There's also a dozen or so groupies milling around, hoping to get lucky.

I don't give them the time of day.

My gaze coasts over the crowd, looking for Willow's golden-blonde head. When I don't immediately spot her, nerves hum along my skin.

Where the hell is she?

It's tempting to dip my fingers inside my pocket and pull out my cell. That's the moment Britt shifts and my attention lands on her. It's like getting smacked in the head with a two by four. My heart stalls at the sight of her wearing my jersey with her long blonde hair styled into two thick braids that rest against her shoulders.

She glances around, as if able to feel the heat of my gaze singeing her skin. When our eyes collide, the air gets knocked from my lungs, making full breaths impossible.

I've never experienced anything like it before.

It takes effort to force my feet into movement as I cut a path straight to her. Hands reach out, patting me on the shoulder as people compliment my game.

Even though I say thanks, I don't bother making eye contact with any of them.

I can't rip my attention away from her.

Once she's within striking distance, my hands slide over her cheeks and I pull her close enough for my mouth to crash into hers.

I don't give a shit who's watching.

All I care about is her.

My tongue sweeps over the seam of her lips before she opens, giving herself over to me. Only then does the beast raging inside calm enough for me to think clearly.

After I've had my fill, I pull away just enough to rest my forehead against hers before staring into her bright blue eyes.

They've turned hazy.

Just the way I like them.

I love that my touch—my kisses—does that to her.

Truth be told, it does the same damn thing to me.

I'm so tightly wrapped up in this girl that I can't see straight.

"Have I mentioned how good you look in my jersey?"

Her lips lift into a smile. "You might have said something about it earlier."

"Good enough to eat," I growl.

The thought of stripping her naked and pushing her thighs apart so I can lick up all her cream has my cock turning to stone.

A groan works its way free from my lips.

It's only when someone clears their throat that I break eye contact and find my parents standing a few feet away. Both of their eyebrows are buried in their hairlines.

I certainly can't blame them for their bewilderment.

The last time they saw me take interest in a girl was with Sabrina back in high school. That was more than three years ago.

I force myself to back away enough to slip my arm around Willow's waist and tug her close.

Not only are my parents staring at us, but so are Ryder and Juliette. A big smile lights up my sister's face, which I take as confirmation that she approves of Willow. Ryder's expression looks eerily similar to my folks'.

When spontaneous applause breaks out from my teammates, I can't help the grin that stretches across my face as Willow's eyes widen. She buries her face against my arm as a tortured groan escapes from her.

"What's wrong, sunshine? You got a problem with everyone knowing that you belong to me?"

"I... We still need to talk," she murmurs.

When fear bubbles up inside me, I stomp it out. I refuse to let anything dampen this moment. "We will. But not before I introduce you to my parents."

POCKETFUL OF SUNSHINE

WILLOW & MAVERICK

01:10   04:10

WILLOW

LEUKEMIA

31

Excitement crackles in the air as we step inside Slap Shotz. With the Wildcats riding high from their win this evening, there's a heightened exuberance to the atmosphere that feels infectious. I've been pinned to Maverick's side ever since he walked out of the locker room, kissed me in front of everyone, then introduced me to his family.

They were all so warm and welcoming. Even though I only spent a short period of time around them, it's easy to see that he, his parents, and Juliette are tight knit. They offered to take us out to eat, but Maverick declined, wanting to celebrate their win tonight with his teammates.

Britt and Fallyn can't stop beaming at me. The rest of the girls I've gotten to know this evening are just as warm and friendly. After the game, I tried cajoling Holland into sticking around, but she declined the offer.

She refuses to come within a fifty-foot radius of Bridger. I wish those two would just bury the hatchet and move on with their lives. But it's doubtful that will happen anytime soon.

Once we settle at a table with all the other players and their girlfriends, he says, "I'm going to grab something at the bar. What can I get you?"

"Just a water."

With a tilt of his head, he studies me carefully. "Do you mind if I have something? If you do, I won't. It's not a big deal."

"I don't mind at all."

"Okay." He rises to his feet before slipping his fingers beneath my chin and pressing his lips to mine for a quick kiss. "Don't go anywhere. I'll be right back."

And then he's gone, navigating his way through the thick crowd. People reach out to pat his shoulder as he saunters past. A few girls jump in his path and attempt to flirt. Giddiness explodes inside me when he doesn't give them the time of day.

"I'm going to be completely honest here—I've never seen my brother like this before."

My gaze slices to Juliette. I was so intent on Maverick that I didn't realize she'd dropped down beside me.

Warmth spreads throughout my chest at the admittance. "Really?"

"Nope." Her smile intensifies, as if she's truly thrilled by the prospect.

"He doesn't normally date?"

Her brow furrows as she shifts before leaning closer. "There was a girl in high school, but..."

I bite down on my tongue to keep everything trapped inside. I hate that he and my brother have this contentious past that sits between them.

It only makes it more imperative that I tell Maverick the truth about who I am as soon as possible. It sickens me that I'm keeping all these secrets when he's been nothing but upfront and honest.

"Did he really like her?" As much as I don't want to pry, I need to know.

Juliette nibbles at her lower lip as her gaze slices to her brother, who's laughing with a few teammates near the bar. I can't help but follow her line of sight. As soon as my attention lands on him, I'm slammed by the emotions that have taken root inside me.

How did I ever think that spending one night with him and walking away in the morning would be enough to satiate me?

He's opened my eyes to so much. There's no way to move forward and pretend that what I've experienced at his skilled hands doesn't exist or never happened.

"Yeah, he did."

I press my lips together, not wanting to ask for more details.

Little does she realize that I had a front-row seat to the fallout from the other side of things.

River was with Sabrina for more than twelve months. They broke up freshman year of college when they couldn't make their long-distance relationship work. Even though she hurt Maverick, I liked her a lot. She'd sit with me when I wasn't feeling well and we became friends. She didn't mention Maverick very often, but even then, I was curious. At the time, her love story with River seemed romantic and meant to be.

In the end, it didn't work out.

We still keep in touch through social media.

I can't imagine what Maverick's reaction would be if he knew that we were friends.

Nausea blooms in the pit of my belly when I think about confessing all of this.

It very well could be the end of us.

When I remain silent, lost in thoughts of the past, she blurts, "But that was a long time ago. Mav's moved on. It's all water under the bridge."

That remains to be seen.

When the last notes of the song currently pulsing through the speakers vibrate through the air, a large man hefts himself onto the makeshift stage and raises his arms in an effort to capture everyone's attention.

I glance around, surprised at how quickly the rowdy crowd has quieted.

"Looks like it's that time of the evening," Juliette says.

My brows pinch as my gaze moves to her again. "What do you mean?"

She nods toward the man. "You've never been here after a Wildcats win?"

I shake my head, intrigued by what's about to happen as a sense of expectation buzzes in the air.

"Any chance you like to sing?" she asks with a smile.

"Only in the shower. Does that count?"

She chuckles. "Sure."

The questions that have gathered on the tip of my tongue are cut off when the man's voice booms through the microphone. "Our boys brought home another win tonight, and you know what that means!"

I squeak in surprise when the crowd bellows back in unison, "Karaoke!"

"You got it!" He points to the drunken college kids with a grin. "Now, who's going to start us off tonight?"

That's all the encouragement three hockey players need to jump onto the stage. They spend a minute or two picking out a song before belting out Bruno Mars's "Grenade."

Color me impressed.

They're not half bad.

"Babe?" Ryder materializes next to Juliette before holding out his hand for her to take. "Are we going to sing our song?"

She pops to her feet before pressing a kiss against his lips. "Would you let me leave tonight without doing it?"

A smile breaks out across his face. "Nope."

With that, he wraps a brawny arm around her shoulders before steering her toward the stage. I'm curious as to what their song is.

Maverick drops down into the chair his sister just vacated before passing me a bottle of sparkling water.

"Thanks."

"Not a problem."

Once the first few notes float on the air, I recognize it.

"Bring Me to Life" by Evanescence.

If I was impressed by the three hockey players, I'm blown away by Juliette. "Wow, your sister has an amazing voice."

Maverick flashes a smile as pride lights up his eyes. "She took choir all through high school. And this has always been one of her favorites."

Her big, blond boyfriend is no slouch in the karaoke department either. All that brawny muscle and the man can actually carry a tune.

I can't help but be drawn into their performance. They stare at one another as if they're unaware of the crowd watching them.

"They're really good together."

Maverick nods before admitting almost grudgingly, "They are. I'm still getting used to thinking of them as a couple, but it's getting easier."

"It'll just take time for your relationship with Ryder to settle into something new." I nudge his shoulder with my own. "I still think you should mention it to him."

He jerks his shoulders. "Maybe. We'll see. It's doubtful they'll be breaking up anytime soon. I think this has been a long time in coming. Plus, he'd be a fool to let her go."

I glance at the couple on stage. The love between them is obvious. It's difficult not to be envious of it. I hope for Maverick's sake that they can find the closeness they once shared. It would be a shame if he allowed his sister's relationship to get between him and his friend.

Applause rings throughout the bar as the final notes of the song reverberate on the air.

The blonde I met at the game takes her place on the makeshift stage.

She sings "Criminal" by Fiona Apple. It's slow and erotic. There's a handsome guy sitting a couple chairs away from me who leans his elbows on the table and smiles, all the while watching her.

I glance at Carina again.

She moves her body as if she knows exactly how to command a crowd. Even I'm entranced by her performance.

It doesn't take long to realize that she's serenading him.

And he is totally here for it.

Fire leaps to life in his eyes. It wouldn't surprise me in the least if he jumped up, stormed the stage, and threw her over his shoulder before stalking out of the bar.

The heat these two generate is combustible and off the charts.

I lean closer to Maverick before pointing toward Carina and the hunky hockey player who's way too good looking for his own good. With those chiseled cheekbones, he could be a model.

"I assume those two are together?"

"Yup. Ford had been not-so-secretly pining for his ex-stepsister ever since I met him." He snorts. "You should have seen the way he'd trail after her like a puppy dog."

I blink, uncertain if I heard him correctly. "Did you say ex-stepsister?"

He chuckles. "Sure did."

"Huh. That sounds like an interesting story."

"If you ask Carina, I'm sure she'd be happy to share all the gory details with you."

I consider the idea. "I might just have to do that."

My earlier suspicions were correct.

As soon as Carina wraps up the song, Ford leaps to his feet and stalks to the stage. He nabs her fingers before towing her to him and laying one on her. The crowd goes even more nuts than before. Whistles and shouts for them to get a room echo throughout the dark bar.

Ford grins at his teammates before throwing Carina over his shoulder and carting her through the thick crowd and out the back door.

My guess is that we won't be seeing them anytime soon.

Maverick shakes his head as a smile simmers at the corners of his lips. "That guy is such a caveman."

Maybe that's true.

But what girl wouldn't want to be whisked away like that?

A few more couples and groups of people make their way to the stage. Some are pretty amazing, although not nearly as good as Juliette or Carina. Juliette knows how to project her voice, and Carina can captivate and command the crowd with sexy moves.

The man who owns the bar and kicked off karaoke returns with the microphone. "Last song of the night. Who's it going to be?"

It's a surprise when Maverick pops to his feet and drags me up with him. "Come on, sunshine."

"What?" I squeak, unable to believe he didn't discuss the situation with me first.

He pulls me closer before pressing his lips against mine. "Let's sing together. You and me."

I groan, indecision spiraling through me. I've been to a couple of bars and watched karaoke, but not once have I ever been tempted to do it myself. I've always been way too shy. The idea of getting up there in front of all these people and embarrassing myself is almost paralyzing.

"It'll be fun," Maverick says, interrupting the whirl of my thoughts. "I promise."

I search his mahogany-colored eyes for a long, silent heartbeat before reluctantly giving in. "All right."

He flashes a grin before pulling me to the stage where Sully waits. "First time up here, McKinnon."

Maverick glances at me before winking. "Guess I was waiting to find the perfect partner first."

That's all it takes for my heart to skip a painful beat.

"Have something in mind?" Sully asks. "I'll cue it up."

Maverick's gaze turns speculative as it slides back to me. "Actually, I do." He leans closer to the bar owner before murmuring something I can't quite catch.

Sully glances at me with twinkling eyes before spinning away. After a minute or two, he shoots a look over his shoulder. "All set."

"This won't go well if you don't tell me what we're about to sing."

"As soon as you hear the first few notes, I promise you'll know. And if you don't, or freeze up, I'll do the heavy lifting and carry us. Sound good?"

I suck in an unsteady breath, holding it captive in my lungs before forcing it out again. "Okay."

My gaze reluctantly scans the crowd, who have quieted and are watching us with interest. The realization that every eye in the house is staring at us is nerve racking. It's tempting to toss the microphone to Sully and race off the stage and out the door into the cool night air.

As soon as the guitar riff opens with the pulsating beat, recognition slams into me.

It's the one I played on repeat during chemo. The positive and upbeat melody never failed to make me feel invincible. As if I could fight my way through whatever obstacles stood in my path.

It was my own personal anthem that helped me battle leukemia.

As silly as it sounds, once I was officially in remission, I emailed Natasha Beddingfield and shared with her just how meaningful "Pocketful of Sunshine" was to me.

Maverick's lips quirk as he croons the first verse.

I blink, surprised to find that, like his sister, his vocals are impressive.

When I continue to stare, he raises his brows.

I force out the second verse as we harmonize together. I've sung this song more than a thousand times and listened to it on repeat for hours. It's not necessary to look at the screen. With my gaze locked on Maverick's, I belt out the lyrics, giving every ounce of energy that I have to them.

Midway through, I realize that I'm smiling so hard that my cheeks hurt. When I sing the chorus for a final time, Maverick repeats it. I throw my hands up and close my eyes as the last notes vibrate in the air. Thunderous applause breaks out as Maverick sweeps me off my feet and spins us in a tight circle. Pure joy bursts inside me like an overinflated balloon as my laughter rings throughout the space.

"You were amazing," he says, smacking a kiss against my lips.

I pull back just enough to meet his gaze. "So were you! You're a man of many talents, Maverick McKinnon."

He smirks. "You haven't seen anything yet, sunshine. Trust me, there's more where that came from."

My body slides down his harder one before my toes touch the stage. That's exactly the way it feels when we're together.

Like my feet don't quite touch the ground.

Being with him is like living in a technicolor dream. One I don't ever want to wake from. I'm so afraid that once I reveal the truth, everything will change, and I'll end up losing what I've only just found.

"You ready to get out of here?"

I jerk my head in a nod, knowing exactly what I need to do.

MAVERICK

McKINNON 28

32

I slip my arm around Willow as we exit the stage.

Without a doubt, this girl has become my sunshine. The more time we spend together, the more she eclipses everything else in my life.

It's why the song fit so perfectly.

I want her to understand that I'm serious about this relationship.

I'm serious about *her*.

And I hope like hell that she feels the same, because I'm all in.

As we're heading out the back door, the last person I expect to see tonight bursts through it.

River fucking Thompson.

Fury vibrates off him in heavy, suffocating waves as his narrowed gaze combs over the crowd before settling on Willow.

His eyes widen before slicing to me. "You motherfucker!"

A growl escapes from him right before he launches himself in my direction. Willow gasps as I shove her from the fray. If he touches one damn hair on her head, I'll bury the guy alive.

Before I can get into position, he lands a punch to my cheek with enough force to snap my head to the side. Stars burst behind my eyes.

Chaos breaks out as people yell, clearing the area and forming a semi-circle around the two of us. From my periphery, I catch sight of Ryder, Hayes, Bridger, and Madden. Ryder steps forward, attempting to break up the fight as I land a quick jab to River's nose. He swears a blue streak under his breath as blood seeps from one nostril.

"River, stop!" Willow yells.

The sound of her voice is just enough to distract me, and the asshole lands a solid hit to the side of my head.

Fuck!

Muted sound rings in my ears as my vision goes blurry. I give my head a little shake to help clear it. I've been in plenty of fights on the ice. Once Ryder and I were in high school, my father signed us up for boxing lessons so we'd know how to take a hit and return them. The training has been invaluable.

It doesn't take long for me to regroup and land a couple more punches before Gerry, one of the bouncers, steps in to break up the brawl. Ryder and Hayes drag me away as Gerry does the same with River.

We're both breathing hard.

It's only now that we've been torn apart and adrenaline isn't pumping through my bloodstream that I realize how much my face hurts.

The asshole landed a few good hits.

Not that I'll be enlightening him to that fact.

My guess is that someone else learned how to box as well.

"Settle the fuck down!" Gerry bites out as River continues to struggle against his ironclad hold.

I take a good look at him.

All the times we've gotten into it on the ice, I've never seen such rage filling his blue eyes. If he could murder me with his bare hands, I think he'd do it.

He turns to glare at Willow. "What the hell are you doing with that guy?"

Fear flashes across her features as she falls back a step. "I'm sorry. I should have—"

"Should have what?" he bites out, voice rising above the din. "Told me that you were sneaking around behind my back?"

My heart pounds a painful staccato in my chest as I still, watching their interaction, waiting for her to tell him that whatever they had is over.

That it has been for a while.

She's with me now.

"It's not like that," she whispers before wincing. "All right, so maybe it is." There's a pause. "I wanted to tell you, but I knew this was exactly how you'd react."

Hurt flickers across his face, and that's all it takes for the fight to drain out of him. "You know I hate it when you keep shit from me."

My brows snap together when she takes a tentative step in his direction.

What the fuck is going on here?

"It's cool now," River grumbles to the bouncer. "You can let me go."

Gerry keeps him locked up tight.

And for good reason.

The guy came in swinging first and asking questions second.

"You cause any more problems and you'll get a nice pair of silver bracelets to wear for your complimentary ride to the station. Got it?"

River's gaze stays pinned to Willow as his lips flatten into a thin line. After a second or two, he jerks his head in a tight nod. Only then does the muscular bouncer release his grip and take a step in retreat, staying close enough to jump in if necessary.

It only takes three long-legged strides for River to eat up the distance between him and Willow.

Just as he reaches out to grab hold of her, I bark, "Don't you dare lay one fucking finger on her!"

He swings around and bares his teeth like a rabid dog before hauling her into his arms. "Or what? What the fuck are you going to do?"

Hayes and Ryder tighten their grip on me, as if they understand my intent before I do.

A potent concoction of fury and jealousy crashes over me as I struggle against my teammates. "You had your chance. Now she belongs to me."

His face scrunches. "What the hell are you talking about, McKinnon? She's my fucking sister!"

The world around me goes eerily silent as my gaze bounces between the pair. Willow's blue eyes flare as her features turn ashen.

Sister?

Willow is River's...*sister?*

It's only now that I see them standing side by side that I realize how much they resemble one another. Both have the same cornflower blue eyes, golden blond hair, and facial features. Although, where River is tall and muscular, Willow is finer boned and more fragile looking.

River's expression turns possessive as his arm locks around her. "Yeah, dumbass. She's my sister. My fucking twin."

Twin?

Holy shit.

It feels like I've entered a parallel dimension. One I never knew existed. My brain continues to somersault.

"I had no idea," I mumble, feeling like the dumbass he just called me.

How didn't I know this?

Better question is, why didn't Willow share this information with me herself?

My gaze slices back to her as the question circles around in my brain.

"Don't you see? He was using you to get back at me! That's all this was! Fucking revenge!"

Even in the dim lighting of the bar, her cheeks drain of all color as uncertainty flickers in her eyes.

Shock spirals through me.

After everything we've shared these past few weeks, it hurts that she would believe the worst in me.

"All he'll do is throw you away like a used-up tissue."

I shake my head when her attention resettles on mine. The questions and doubts that have mushroomed up within her eyes are nearly enough to kill me.

"You know that isn't true, sunshine. I didn't know you were related to that assho…" My voice trails off before I correct myself. "*River.* I didn't know he was your brother."

"No, it's worse than that," River interrupts. "You thought she was my girlfriend. Someone I cared about."

It takes a moment to realize how silent the bar has grown. A pin drop could be heard as the crowd that rings us swells in size.

I hate that everyone is standing around listening to our personal business being hashed out.

She straightens to her full height as emotion floods her eyes. "Is that what this is? Were you only trying to settle an old score with River?" Her gaze studies mine, attempting to pick through my private thoughts. "Just be honest." She gulps. "Please."

Even though she lied to me, I find that I'm unable to be anything less than truthful with her.

"Maybe in the beginning—"

"See!" River pounces on the admittance. "It was all a fucking game!" he snarls before stabbing a finger in my direction. "Stay the fuck away from Willow. She's not like other girls. She's…" He pauses, almost as if searching for the right word to use. "*Vulnerable* and doesn't need you playing head games with her."

My brows jerk together. "Vulnerable?"

What the hell does that mean?

River opens his mouth only to snap it shut a second later. The ruddy color filling his face drains as he shoots an uncertain look at Willow.

Just when I think he'll refuse to answer, his voice dips, turning husky. "She had cancer."

Air gets knocked from my lungs, making it impossible to breathe.

My attention shifts to Willow as the bomb River just dropped reverberates throughout my entire being.

Cancer?

My brain cartwheels, making it difficult to hold on to a single thought.

Before I can come up with a response, River beats me to the

punch. "You come near her again and I'll finish what I started tonight, understand?"

Then he's gone, disappearing with his sister through the exit and into the night.

And still...

The only thing I can do is stare at the last place I saw her standing.

Willow had cancer?

POCKETFUL OF SUNSHINE
WILLOW & MAVERICK
01:10 04:10

WILLOW

LEUKEMIA

33

I stare sightlessly out the windshield as River stabs the ignition button and the SUV roars to life. A heavy silence blankets us as he squeals out of the parking lot and onto the main road that leads back to campus.

In less than five minutes, my life has been turned upside down.

My head spins as shock reverberates throughout my entire being.

It takes effort to force the words through stiff lips. "Why did you do that?"

River's angry gaze slices in my direction before glaring back at the ribbon of road stretched out in front of us. "Do what? Protect you from the asshole who was only using you to get back at me?"

His words are like a punch to the gut, robbing the air from my lungs.

Everything that happened between Maverick and me flashes through my brain like a slow-motion picture show.

No.

It wasn't like that.

At least...I don't think it was.

He shoots another glare at me as his voice rises. "He fucking admitted it." There's a pause before another outburst. "You heard him!"

Tears sting the backs of my eyes as I wrap my arms around my middle and stare sightlessly out the passenger side window.

My brother isn't wrong.

Maverick did admit that he wanted to steal me from River because of what happened in high school.

Even though that acknowledgment hurts, it's not nearly as painful as what River did. Whether my brother realizes it or not, there are bigger issues at play.

"You have to stop outing my cancer diagnosis." Before he can respond, I snap, "I'm not a fucking disease. Not every person I meet needs to know my medical history, and you do it all the time!"

His intake of breath is sharp and audible as his expression twists, turning pained. "I never meant—"

"Bullshit. You always pull out the cancer card anytime a guy shows interest, and I'm tired of it." There's a pause before I tack on, "It needs to stop!"

His wide eyes fasten on mine in the darkness. "I... I'm sorry. All I've ever wanted to do is protect you, Willow. You're my twin. A piece of me." He swallows as his eyes turn shiny in the darkness. "There were times when I thought we'd lose you." He shakes his head. "How the fuck could I go on if the most important piece of me was gone?"

Some of my anger melts away at the thick emotion that clogs his deep voice.

Unable to help myself, I wrap my hand around his before giving it a squeeze, wanting to draw him out of those painful memories.

All the love that fills my heart is silently conveyed in that one touch.

It only takes one shared look, a brush of hands, or even a thought popping into one of our heads, to understand what the other is thinking or feeling.

It's the kind of bond that can never be severed.

Even though it would be far easier to drop the topic and move on to something else less painful, I can't. I despise arguing or being at odds with River, because it feels as though I'm not right with myself.

But the only way for me to move on is to finally air it out.

I need to do something with my twin that I never expected.

Set boundaries.

The thought saddens me. In a way, it's like hacking off a limb. But I need to be my own person. I can't continue living in the shadows and allowing the people around me to hold me back.

As much as they love me, they're smothering me.

Hampering me.

They're not allowing me to spread my wings and fly.

That's all I've ever wanted to do.

As much as I know this will hurt him, he needs to understand my feelings on the matter.

Not only that, he needs to accept them.

"Mom, Dad, and you are the ones who make me feel sick. There are times when I actually forget that I had cancer, and you know what? Those are amazing days. But then Mom calls or you out me to someone I just met, and it's like the candle has been snuffed out and I'm dragged back into the darkness. Alone. It's isolating, and I hate it. I really fucking hate it." I let that sink in before adding, "It makes me not want to be around any of you. And that just breaks my heart because I love you all so much."

His face turns ashen as anguish floods his eyes. "God... I'm sorry, Willow." He opens his mouth as if to say something more before slamming it shut with the next breath.

His pain has always been my own.

When I hurt him, I cause the same damage to myself.

We're so tightly connected and intertwined.

As much as I've always loved that feeling of never truly being alone in this world, especially during my darkest hours, I need the separation.

I need boundaries.

"I've never wanted to see you hurt," he mutters, thick emotion invading his voice.

It's so tempting to crumble and offer forgiveness the way I have in the past. Instead, I force myself to hold strong. Nothing will change between us if I don't.

"Right now, you're the one who's causing me pain."
Those charged words hang heavy in the air.
The remainder of the drive is silent.
Bursting with unease.
The one thing it never is between us.

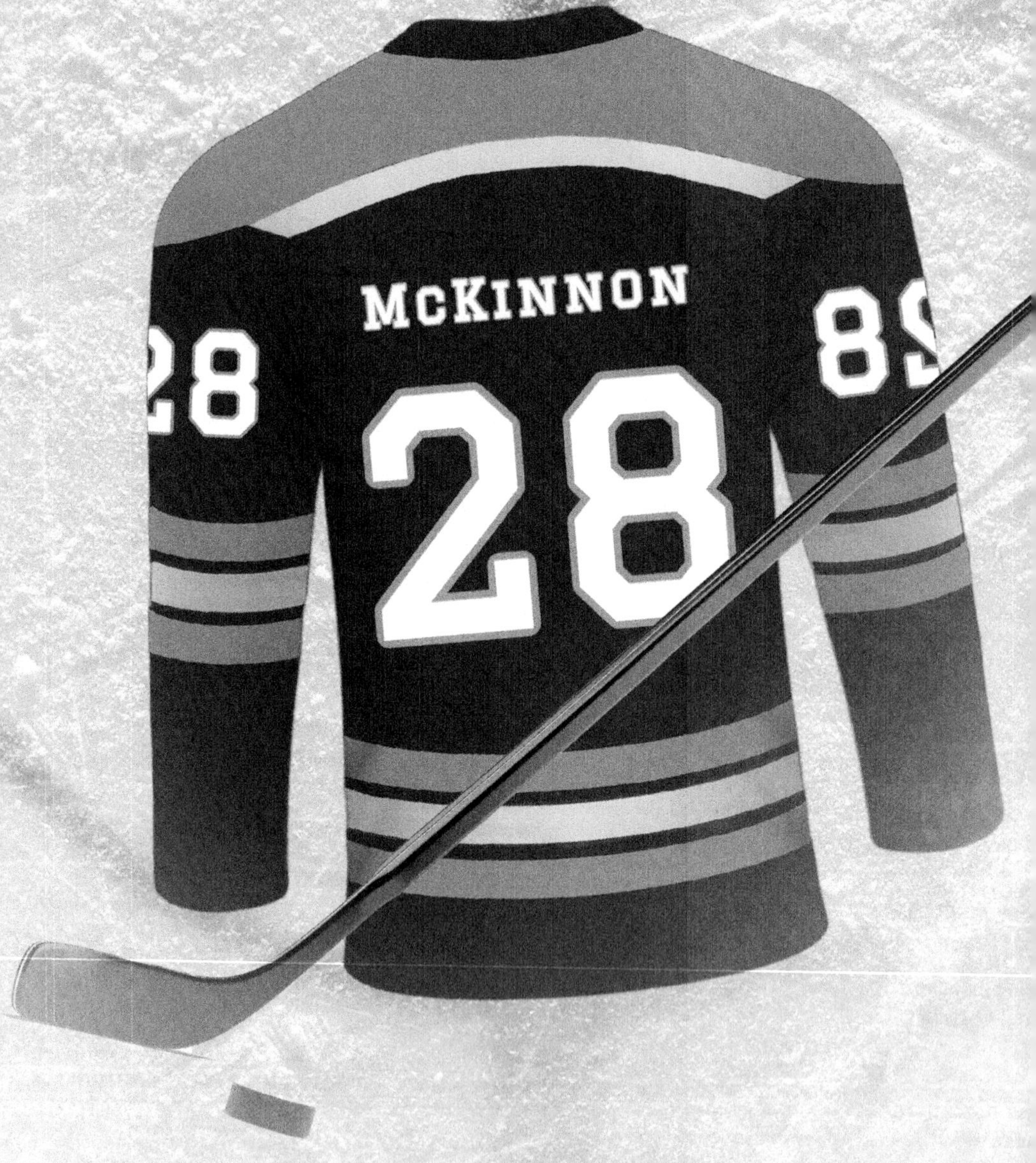

MAVERICK

WILDCATS

34

I slam into the locker room and throw my stick into the holder before stalking to the bench and chucking my gloves. Only then am I able to unsnap the chin strap and rip the helmet off my head.

Sweat drips from my hair as I draw a lungful of fresh air into my body and bury my head in my hands.

It was a shitty practice.

The worst I've had since starting at Western.

I was off the entire time, and no matter what I did, I couldn't get back into the flow. I wasn't focused on the scrimmage. When I should have capitalized on scoring opportunities, I missed a handful of easy shots. Then there were the defensive lapses and turnovers. Instead of battling Hayes against the boards when he was driving the puck toward the net, I hesitated and backed off.

Thoughts of Willow have been fucking with my head ever since Saturday night at Slap Shotz.

Before I can calm the chaotic whirl of my thoughts, Coach bellows, "McKinnon, in my office after your shower!"

"Looks like you screwed the pooch this time," Colby says after the frosted glass door stops vibrating on its hinges.

"Tell me something I don't know," I mutter as other players stop and stare at the now closed office door and then at me.

Looks of pity fill their expressions as they return to their convos.

I'm sure they're just glad it isn't their asses he'll be crawling up.

Ryder strips off his pads.

A couple months ago, he would have given me shit like Colby and rubbed the predicament in my face. Instead, he remains quiet, his thoughts hidden behind a mask. There's an unease between us that wasn't there before.

Not only do I fucking hate it, I have no idea how to move past it.

Especially when the silence that stretches between us turns unbearable.

For a few seconds, I consider heading to Coach's office now and getting this convo—or, more than likely, ass chewing—over with. It's better than sitting here and drowning in this awkwardness.

"I didn't even know you were seeing that chick," he mutters, staring straight ahead at his locker.

"Willow," I grumble, irritated that he'd refer to her as "just some chick."

No matter what happened the other night, that's the last thing she is.

His gaze flickers in my direction as he shifts. "Sorry. Willow." After removing his chest and elbow pads, he bends down to unlace his skates. "Why didn't you mention it? I had to hear about it from Juliette."

I shrug as anger bubbles up inside me. It takes effort to keep it under wraps. "What else do you expect when you spend all of your time with her?"

I wince, hating how butthurt that came out sounding.

If I could snatch the words from the air, I'd do it in a heartbeat.

But that's not possible.

They're out there, demanding acknowledgment.

His brows knit as he frowns before glancing up to meet my gaze. "I didn't think you had a problem with us being together."

Oh, for fuck's sake.

Why does everything need to be spelled out?

I huff out an irritated breath and try to wrap my brain around my thoughts in order to express them. "I don't."

Well, not really.

When he remains silent, I blurt, "Guess I didn't expect that you'd drop me like a bad habit. The only time we see each other is on the ice."

Heat stings my cheeks as I glance away.

Now I really do sound like a needy bitch, and that's the last thing I want.

I squeeze my eyes tightly closed and suck in a deep breath before expelling it from my body. This whole talking-about-my-feelings thing sucks even more than I assumed it would. But I'm knee deep in it. The only thing I can do at this point is wade all the way in before reaching the other side.

And who knows? Maybe the guy who's always been my best friend will be nothing more than my sister's boyfriend.

The sadness that floods my system at that thought is more anguishing than a gunshot wound.

"Look, I know it doesn't sound like it, but I really am happy for you and Juliette. In hindsight, I should have seen what was right in front of my face and realized that you two had feelings for one another." I jerk my shoulders. "Maybe I just didn't want to see it. Maybe deep down inside I knew on some level that everything would change between us."

Ryder blinks as he stares at me like I just sprouted a horn on my forehead. "I..." His voice fades as he glances away with a frown.

Well, fuck.

I've just bared my damn soul to this guy, and he's at a total loss for words.

He can't even look at me.

I want the floor to open up and swallow me whole.

There is definitely no coming back from this.

Even though guys are joking and talking shit in the locker room, it doesn't infiltrate the bubble of silence that has settled over us.

Just when I'm about to tell him to forget the conversation, he mumbles, "I'm sorry. I had no idea you felt that way. I wish you'd said something sooner about it. I hate that you've been holding all this inside. I promise I'll make more of an effort to hang out." His lips quirk as he tosses his skates into the locker and meets my gaze. "Like we used to."

Air leaks from my lungs as my heart pounds a steady tattoo against my chest. Inside, I'm fist pumping. Outwardly, I jerk my head into a nonchalant nod. "Yeah, that would be cool."

"Whatever it takes, we'll get it figured out."

After a few minutes, I clear my throat. "It's not like I don't want you spending time with my sister."

"Yeah, I know." His voice turns pensive. "Guess I didn't realize we'd gotten so wrapped up in one another that we were excluding our friends. It's something we should probably talk about." He jerks his chin toward me before smiling. "Who knows, maybe once you iron out everything with Willow, the four of us can go out sometime."

That's all it takes for thoughts of her to crash over me again.

I drag a hand through my sweat-soaked hair. "Yeah... I'm not sure what will happen with that."

For all I know, we're over before we ever really started.

That thought is like an arrow piercing my heart. The pain of it is almost enough to have me doubling over.

His voice gentles. "Have you talked to her about what happened at the bar?"

I shake my head. "No."

"Why not? From what I saw, it seemed like she really meant something to you."

"She did." I wince and correct myself. "I mean, she does."

More than anyone else has in a long time.

Maybe more than anyone else ever has.

He jerks a brow. "But?"

"The situation is...complicated."

His expression turns curious. "How come?"

I roll my eyes. "I think we both know the answer to that one. In three words—River fucking Thompson."

He shrugs. "I know you hate the dude, but what does that have to do with Willow?" His eyes search mine. "One of the reasons I stayed away from Jules for so long is because I knew you wouldn't like it. But it got to a point where I couldn't let our friendship stand in the way of something that could be amazing. If you really care about this girl, then don't let your issues with River be what stops you."

He's not wrong.

I stare down at my hands. "There's the other thing," I mumble, unable to meet his eyes.

"The C word."

It's not a question.

Ryder was there through it all when Mom battled cancer. He knows exactly how much it affected all of us.

Me especially.

Can I open myself up to potentially losing someone else I care about down the road?

I don't know.

As that question circles through my brain, I glance around, only to realize that Hayes is eavesdropping on our convo.

When I frown, he pops a shoulder. "Just wanted to make sure you two hugged it out. I was thinking about gathering the guys for an intervention."

With a shake of my head, I mutter, "Shut the fuck up, dude."

I'm embarrassed that our private convo wasn't so private after all.

Then again, maybe we shouldn't have done this in a locker room full of our teammates.

"He's totally serious," Colby says, using the towel to dry his hair. "We talked about it the other night. We were thinking of catering the affair with barbeque." He pats his belly. "I could have gone for that while you two hashed your shit out." He shrugs. "Guess that won't be necessary. Bummer."

"More important than barbeque is all those good vibes we need gelling on the ice," Hayes adds with a grin.

Ryder shakes his head. "You guys were stressing over nothing." His gaze settles on mine. "We're all good. Right?"

For the first time in a while, our friendship feels as if it's back on solid ground. "Yup. So feel free to move it along. There's nothing to see here."

"Glad to hear it." Colby hauls his boxers up his legs.

"You never answered Ryder's question about Willow," Hayes cuts in, some of his humor fading.

As our gazes collide, I'm struck with the realization that he had insider intel he didn't bother to share with me.

My brows jerk together as I growl, "Why the fuck didn't you give me a heads-up and tell me she was River's sister or that she was sick?"

He shrugs. "It didn't really seem like my place."

Is this guy being serious?

"When the hell have you ever been concerned with minding your own business or staying in your *place*?" I ask with a disbelieving snort, using my fingers to make air quotes around the last word.

He folds his arms across his brawny chest. "I've known River for a long time. I consider him a friend in the same way that I consider you one. I know what happened between you two and I didn't want to get caught up in the middle of it. I told Willow she needed to come clean, but that was her story to tell, not mine. And she doesn't have cancer anymore." There's a pause as his brow furrows. "At least, I don't think she does. What I do know is that she was diagnosed in high school, and by the time we graduated, she was in remission. That girl has been to hell and back. She deserves all the happiness she can grab hold of. And if you can't be a part of that, then don't mess with her."

Hearing about her cancer is like a kick to the balls, and sucks the air from my lungs as icy fingers wrap their way around my heart before squeezing. It takes a few seconds to realize that it's the very same kind of fear and anxiety that takes hold of me when I worry about Mom.

I've spent years trying to keep these emotions at bay.

Somehow, Willow has managed to sneak past all of my defenses and burrow deep inside my heart.

I have no idea if there's a way to evict her.

And I'm no longer sure if I want to.

Our relationship was complicated from the moment I saw her sitting in the visitor's section, wearing River fucking Thompson's jersey, cheering for him when he scored a goal.

How is it possible that it's become even more convoluted?

We're supposed to meet up for a tutoring session tonight. It was set up before everything exploded over the weekend. I'll admit that I considered blowing it off until I was able to get a better grasp on my feelings.

But if I do that, I'm running away from my problems. What I've learned over the years from having dyslexia is that nothing good happens when you do that.

In fact, it only makes everything worse.

Uncertainty spirals through me as I strip off the rest of my gear and hop into the shower before getting dressed.

Then I head to Coach's office to get my ass chewing over with.

Ryder glances at me as I huff out a breath.

"Want me to wait around?"

I shake my head. "Nah, I'll see you back at the house. I've got something to take care of."

The guy who I've always considered my best friend smirks. "Something or *someone*?"

"Someone."

As I say it, a sense of rightness settles over me.

He nods. "Good. We just might be able to make that double date happen after all."

"I hope so."

I realize I've never meant anything more as I straighten my shoulders and rap my knuckles against the frosted glass door.

"Come in."

I poke my head inside the small space. "You wanted to see me, Coach?"

"Yeah." He glances up from the paperwork strewn across his desk. "Close the door and take a seat."

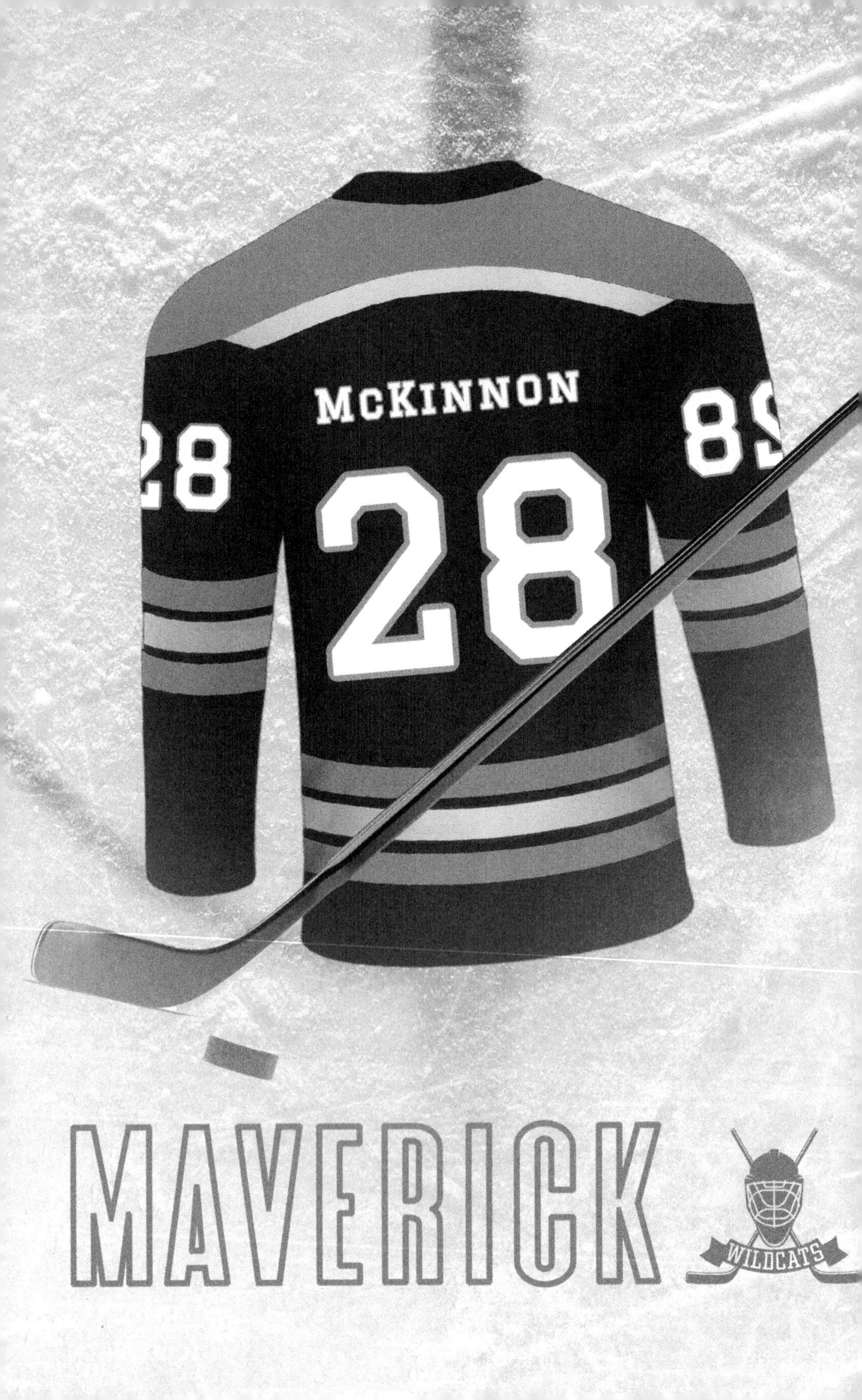
McKINNON
28
MAVERICK
WILDCATS

35

Twenty minutes later, I'm hustling my ass across campus, hoping to make it to the library by six o'clock. I considered calling or texting Willow a million times throughout the week, but ultimately, it's better if we have this conversation in person.

The entire time Coach had been yapping, I'd snuck quick peeks at my phone, hoping he'd bottom line his long list of grievances.

No such luck.

He'd gone on for another fifteen damn minutes before finally wrapping up his spiel.

And now I'm late.

At ten minutes past six, I yank open the door and rush through the lobby to the staircase before taking the risers two at a time. The closer I get, the more anxiety crashes through me.

Even though it's only been a handful of days since we last saw each other, it feels more like weeks. I'm starving for the sight of her. Once I reach the third floor, my gaze coasts over the area before spotting a blonde with her back to me. Her head is bent and her hair is in a messy bun at the top of her head.

I suck in a deep breath, hoping to steady everything that rampages inside me. Sweat springs to my palms as I beeline to the table she's parked at.

"Hey." The greeting bursts from my lips before I can stop it.

I spent most of practice thinking about how I wanted this conversation to go. It's the reason I was such a shitshow on the ice.

And Coach let me know it.

His advice was that I needed to focus on what's important—my future.

And that's exactly what I'm doing.

Willow has become a bright spot in my life, and I refuse to lose that.

Or her.

The moment she glances up and meets my gaze, a large smile breaks out across her face. "Hi!"

I blink, thrown off guard at finding a stranger. The longer I stare, the more I wonder how I ever thought she was Willow. Upon closer inspection, other than the fact that their hair color is a similar shade and they're roughly the same size, she looks nothing like my girl.

"Um, sorry," I mumble, taking a hasty step in retreat. "I thought you were someone else." I shift and glance around the third floor, hoping to spot her.

Just when I'm about to swing away, she chirps, "Maverick, right?"

My heart picks up tempo. "Umm, yeah."

"I'm Stacie. Willow asked me to take over your tutoring sessions for the remainder of the semester." With a tilt of her head, she eyes me up. "I thought she would have mentioned it."

The tossed-out comment is like a kick to the balls. "No, she didn't."

"That's all right." Her smile widens as she points to the chair across from her. "Why don't you take a seat and we can get started?"

"Sorry, I just remembered that I have a thing and need to reschedule."

Her brows draw together as she frowns. "Are you sure? I probably won't be able to squeeze you in again for a couple of days."

"Yeah, I am."

Before she can come up with another way to detain me, I take off.

Did Willow really think she could send someone else in her place in hopes of avoiding me?

Ha!

That's not about to happen.

POCKETFUL OF SUNSHINE
01:10
WILLOW & MAVERICK
04:10
WILLOW
LEUKEMIA
SURVIVOR

36

I curl up in a ball on the bed and screw my eyelids closed. Every time a shiver racks my body, I drag the comforter up around my neck to ward off the chills. A few minutes later, it'll feel like I'm burning up and I'll toss off the blanket. This scenario has been playing on repeat for hours.

When Holland hovers near the threshold of the room, my eyelids flutter open to meet her concerned stare.

"Are you sure there isn't something I can get for you? A drink? Maybe some crackers? How about a bowl of soup?"

The thought of food makes me nauseous.

But I keep that to myself.

I don't want Holland to realize just how miserable I feel.

Instead, I shake my head and close my eyes, only wanting to sleep off whatever virus I've picked up. "No," I mumble. "I'm not hungry."

"You need to at least drink and stay hydrated."

I point to the bottle of water on my nightstand. "I'm trying."

A heavy silence settles over us.

It's almost a surprise when she mutters, "As much as I hate to even speak her name, maybe we should call Becks."

I force my eyelids open again and shoot her a scowl. "Don't you dare. It's just a little bug. A day or so of rest and I'll be fine. You'll see."

"I don't know..." She creeps closer before staring down at me. "You're really pale."

"We both know that I've always been pale. Don't you remember the way Jonnie Decker teased me in fourth grade? He tried to convince everyone that I was an albino."

"That kid was such a little fucker."

"Truth." There's a beat of silence. "And he never said another peep to me after you broke his nose."

For the first time since Holland stepped into my room, a smile lifts the corners of her lips. "That's one of my favorite memories from elementary school."

"You're lucky you didn't get suspended."

She shrugs. "I could have used a little R and R. That unit on the Revolutionary War was a killer." When the humor fades from her expression, I realize that my distraction technique hasn't worked. "I know you don't want to hear it, but I'm worried."

This conversation has become exhausting. I just want to sleep. "Don't be," I mumble around a yawn. "Everybody gets sick."

"Yeah..." Her voice wavers before trailing off. "But not everybody has a weakened immune system."

I huff out a sigh. "Always have to throw that in my face, don't you?"

My bestie settles tentatively on the edge of the bed. "That's not what I'm trying to do."

"I know."

"I think we need to—"

Her voice dies a quick death when the doorbell chimes throughout the townhouse.

My eyes lock on hers before narrowing. "If that's my mom, you're in deep trouble."

With a frown, Holland rises to her feet. "I didn't call her. But I wouldn't put it past Becks to have a sixth sense where you're concerned."

That sad piece of truth is enough to have a weak chuckle escaping from me. "You're one hundred percent right about that. Sometimes it's scary."

"What are you talking about? It's always scary." When the doorbell peals for a second time, she says, "I'll be right back."

It's only when she slips from the room that my eyelids drift shut again.

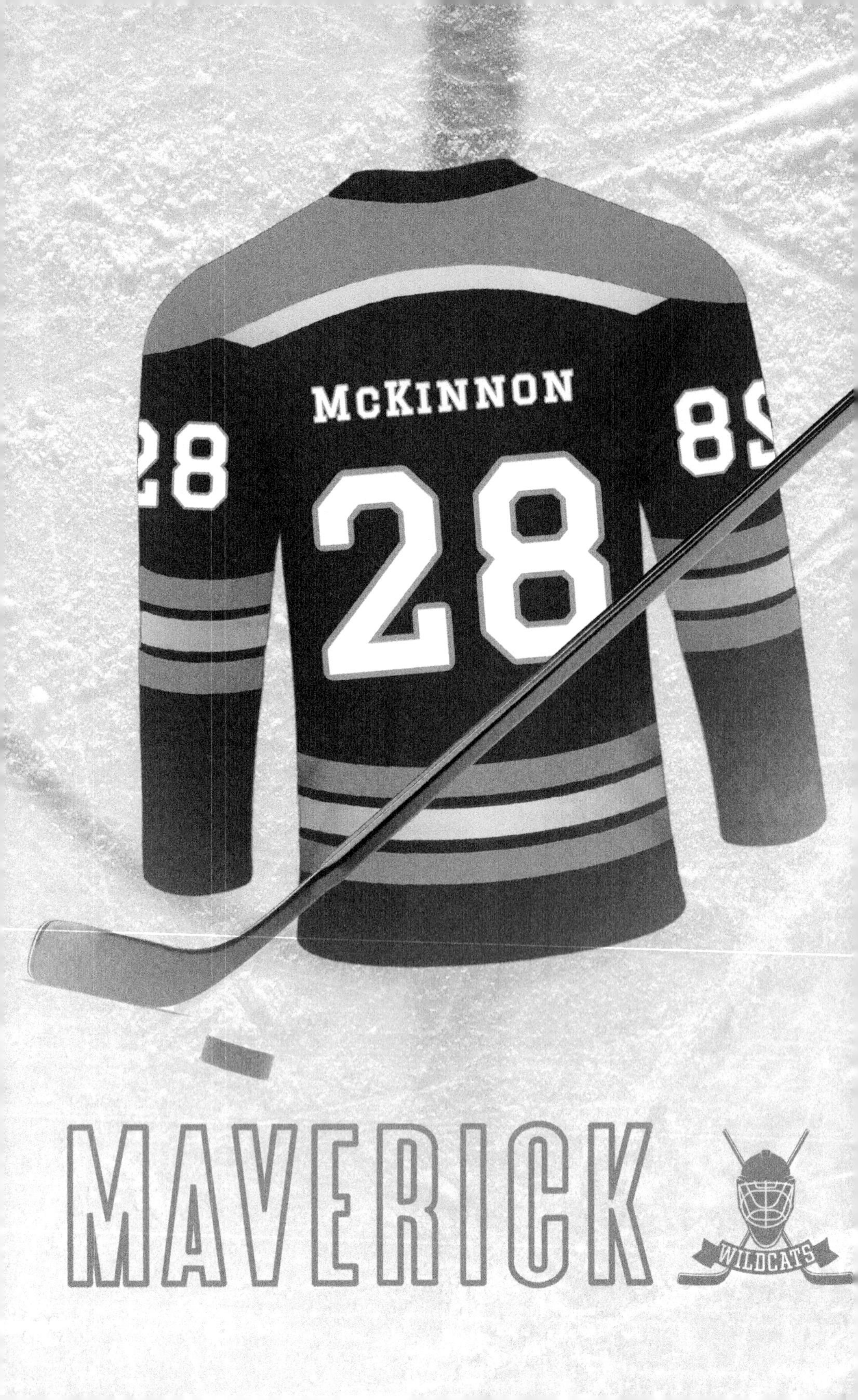
McKINNON
28
28
MAVERICK
WILDCATS

37

I'm about to hit the bell for a third time when the door swings open and I find a tall girl with strawberry-blonde hair standing on the other side. Even though I stopped by a couple days ago, we never introduced ourselves.

When she continues to stare in awkward silence, I lift a hand in greeting. "Um, hey. I'm Mav—"

"I know who you are." Her voice turns impatient. "What do you want?"

I peek past her into the townhouse. "Is Willow around?"

She shifts, blocking my view. "She's busy at the moment, but I'll be sure to let her know you stopped by."

When she takes a step in retreat and tries to slam the door in my face, I flatten my palm against the thick wood. "Busy with what?"

Her narrowed eyes slice to my hand. "You're going to want to move that appendage unless you'd like it broken."

My brows shoot up at the hostility that pours off her in heavy waves. "For someone who doesn't know me, you sure seem to have a problem with me."

Her nose scrunches. "You play hockey for the Western Wildcats, right?"

"Yeah."

"That's all I need to know."

When she attempts to slam the door in my face for a second time, I lose my patience and bark, "I'm sure you won't believe this, but I'm actually not trying to piss you off. I just want to talk to Willow and straighten things out between us. I..." My voice trails off as I swallow past the thick lump in my throat.

It would be so much easier to tell this angry girl to go fuck herself, but the most important thing is clearing the air with Willow. I'm not leaving until that happens. So, if that means I need to drop to my knees and beg Willow's guard dog, who'd much rather take a chunk out of my ass than to let me speak with her—even for five damn minutes—then that's exactly what I'll do.

My shoulders wilt as my eyes plead with hers. "Look, I really care about Willow. We had a misunderstanding, and I want to make sure we're good. If you're afraid I'm going to come in here and upset her, I won't. Promise."

I hold my breath and wait for the verdict.

It takes a handful of seconds for her expression to soften.

Marginally.

For all I know, it's a trick of the light.

She searches my face for a long, silent moment that leaves me fidgeting beneath her steady stare. I get the feeling this girl sees way more than I'm comfortable with.

Just when I think everything I've confessed has fallen on deaf ears and she'll slam the door in my face one final time, she surprises me by poking a finger at my chest.

"If you say anything to upset her, I'll personally make sure that you never play hockey again. Are we clear?"

"Crystal."

The scary part is that I believe her. This girl is no joke. She'd happily fuck me up.

After another hard look, she grudgingly steps aside, allowing me into the tiny entryway.

As soon as I walk by, she slams the door closed before pushing past me. My gaze flies over the compact living room, taking in all the homey touches as we cross through it to a hallway on the other side. Just as we reach a closed door, she spins around to face me.

"Willow isn't feeling well."

I frown, thrown off by the warning. "What do you mean?"

Only now do I pick up on the anxiety wafting off her as she jerks her shoulders. "She caught a cold or the flu. I'm not sure which. She's been sleeping for most of the day." There's a pause. "I threatened to call her mother if she gets any worse."

A chill slithers down my spine. It's the same feeling I get when Mom isn't feeling well. My chest will constrict, making it impossible to suck in a lungful of air.

I don't realize that I've hesitated outside the door until her roommate clears her throat. "Don't stay long."

I glance at her again, only to find concern etched across her expression.

"I won't."

With that, she spins away, retreating into the living room.

I stare at the closed door. I fucking hate the ball of nerves that has settled in the pit of my belly along with the memories mushrooming up inside me.

The fear.

The lack of control.

The anger.

I have to mentally prod myself into rapping my knuckles against the door. I wait a beat. Then another. When a response isn't forthcoming, I push open the thick wood and peek inside the dimly lit space.

Every muscle constricts when I find Willow curled up on the bed under the covers with her eyelids closed.

She doesn't bother to open them. "Who was it, Holl? Not the holy rollers again?"

I step inside the room before closing the door and clearing my throat. "Nope, it wasn't them."

Her eyelids flutter open and her tongue darts out to moisten her lips. "Maverick?" She glances at the clock on the nightstand next to the bed. "What are you doing here? Shouldn't you be at the library?"

I cock my head. "Hard to do when my tutor bailed on me."

"She did?" Her brow furrows. "That doesn't sound like Stacie."

"I meant you."

There's a beat of silence before her gaze shifts and understanding dawns. "It seemed like it might be better for both of us if you worked with someone else."

I take another step closer. It feels like there's an invisible thread binding us together. "What if that's not what I want?"

"Maverick…"

"What?" The mattress dips as I tentatively settle on the edge. Unable to stop myself, I reach out and run my hand over her cheek.

Her skin is surprisingly hot to the touch.

There's a beat of silence before her solemn gaze flickers back to mine. "I have to know… Did you only sleep with me to get back at River? Is that all it ever was? A game?"

POCKETFUL OF SUNSHINE
01:10
WILLOW & MAVERICK
04:10
WILLOW
LEUKEMIA

38

His featherlike touch drifts over my face, pushing the sweaty strands of my hair away from my forehead. All I want to do is press my cheek against his cool palm.

The silence that stretches between us sets my nerves on edge.

"The first time I saw you sitting in the stands, I couldn't stop staring. As corny as it sounds, it felt like time stood still. I was afraid that if I looked away for even a second, you'd disappear." His lips quirk. "The fact that you were wearing River's jersey pissed me off. It's the reason I went after him."

Air leaks from my lungs as a shiver dances down my spine.

The moment I saw him on the ice during the game will forever be singed into my brain for all eternity. Even though I should have been focused on my brother, I couldn't take my eyes off Maverick.

He eclipsed everything and everyone around him.

"Afterward, I figured I wouldn't see you again. But you showed up at the bar and I knew at that point, I had to have you. It didn't matter who you were with or belonged to. I wanted you to be mine. At least for one night." He jerks his shoulders. "Long enough to fuck you out of my system. Instead, I woke up the next morning only wanting to get my hands on you again, and you'd disappeared, leaving behind your necklace. No matter how hard I tried, I couldn't get you out of my head. All I wanted to do was find you. See you again."

His eyes sear mine as he continues to stroke my cheek.

"What I feel for you has nothing to do with your brother. After all these years, I don't give a shit about what happened with Sabrina. You're the only one who matters, sunshine."

As tempting as it is to believe him, doubt bubbles up inside me, making it impossible.

"You admitted at the bar that you wanted to get back at my brother by sleeping with me."

He squeezes his eyes tightly closed and bows his head. "*You're* what I wanted. Just you. I'll admit that hurting River was a bonus. I wish it hadn't been. More than anything, I hate that it tainted the beginning of our relationship, because that's exactly what it was."

My heart flutters as I weigh his soft words.

When I remain silent, his thumb strokes over my lower lip. "Your silence is killing me. Tell me what you're thinking."

I release the pent-up air from my lungs as our conversation circles through my brain.

Maverick is the first guy to come along and make me feel like I'm not made of spun glass that will break when the slightest bit of pressure is applied. And I've loved every minute of it. Even—or maybe especially—when he pushed me out of my comfort zone.

I've relived every single time he laid his hands on me.

The idea of going back to a pale imitation of what we've explored together is depressing.

My teeth scrape across my lower lip as I shake my head. "I don't know, Maverick." Even though it guts me to say it, I force out the truth. "I'm not sure if there's a way for us to move forward."

He scoots closer before snaking his hand around the nape of my neck and tipping my head upward until his lips can hover over mine. "Don't say that. The past couple days without you have been shit, and it only drives home how much you mean to me." He gulps. "How much I need you in my life. I don't want to lose what we've only just found. I don't want to lose you."

His warm breath ghosts across my lips.

It's intoxicating.

All I want to do is inhale a deep breath of him and hold it hostage in my lungs forever.

To always keep him close.

Even if this is the only way to do it.

"I'm scared," I admit. "Scared that even if we try to make it work between us, you'll treat me differently. Or worse, you'll decide that you need someone with less baggage, and you'll walk away."

His brows furrow. "That's not going to happen, sunshine."

"How can you be so sure?"

"Because I've never cared for anyone the way I care about you. When we're apart, I think about you all the time, and when we're together, I don't want to let you go. You might not realize it, but your nickname fits you perfectly, because you fill my world with bright sunshine. And when we're not together, everything feels blanketed in darkness. I just want to bask in your presence so your light can shine down on me."

Tears prick the backs of my eyes.

No one has ever said anything so beautiful to me.

"Are you sure?" The question is out of my mouth before I can rein it back in.

With a shake of his head, his lips quirk. "I've never been more certain about anything in my life."

"Okay." Joy explodes inside me before rushing through my veins until the tips of my fingers and toes tingle with it.

When he presses a kiss against my lips, I whisper, "Will you promise me one thing?"

"Anything."

"I don't want you treating me like I'm some kind of fragile flower. I loved everything we did together." I straighten my shoulders. "And I refuse to accept anything less."

"Trust me, sunshine, that's not going to happen. I love the way we fuck, and as long as you tell me that you're good, we'll keep doing it."

My heart flip flops in my chest.

It's exactly what I needed to hear.

Better than that—I can see the sincerity shining in his eyes.

"Now I'm going to ask something of you."

"Okay."

"I don't want any more secrets between us. Do you understand?"

I jerk my head in a nod. "I'm sorry about lying. I should have been upfront about everything right from the start."

He releases a long slow breath. "It's okay, sunshine. In a way, I get it. But no more. And if I find out that you've been keeping secrets, I'll spank that gorgeous ass of yours and love every damn minute of it."

My mouth turns cottony.

A mixture of heat and humor flares to life in his eyes. "Or maybe I'll just spank your ass whenever I damn well please. How does that sound?"

"Promises, promises," I tease, thrilled that we've somehow managed to find a way to the other side. I wasn't sure if it was possible.

"Just wait until you're feeling better," he growls.

His lips drift over mine one more time before he rises to his feet and strips off his sweatshirt, tossing it to the floor until he's left in a pair of dark wash jeans.

Even though I feel run down, I can't stop from watching him flip open the button and lowering the zipper before shoving the thick denim down lean hips and thighs until the only piece of clothing that covers him is a tight-fitting pair of boxer briefs.

My gaze dips to his thick length.

"Yeah, there'll be none of that while you're sick." His deep voice smolders with pent-up heat.

My eyes widen, slicing to his face. "I wasn't—"

He arches a brow. "Lying to me already?"

A small smile curves my lips as I release the breath clogged in my lungs. "Fine. Maybe I was."

"Oh, there's no maybe about it. Trust me, as soon as you're well enough to be fucked, that's exactly what we'll do. My cock needs inside that sweet little pussy. It's been way too long. But for now, I'm just going to hold you in my arms while you sleep. And hopefully, you'll feel better in the morning."

He lifts the sheet and comforter before sliding in beside me. The mattress dips beneath his heavy weight. There's something so comforting about his presence.

"Roll onto your side and I'll spoon you," he orders.

I hesitate as uncertainty spirals through me. "I'm not sure what I've caught, but I don't want you to get sick. Especially now. The last thing you need is to miss practice or any of your games."

"I appreciate the concern, but I'll be fine."

When a silent war continues to rage in my head, he jerks a brow. "Turn over, Willow. Do I have to threaten to spank that ass already?" There's a beat of silence as his voice dips. "Unless that's not a threat at all?"

My face warms as I roll onto my side.

The deep chuckle that reverberates from his chest only makes it flame more as he slides behind me and slips his arms around my waist until our bodies are pressed tightly together.

"Go to sleep, sunshine. We'll talk more in the morning."

He tugs me even closer before brushing his lips across my temple.

A sigh of contentment escapes from me as I drift off wrapped up in his arms.

McKINNON 28

MAVERICK WILDCATS

39

As soon as my eyelids open, I realize I'm not alone. Willow's warm body is nestled against my chest. And just in case she tried to put a little distance between us during the night, I kept my arm locked around her. Now that we've cleared the air, I don't want anything coming between us.

My morning wood stirs against her perky little ass.

That's all it takes for my mind to tumble back to yesterday and the way arousal had flared in her eyes when I'd threatened to spank it.

Yup...we'll definitely be exploring more of that.

Even the thought of laying hands on her has my erection turning painful. I can't help but nudge it against her backside.

There's nothing better than waking up with Willow wrapped up tight in my arms.

It's the perfect way to start the day.

To start every day.

I promised her last night that we would talk when she woke up, and that's exactly what we're going to do.

Hash everything out and come to an understanding.

And that understanding is that Willow Thompson belongs to me.

Everything loosens inside me as that thought reverberates through my brain.

Unable to resist touching her, I brush aside the long mass of golden strands to kiss the side of her face. As soon as my lips sweep over her temple, I realize that she's still hot.

No, not just hot…burning up.

It's like being scalded.

The jolt of fear that sizzles through my veins is more than enough to shake off the last dregs of sleep.

And then I'm wide awake.

I haul myself into a seated position before rolling Willow onto her back. Her eyelids remain feathered closed as color stains her cheeks.

I lay my palm against her forehead, hoping I'm wrong and it's not as bad as I think it is.

Fuck.

She feels even hotter than I first thought.

"Willow?" Fear weaves its way through my voice until I hear the fine tremble in it. "Wake up, baby."

She remains unresponsive.

If it weren't for the rapid rise and fall of her chest, I'd be freaking the fuck out.

It takes effort to remain calm and figure out the best course of action before rolling from the bed and hauling on my jeans. After that, I drag my sweatshirt over my head and shove my feet into shoes.

Willow is dressed in a loose T-shirt and shorts. I scoop her limp body into my arms before heading to the door.

Her roommate's eyes widen and her mouth falls open as she steps out of the bathroom and grinds to a halt.

"Oh my god, what happened?"

I shake my head. "I don't know. She's burning up. We need to get her to the hospital."

Indecision flashes across her face. "Should we call an ambulance?"

"The closest hospital is ten minutes from here. Let's just get her there, all right?"

Thankfully, Willow's guard dog doesn't argue.

"I'll grab my keys."

Her car is parked in front of the townhouse. It's a rusty piece of crap that has seen better years. Make that decades. But as long as it gets us to the hospital as quickly as possible, I don't give a shit.

She races ahead of me and opens the door so I can slide onto the back seat, all the while holding Willow against my chest. Then she hustles around to the driver's side and starts up the vehicle. A handful of seconds later, we're hauling ass out of the parking lot and into early morning traffic. That's when I realize the sun is barely peeking over the horizon.

"I don't even know your name," I mutter, stroking my fingers over Willow's cheek, trying to rouse her before we reach the hospital. I'd feel so much better if she'd just open her eyes.

Her roommate's gaze meets mine in the rearview mirror for a heartbeat. After our terse convo yesterday, I'm prepared for her to bare her teeth.

"Holland."

"Interesting." I say it more because nothing else comes to mind. This girl isn't exactly the chatty sort.

She's more the piss-me-off-and-I'll-shank-you-in-the-eye sort.

What can't be denied is how protective she is of her friend. Even though this girl is as prickly as a cactus, I can't help but like her for that alone.

Just when I think the rest of this ride will be made in silence, she clears her throat. "We've known each other since elementary school."

My gaze roams over Willow's face as Holland continues to talk.

Her voice wavers as she admits, "I honestly don't know what I'd do without her. No one else gets me the way she does."

I glance at the rearview mirror and notice that moisture has gathered in her eyes.

"She'll be fine." I have no idea if it's the truth, but, in this moment, it's what we both need to believe.

Holland swerves into the hospital parking lot before pulling into a space and cutting the engine. She jumps out of the car and jogs around the hood to the other side before yanking open the door. It doesn't take much jostling before I'm out of the vehicle and we're both racing through the glass emergency room doors. As soon as we step inside the vestibule, hospital staff descends on us. As much as I want Willow to get the medical care she needs, I'm reluctant to let her go. Memories of my mom getting wheeled off to surgery flood my brain and try to take hold.

"Sir? You need to hand her over," a woman says. The briskness of her voice is enough to snap me from my thoughts.

I jerk my head in a nod before gently setting Willow's limp body on the gurney. The moment I release her, she's whisked away, disappearing through a set of double doors. A woman sitting behind a glass partition fires off questions, trying to understand what they're dealing with so they can figure out the best course of treatment.

Holland fills in more details along with her medical history, which I quietly listen to. My gaze is continually drawn to the doors Willow disappeared through. Every second that ticks by only ramps up my agitation.

I plow a hand through my disheveled hair. "Can I go back with her?"

The woman looks up from the computer screen. "Are you family?"

Fuck.

When I glance at Holland, she pops a brow.

"Yeah, I'm her fiancé."

The woman peers at me from over the rim of her reading glasses. "Are you sure about that?"

I straighten to my full height. "Yes."

Air gets trapped in my lungs when Holland jerks a thumb in my direction. I'm afraid of what's going to come out of her mouth.

It wouldn't surprise me if she outed the lie.

Security would get called and then I'd get tossed out on my ass.

"This is Maverick McKinnon. You know, the hotshot defenseman for the Western Wildcats? The one turning pro next year?" When the woman doesn't blink, she adds, "His father is Brody McKinnon?"

Apparently, that means something, because her expression transforms as she sucks in a deep breath before gushing, "I had the biggest crush on him when he played in the NHL. He was so big and blond..." Her voice trails off as she gets lost in the memories.

Yikes.

When Holland side-eyes me, I clear my throat. "So… I can go back and sit with her?"

"Sure, sweetie. Follow me."

I huff out a relieved breath.

As I turn to follow her, I mouth to Holland, "*thank you.*"

She jerks her head in a nod. "I'll call her parents and let them know what's going on."

POCKETFUL OF SUNSHINE
WILLOW & MAVERICK
01:10
04:10
WILLOW
LEUKEMIA
SURVIVOR

40

The voices are what first capture my attention and tug me toward the surface. It's a struggle to make sense of the words. My eyelids feel like they're weighed down by cement blocks. After a minute or so, exhaustion creeps back in at the edges and I give up, happy to be sucked back under.

The second time it happens, my eyelids flutter and I squint against the light that pours in through the windows. It takes a moment to focus on my surroundings. My brows draw together when I realize nothing looks familiar. Everything is white or cream colored and sterile.

The beeping of machines is all too familiar and slams home exactly where I am.

The hospital.

The strangest part is that I have no memory of how I got here.

"I think she's finally waking up."

Mom.

I would recognize her anxiety-riddled voice anywhere.

Truth be told, it's a relief to know she's here and that I'm not alone.

"Hey, sweetheart," Dad murmurs. "Look who's returned to the land of the living. We've been worried about you."

Only now do I realize that my head is throbbing a steady beat. "It kind of feels like I've been run over by a truck." I search my memory for more information but come up empty. "What happened?"

"You caught the flu and got dehydrated."

I glance at the IV taped to the back of my hand.

It's a sight I'd hoped to never see again.

Mom slips her fingers around mine, drawing my attention to her. "Honey, why didn't you call me when you didn't feel well? I would have come over and taken care of you. I knew you weren't being careful and sanitizing. And look what happened." When her voice continues to escalate, I wince. "You ended up in the hospital!"

I squeeze my eyes tightly closed in an attempt to block her out.

"Rebecca," Dad says with a heavy sigh. "Let's save that conversation for a later date. This isn't the time or place."

Mom sends him an icy glare. "Of course it is. It's the perfect time for Willow to realize that she can't take these kinds of foolish risks with her health. She needs to be more vigilant."

My tongue darts out to lick my chapped lips. "I refuse to spend my life living inside a bubble."

"That's not what I said." She huffs.

"Yes, it is. You'd be much happier if I lived at home and didn't attend college or get a job."

"That's not true!" Her voice falters as tears gather in her eyes. "I just want you to stay healthy. Is that such a crime?"

I force myself to meet her searching gaze and say the things I've wanted to get off my chest for the past couple years. "No, it isn't. But it feels like I've been given a second chance, and what I want most is to live every day to the fullest without regret." I pause and allow those words to sink in. I need her to hear me. Really hear me this time. "And you don't want me to do that."

She gasps. "Willow!"

I struggle to pull myself up to a seated position. "It's true, Mom. I'm tired of watching everyone do all the things *I* want to experience. I'm tired of being the sick girl. I played that part enough in high school. I don't want to do it anymore." As much as I know this will hurt, it needs to be said. "Sometimes it feels like that's what you want me to be so you can continue coddling me."

A single tear treks down her cheek. "I..." Her voice trails off as she glances away before swiping at the moisture. "I'm just so afraid of losing you. When the doctors first diagnosed you with leukemia, it felt like the floor was ripped out from beneath us. I don't think I've ever been more scared or prayed so hard in my life." A suffocating silence falls over us as she chews her lower lip. "I'm sorry if that's the way I came across. It was never my intention."

Guilt rushes in to drown me. As much as I don't like the sight of her tears, there's relief in finally getting my feelings out in the open.

"I just...love you so much."

I suck a fresh breath of air into my lungs before gradually releasing it back into the atmosphere. "I know, Mom. And when I was diagnosed, you quit your job and put your life on hold to care for me. I'm appreciative of that. But right now, what I need most from you is a little bit of space. Not everything is a catastrophe. Sometimes, I'm going to mess up and make mistakes. And, just like everyone else, I'm going to get sick. All I can say is that I'll do my best not to die on you."

When her expression turns to one of horror, the corners of my lips tremble. "That was a joke."

She glares. "Not funny. But I get it, and I'll try to do better. Promise."

I nod.

That's all I can ask for.

My gaze settles on my brother, who's been strangely quiet throughout our conversation. We haven't spoken much since the night he drove me home from the bar.

And I hate it.

"Hey, sis. We were worried about you." He flicks a glance at our mother. "Mom nearly shit a brick."

"River," she snaps. "Watch your language."

"What?" He gives me a conspiratorial wink. "It's true."

She purses her lips.

Now seems like a good time to cut in. "How'd you find out I was here?"

"Holland let us know."

My memories of what led up to my trip to the hospital are still murky around the edges, but I seem to remember Maverick stopping by the townhouse.

Did we talk?

I could have sworn he crawled into bed with me.

Unless I was already delusional by that point.

For all I know, it was a hallucination.

Or wishful thinking on my part.

A puff of air escapes from me. It would be impossible to shake off the disappointment that has taken hold.

"Just in case you were wondering, he's the one who brought you here," my brother murmurs, drawing my attention back to him.

Our gazes lock and hold.

My mouth turns cottony as every cell in my body goes on high alert. My voice comes out sounding raspier than intended. "Who?"

"McKinnon."

"He did?" My eyes widen as my heart picks up tempo. "He was here?"

River's expression remains inscrutable as he dips his head in a nod.

If Maverick wasn't already frightened away by me passing out, I'm sure a run-in with River hammered the final nail into the coffin.

Sorry, bad joke.

As soon as my parents arrived, he probably got the hell out of Dodge as fast as humanly possible. It's doubtful I'll hear from the guy again.

"Yup." My twin's expression turns cagey. "He told the staff that you were his fiancée so he could stay with you. He didn't want you waking up alone and not knowing where you were."

Warmth blooms in my chest before slowly spreading outward until it reaches the very tips of my fingers and toes.

I can't believe he did that.

River clears his throat. "As much as it pains me to say this—he seems to genuinely care about you."

I blink, thrown off by the admittance.

I can only imagine how difficult that was for River.

A kernel of hope tentatively rises within. "Do you really think so?"

My brother jerks his shoulders as he shifts from one foot to the other. "Yeah, I do."

Some of the heaviness pinning me to the earth lifts, making it easier to breathe.

My lips twitch as I tease, "You don't have to sound so happy about it."

"Trust me, I'm not."

I raise a brow, hoping that's not his final word on the matter. "But?"

He rolls his eyes before grumbling, "I guess there are worse guys you could get involved with than Maverick McKinnon."

"That's progress, and I'll take it." I tilt my head and study him. "Would you believe that you two actually have a lot in common? If you weren't always at each other's throats, you'd probably be friends."

It's almost comical the way his face scrunches. "Sorry to disappoint, sis, but that's *never* going to happen."

A small smile simmers around the corners of my lips. "Anything's possible."

He shakes his head. "Nope. Not a snowball's chance in hell."

Our mother sighs. "River...language."

Before my brother can shoot back a response, there's a knock on the hospital room door. A second or two passes before it opens and Maverick pokes his head inside.

Our gazes fasten.

It would be impossible not to notice the concern etched across his expression. I feel terrible that he was so worried about me.

But...is that all it was?

Concern?

The kind you feel for a friend?

He glances at my brother and then my parents. "Is it all right if I come in?"

In a surprising plot twist, they turn their attention to me for an answer.

I nod as a fresh burst of nerves detonates at the bottom of my belly.

Mom rises from the chair parked next to my bed in one swift movement. Her fingers are still clasped around mine.

Even though I don't want to, I rip my gaze away from Maverick to meet her eyes.

She clears her throat. "We'll go home and grab something to eat. And then we'll return in a few hours. Hopefully, once we get back, you'll be released."

"If you don't mind, Mrs. Thompson, I'd like to take Willow home."

Indecision flickers across Mom's face. He's unwittingly crossed into her domain.

When she remains silent, Dad says with a meaningful look aimed in her direction, "I think that would be fine, Rebecca. Don't you?"

Mom straightens her narrow shoulders before reluctantly relinquishing my hand and forcing a slight smile to her lips. "Sure. Will you at least text me when you get home?"

A lump of emotion settles in my throat. "Of course I will."

She chews her lower lip before nodding.

In a way, I understand how difficult it is for her to loosen the reins and let me take control. Mom is the one who kept track of all my appointments and medications. When I was too sick to take care of myself, she's the one who did it for me.

And I'm so appreciative of her love.

But I'm not a child anymore.

And I don't want to be treated like I'm on the verge of relapsing.

She needs to give me the space to grow into the adult I was always meant to be. No matter how difficult that is for her.

"Okay then," she murmurs, tucking a stray lock of blonde hair behind her ear.

Dad slips his arm around her waist before gently steering her from the room.

Rather than trail after them, River waits for our parents to disappear into the corridor before eating up the distance between him and Maverick. It only takes three strides to bring them toe-to-toe.

When they're no more than a foot away, my brother pauses to search Maverick's eyes. "I'm only going to say this one time—you hurt her and I'll bury you where no one will ever find your carcass again. Are we clear?"

Tension crackles in the air between them.

The last thing I want is for a fight to break out and security to get called.

Maverick straightens to his full height as he stares right back. Although, his expression lacks the animosity that's usually present when he's around River. "The last thing I want to do is hurt Willow. You have my word."

My heart constricts at the sincerity that rings through his deep voice.

The heavy tension wafting off River gradually dissipates.

When he hesitates, I realize he wants to say more, but for whatever reason, he decides to hold his tongue. Instead, my brother turns to meet my gaze.

Both his tone and expression soften. "Call me if you need anything, all right?"

A smile breaks out across my face as a potent concoction of relief and joy crashes over me. The fact that these two actually engaged in a civil interaction is more than I could have expected, and it gives me hope for the future.

"I will. Love you."

"Love you too."

And then he's gone, disappearing into the hallway.

Now that it's just the two of us, Maverick settles in the chair near my bed. Our gazes stay locked as his fingers slip around mine before giving them a gentle squeeze.

"You really scared the shit out of me," he admits.

Heat slams into my cheeks. "I'm so sorry about that."

"You don't have anything to apologize for. I'm just relieved that you're all right and it was a matter of being dehydrated rather than something being wrong."

"I should have taken better precautions and made sure I drank more fluids."

He lifts my hand to his mouth before brushing his lips against my knuckles. "I don't know what I would have done if something happened to you."

Bits and pieces of our conversation from last night float back to me.

My tongue darts out to moisten my lips. "Mav?"

"Yeah, sunshine?"

I wave to the hospital room around me. "Are you sure you can handle all this? There are no guarantees I won't end up back here again."

His eyes soften as his lips stroke over the back of my hand for a second time. "I guess what I've come to realize is that there are no guarantees in life." There's a pause. "And I need to be all right with that, because the only other option is to not have you by my side. That's not a choice I'm willing to make. So, if that means opening myself up and risking my heart, then I'm willing to do it." He searches my eyes, and his voice dips. "For you, Willow. I'm willing to do it for you."

A weight I hadn't even realized was pressing on my chest, constricting airflow, disintegrates.

Maverick rises to his feet and looms over me before capturing my lips with his own.

He only pulls away long enough to meet my eyes. "I think you might be it for me, sunshine. I think you might just be my everything."

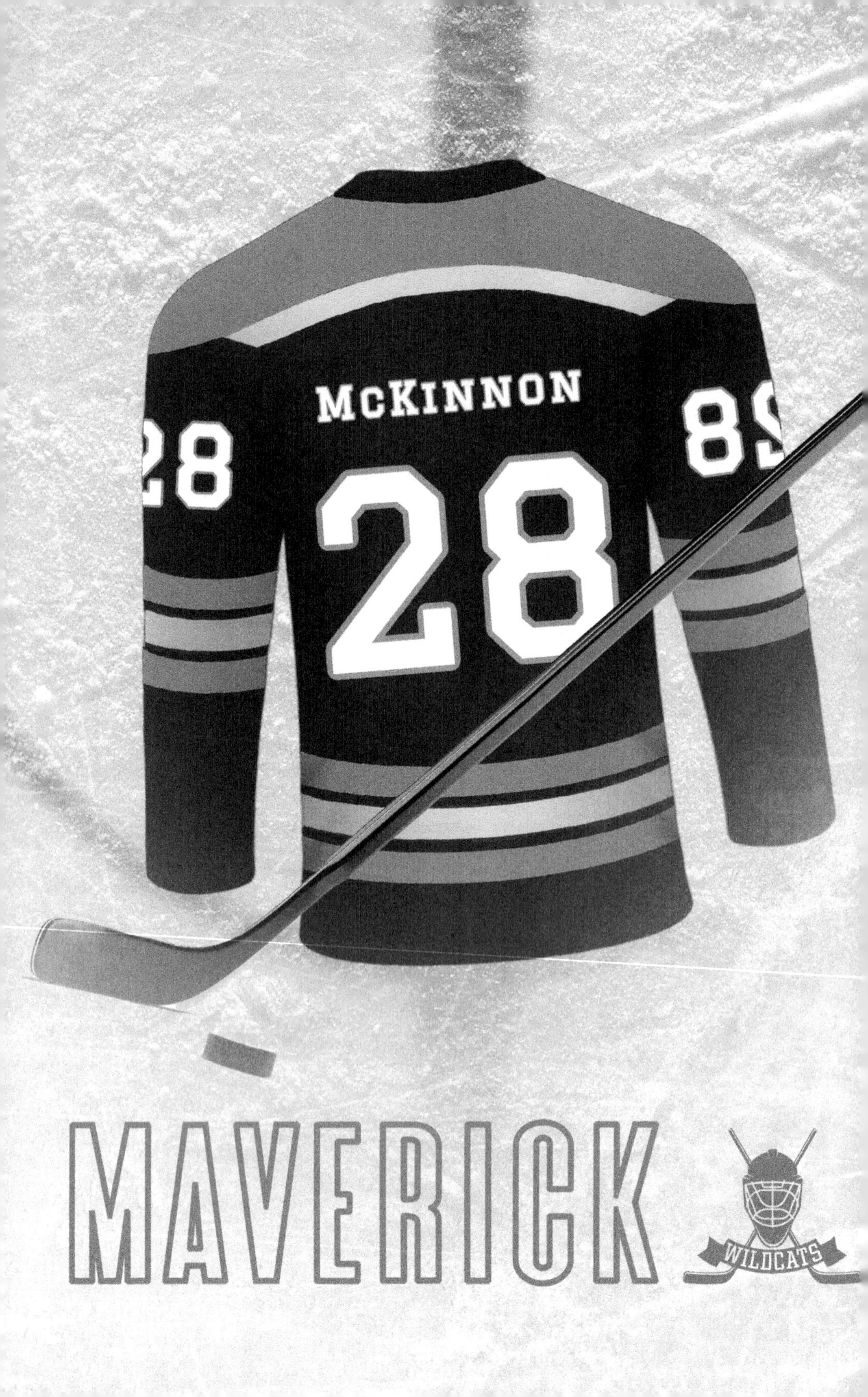
McKINNON
28
28
MAVERICK
WILDCATS

41

My arms are wrapped around Willow as Britt and Colby belt out one of the songs she's written on stage. The Wildcats took home another win tonight, and you know what that means...

Yup, you guessed it—karaoke.

This was our final conference game. Next week, playoffs begin. We've been working hard all season to get to this point, and now it's here. I glance at Ryder, Wolf, Bridger, Hayes, Madden, Riggs, and Ford. These guys were already a unit when I came in freshman year. I was lucky enough to be accepted into their brotherhood so easily.

After this season, they'll graduate. For some, they'll go on to play in the pros. For others, their hockey playing days will be behind them and they'll jump into their careers and families.

I'm going to miss them.

Coach was impressed with the way I've turned my grades around, and he talked to me about being captain next season. With the added responsibility, I'll need to step more into a leadership role for the team.

I press a kiss against the top of Willow's blonde head.

It's amazing how easily everything has fallen into place now that the air has been cleared and there are no more secrets.

She might not remember it, but I was serious when I said that I'd spank that gorgeous ass if she ever hides anything from me again.

Although...here's a secret—I think my little sunshine enjoys having her backside smacked. Especially when she's on all fours and I'm fucking her from behind, teasing her until she screams out her orgasm.

My cock stirs at the thought.

Willow tips her head until our gazes can collide. Her eyes search mine in the darkness of the bar, as if she's able to sense my thoughts.

"Whatcha thinking, sunshine?"

There's zero hesitation on her part. "Just how perfect everything feels."

It really does.

Instead of waiting for the other shoe to drop or worrying about what might happen in the future, I'm learning to let go and simply enjoy the moment. The greatest gift we can give ourselves is to live life to the fullest and appreciate the people we choose to let in.

She tilts her head enough for our lips to align. That's all the invitation I need to take her mouth. When my tongue sweeps across the seam, she opens, allowing me entrance. And then I'm delving inside to plunder her sweetness.

There's nothing better than the taste of her flooding my system.

"For fuck's sake," River grumbles from a few chairs away.

My lips twitch as we break apart. "Problem, Thompson?"

"Yeah, stop mauling my sister in front of my face. Can't you save that shit for behind closed doors?" There's a pause. "On second thought, just don't do it at all."

"Maybe I should remind you that no one invited you here to—"

Willow swats my chest. "I invited him so you two can get to know each other better."

I watch River from the corner of my eye, only to find him giving the same look right back at me. The truth of the matter is that I know exactly how it feels to watch your sister making out with some dude.

It's borderline uncomfortable.

Then consider that it's the guy you've always had beef with...

So, maybe I understand River fucking Thompson better than I want to.

That's all it takes for the tension filling my muscles to loosen.

My attention is drawn back to the stage as Colby tugs his wife into his arms and smacks a kiss against her lips. The crowd roars their approval as they splinter apart and my teammate escorts her back to the table.

My gaze settles on River, who still looks none too happy to be here. Other than Hayes, most of my teammates are ignoring him. I'm sure it feels a little like being in enemy territory for him. As easy as it would be to carry our grudge forward and be a jerk, I don't want to do that.

Even though we've been at odds from day one, this guy is important to Willow.

And if he's important to the girl who's turning out to be my everything, then the relationship I have with him matters.

End of story.

"You any good at karaoke?"

He glances in my direction. "I'm sorry, are you talking to me?"

"Yup." I nod toward the stage. "Instead of hugging it out, maybe we can sing it out?"

Hope brightens Willow's expression as she sits up and stares at her brother.

"Come on, Will, don't do this to me," he grumbles.

She doesn't have to say a word before he's caving.

"Fine."

"I don't know how you did that," I whisper in her ear, "but it was impressive. And a little bit scary."

"It's a twin thing," she says, eyes twinkling with mischief.

I pluck her off my lap and settle her on the chair next to it before rising to my feet. "So... What are your thoughts when it comes to the Backstreet Boys circa 1997?"

"Hate them."

I grin. "Perfect. I know exactly what we're going to sing."

"Last song of the night," Sully booms into the microphone as we make our way to the stage.

As soon as we arrive, I let the bar owner know the selection I've chosen for the occasion.

I pick up one of the microphones before tossing the other to River.

He catches it with one hand. "Are you going to tell me what we're doing or am I supposed to guess?"

My shoulders shake with silent laughter. "Trust me, you'll know what it is when you hear it."

He huffs out an irritated breath before shaking his head.

"All cued up," Sully says.

As soon as the powerful rhythm drum pattern, accompanied by a driving beat of "Everybody (Backstreet's Back)" by the Backstreet Boys echoes throughout the bar, River swears under his breath.

"You're such a dick."

The crowd cheers as some of them jump to their feet. We haven't sung one lyric yet and already hands are raised in the air.

I'm half prepared for him to toss the microphone to Sully and storm off the stage. Instead, he belts out the opening verse along with me. And I have to say, we're in perfect harmony.

About a dozen girls nearly swoon as my gaze fastens on Willow, who beams from the chair I set her on. And that's exactly when I know that I'll do whatever it takes to keep that expression on her face.

Just call it my new mission in life.

By the time we finish, the entire bar is screaming the lyrics back at us, and it's a standing ovation as the last notes reverberate throughout the dark space.

I rip my gaze away from Willow to stare at her brother. A reluctant smile has settled on his lips.

"See, you had fun."

He shrugs. "Maybe so, but you're still a dick."

With a chuckle, I jump off the stage and make my way back to Willow. All I can think about is getting her alone.

Once I reach the table, I pull her out of her seat and wrap her up in my arms before whispering in her ear, "You ready to go, sunshine? All I want to do is get my hands on you, and I can't do that in front of your brother."

"Thanks for including him. You have no idea how much it means to me."

"That's where you're wrong. I know exactly how much it meant. It's why I did it. Why I'll do whatever it takes to make you happy."

The softness that fills her eyes is enough for me to drown in.

Happily so.

Her teeth scrape across her lower lip. "I love you, Maverick."

Those words steal the air from my lungs. I've been wanting to tell her I love her for the last week or two, but I was worried that she wasn't there yet. I'm trying to take our relationship slow so I don't scare her away with the enormity of my feelings. It's a relief that I don't have to hide them anymore.

"I love you too."

With a smile, she presses her lips against mine. "Let's go home so you can show me exactly how much."

"Deal."

POCKETFUL OF SUNSHINE
WILLOW & MAVERICK
01:10
04:10
WILLOW
LEUKEMIA
SURVIVOR

EPILOGUE

Two years later...

"Ms. Thompson? I have a question."

I turn away from the smartboard where I'm writing out the math problems we'll be tackling for our lesson this afternoon.

"Yes, Alice?"

"Are we having a guest today?"

My brows draw together, wondering where the question came from. One of the first things we do in the morning is go over our schedule for the day. If there's a change to the itinerary, that's when we talk about it. Our second-grade class runs smoother when everyone understands what to expect and there aren't any surprises.

"Nope. Today's a normal day. No speakers or assemblies." I tilt my head. "Why do you ask?"

When the little girl points toward the classroom door, I follow the movement. A burst of happiness explodes inside me when my gaze collides with mahogany-colored eyes.

Maverick.

That's all it takes for a smile to break out across my face as he lifts his hand in a wave.

Some of the kids who play hockey jump to their feet.

"That's Maverick McKinnon," Devon Richfield yells, body vibrating with excitement.

"He's so cool!" Brett Samson adds.

Alice swivels toward the boys and chirps, "My mom says that Ms. Thompson is a very lucky lady."

My brows shoot up before my gaze slices back to Maverick.

His shoulders shake with humor, because he knows exactly what that little girl's mom is implying.

And, yeah, it's true.

I am *very* lucky.

It's so tempting to close the distance between us and throw myself into his arms. Even though it's only been five days since I saw him, it feels like forever. I want to soak up every little detail and commit it to memory.

It's only when he steps farther inside the classroom that I realize he's not alone. My parents and River are crowded behind him.

I blink, surprised to see them.

The only time they've been here is when I was first hired as a second-grade teacher. The three of them stopped to check out my classroom, and I gave them a tour of the building. Mom cried the entire time. Not because she was worried about me getting sick but because she was so proud.

"Hi." My gaze touches upon each of them. "What are you all doing here?"

It's tempting to tack on *during the middle of a school day*.

The four of them step farther inside the classroom.

"I thought it was important that your family be here," Maverick says.

My brows draw together. "For what?"

When he's standing directly in front of me, he drops to one knee.

It takes a moment to process what's happening. My eyes widen as my hands fly to my mouth. When I'm finally able to force out my voice, it sounds like it's being choked from my body. "Maverick?"

"Yeah, sunshine?"

"What are you doing?"

"Asking the love of my life to marry me. After being away from you for five days, it only reinforced that you're it for me. The beginning and end of my world. I want us to take that next step together. The one that leads to the rest of our lives. What do you say, Willow? Will you make me the happiest man in the world and become my wife?"

Tears flood my eyes as I nod. "Of course I will. I love you, Maverick. More than anything."

River clears his throat. "Ummm... Weren't you supposed to ask that question with a nice piece of bling? You know, something to sweeten the deal for having to look at your ugly mug for the next fifty years?"

"Well, hell. He's right." Maverick winces. "I was so nervous, I forgot to show you the ring."

All the kids make ohhhing sounds.

"That's a bad word, Mr. McKinnon."

"Yeah, Ms. Thompson doesn't allow us to say that."

Another girl pipes up, "Ethan said it in the library last week and Ms. Thompson told him that she'd send him to the principal's office if it happened again."

Ethan uses his fingers to make a zipping motion across his lips.

"It sounds like your teacher is a real stickler," Maverick says with a smirk.

Heat floods my cheeks when the kids all nod in agreement.

"However, Ms. Thompson is right about that. And she can deal with my punishment once we get home."

He gives me a little wink before slipping his hand into the front pocket of his jeans and pulling out a light-blue box. My heart spasms when he pops open the lid.

That's all it takes for another gasp to slip free as I catch my first glimpse of the ring nestled on the cushy pillow inside.

The piece of jewelry is so stunning, it robs the air from my lungs.

The band is platinum with a sparkling diamond set between two equally dazzling sapphires that are polished to a high shine.

A heavy silence falls over the classroom.

Even the children hold their conversation as the scene plays out in front of them.

Maverick has no idea the miracle he's been able to accomplish.

But I can't focus on that right now.

The only thing that fills my vision is Maverick staring up at me from his bent knee.

When I say nothing, his brows pinch together and uncertainty flickers in his dark eyes. "Sunshine?"

It takes effort to blink away the haze that has settled over me.

My tongue darts out to moisten my lips. "Yes."

His eyes widen. "Yes?"

I nod as a grin breaks out across my face. "Of course I'll marry you!"

In one swift motion, he leaps to his feet and wraps his arms around my body before lifting me up and swinging me around in a tight circle. Excited voices explode around us as the children cheer and my family claps.

"You need to kiss her," one of the boys shouts.

"Yeah, Mr. Maverick, you need to kiss Ms. Thompson!"

"Well, if you all think I should kiss my fiancée, then I probably should do it." Maverick grins. "Are you good with that, Ms. Thompson?"

I glance at the kids before flicking my gaze back to the man of my dreams. "Maybe just one."

"I'll try to keep it PG."

"That would probably be for the best."

His lips sweep over mine. The chasteness of the peck only makes me hungry for more. The glint filling his eyes tells me he knows it.

"I promise I'll show you exactly how much I missed you when we don't have an audience," he murmurs.

"I love you so much and can't wait to spend the rest of our lives together."

He rests his forehead against mine so our gazes can cling. "I love you too, sunshine. More than I'll ever be able to put into words. But if you let me, I'll spend the rest of my life doing my best to show you."

When another cheer goes up around us, we break apart with a smile.

My mind tumbles back to the very beginning—the moment our eyes connected while he was out on the ice—and then everything we went through to get to this point.

What I realize is that there's not a damn thing I'd change about how our story unfolded.

Because in the end, it's ours.

The one we'll share with our own children someday.

And maybe even grandchildren.

What could be more amazing than that?

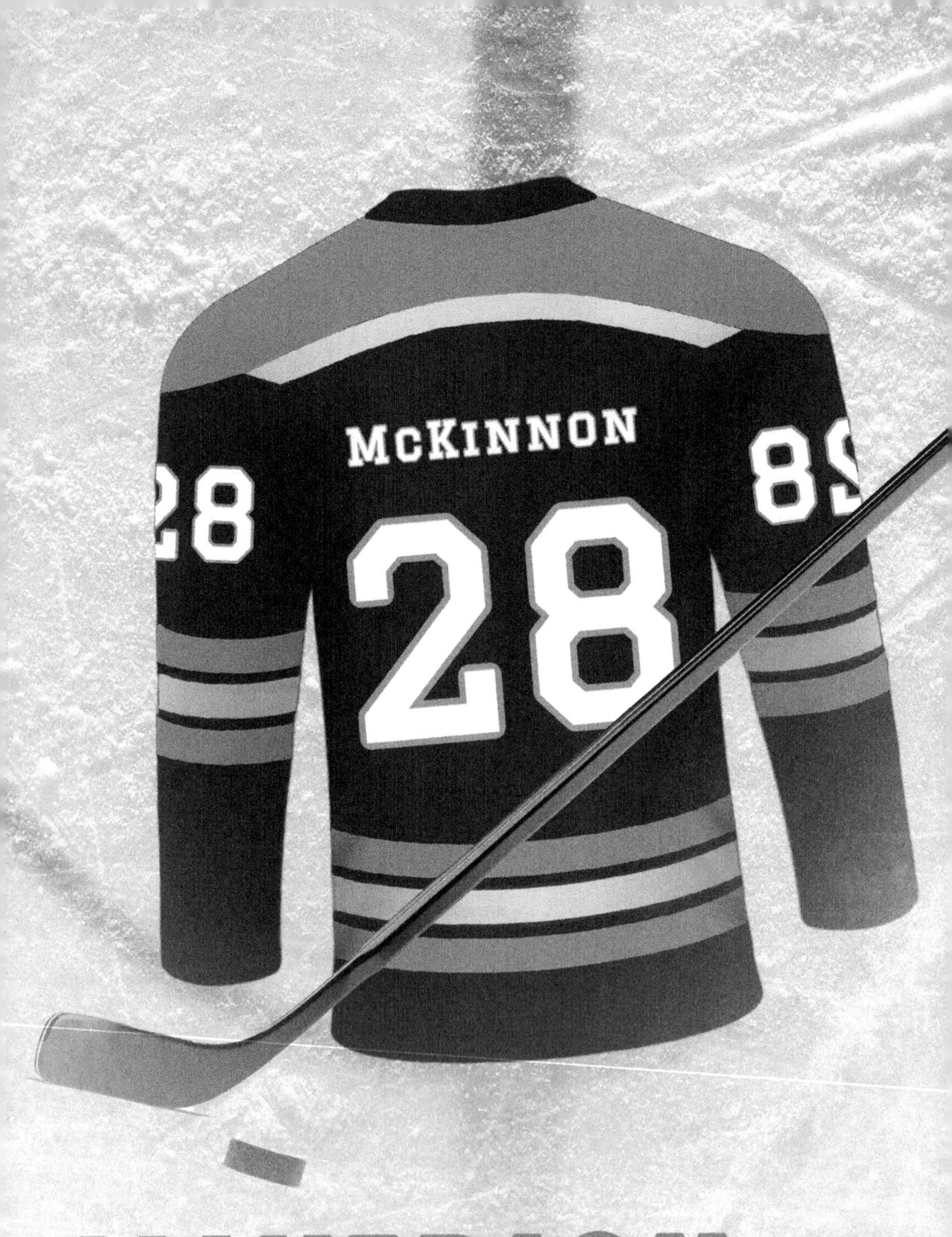

MAVERICK

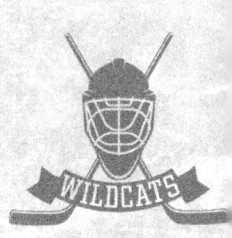

bonus EPILOGUE

Three years later...

I tip my face to the spray and let it rain down on me. The hot water washes away the last of the coiled tension filling my muscles from the game we just played. Instead of heading to the locker room like everyone else, Coach pulled me into the pressroom to field a few questions. He hates talking to reporters. The man only seems capable of grunting and yelling.

In that order.

Unfortunately, the press loves me. They've always had an affinity for my father, and that seems to have transferred over to yours truly.

It's both a blessing and a curse.

Especially when all the other guys have taken off either to party with groupies or go home to their families. There's an equal number of both on this team.

I fit in with the latter.

The only person I'm interested in partying with is my gorgeous wife.

And I scored a hat trick during the game, so you know what that means...

Oh yeah.

Someone's getting on her knees tonight and worshipping her god.

As soon as that third goal hit the back of the net, I stared up at where she was sitting with the other WAGS, and grinned. Even from the ice, I could see the pretty pink color that suffused her cheeks and the smirk that lifted her lips.

She loves it just as much as I do.

Even the thought of deep throating Willow's warm mouth all the while tangling my fingers in her golden-blonde hair is enough to have me stiffening right up.

It's definitely time to get my ass in gear and find my woman.

Just as I'm about to twist the handle and turn off the shower, slender hands wrap around me from behind before a naked body is pressed against my back.

For a heartbeat, my muscles tighten and I wonder who the hell has snuck into the locker room. It wouldn't be the first time a groupie or two have slipped inside our private space.

"You played an amazing game tonight," a husky voice whispers before brushing a kiss against my shoulder blade. Air gets clogged in my lungs when her teeth scrape across my flesh. "It made me hot just watching the way you took command out there."

A fine tremble slides through her.

Everything inside me loosens as her hands roam over my chest, massaging the muscles before tweaking my nipples.

A groan slides from my lips as my head falls back.

There's nothing better than the feel of Willow's hands.

Even with our entire lives stretched out ahead of us, I have no idea how I'll ever get enough of her.

She's the light that fills my entire existence.

Without her, my world would be a dark place.

Willow will forever be my own personal ray of sunshine.

She peppers kisses along my wet back.

"How'd you get in here? Did security already take off for the night?"

"Nope." Sharp teeth nip my flesh. "I told them you needed a little help washing up after such a hard-fought game."

I grunt. "Liar."

She chuckles. "You're right. I slipped past while they were fending off a couple of girls who wanted to see the great Maverick McKinnon in all his naked glory."

Even though she can't see it, I roll my eyes.

Ever since Willow came into my life, I don't notice other women.

Although, from what my teammates have said, that's only made me more desirable to the female fans.

I hiss out a breath when her hands trail down my belly before one wraps around the thick length of my cock and the other caresses my balls.

Fuck.

Fuck.

Fuck.

There's nothing better than this.

All right, maybe that's not completely true, but this is a close second.

"Mmmm, so hard."

"I was thinking about you and what you owe me when we get home."

"Same, but I couldn't wait that long."

And just like that, my dick grows unbearably stiff.

"Although…if you'd prefer, we can wait until later."

"Don't you dare." I growl at the idea of her leaving me high and dry.

A throaty chuckle escapes from her as she continues stroking my hard length. It wouldn't be the first time I've come from this alone. The woman has magic hands.

Just as my balls begin to tighten, she releases her hold. I didn't realize my eyelids had drifted shut until they fly open and I find Willow standing before me with a sexy little smile on her face. I can't stop my gaze from sliding down her naked body as water sluices over her. Willow is curvier than she was in college, and I love it. Both her hips and breasts have filled out.

There's a healthy glow about her.

Ever since signing my contract with Boston, I've made it my mission in life to keep her as healthy as possible. The first thing I did was hire a private chef who could prepare balanced meals that were packed with plenty of vitamins, nutrients, and antioxidants. We exercise with a trainer several times a week and have discovered the power of meditation.

Being in tip-top physical condition is important, but so is taking care of your mental health.

This woman is the most important person in my life, and I'll do whatever it takes to make sure she's both happy and healthy.

Unable to resist, my fingers reach out to play with her nipples. I love when they stiffen before my very eyes. Her pupils dilate as soon as I lay hands on her.

One of these days, I'm going to knock her up and then her breasts will swell even more. The thought of her nourishing our baby from her pretty little titties is such a fucking turn-on.

Before my hands can meander farther down her body to her soft pussy, she drops to her knees.

As much as I love the way she looks staring up at me with her big blue eyes and a mouthful of cock, I say, "You don't have to do this now. I don't want you scraping yourself up, sunshine."

"I'm fine." She smirks before adding, "And it's unlikely I'll be here long."

I snort.

She's not wrong about that.

Within minutes of her wrapping her lips around my dick, I'll be ready to blow.

The warmth of her mouth feels way too damn good.

When my erection bobs in front of her face, her tongue peeks out to lick the crown.

A groan escapes from me. "Don't tease me, woman."

Her lips lift into a smile before she tightens her fingers around my girth and draws me into her mouth to suck the tip. Her tongue swirls over the bulbous head as my fingers tangle in her wet strands, tugging her closer.

It doesn't take long for Willow to fall into a steady rhythm of drawing me in deep until I'm nudging the back of her throat and then sliding along the length to the crown. Her gaze stays pinned to mine the entire time.

It's exactly where I want it.

I always want her eyes on me.

And only me.

I want to be this woman's entire world.

The same way she's mine.

When her other hand rises to massage my sac, I know it's game over. As much as I enjoy coming down her throat when it constricts around my thick length, what I want right now is to bury myself in her sweet heat. I want to feel her inner muscles spasming around me, milking every drop as she finds her release.

Just as she turns voracious, I carefully slip my cock free.

Her brows furrow as she stares up at me. "You didn't like that?"

My fingers stroke over the curve of her jaw. "Baby, you know I loved it. Just like I always love when you take me in your mouth." My hands slip around her ribcage before pulling her to her feet. "But what I want more than anything is to sink inside your perfect little cunt. I've missed it." I press a kiss against her lips and taste myself there. "I need to feel it wrapped around my cock. You good with that, sunshine?"

Her eyes darken with my dirty talk. "I love when you're inside me."

I force her backward until her spine hits the tile wall before pinning her against it and drawing her arms upward.

"I want you to grip the pipe of the shower head."

I nod when her fingers tighten around the metal and she watches me with wide eyes. I can't help but take a step in retreat and stare at what a stunning picture she makes, stretched out against the wall with her nipples standing at attention as the shower continues to run, filling the room with steam.

Unable to help myself, I close the distance between us before tweaking one puckered bud and then the other. There's a quick inhale of breath from her. When she shifts, her hands loosening, I give her breast a little tap. It's nothing hard. I'd never want to hurt

Willow. Only heighten her pleasure. We've spent enough time experimenting, discovering what each other likes. And I've learned exactly what will get her off.

"Keep your hands on the pipe."

Her eyes flare wide when I give the other one a little slap.

The way her breasts jiggle makes me want to come all over myself.

When she follows the directive, I stroke my hands over each full tit. "Such a perfect girl." There's a pause before I add, "*My* girl."

Her expression softens as a whimper escapes from her.

I know exactly how much she loves hearing the praise. It's almost as much as I enjoy saying it.

I suck one nipple into my mouth before giving the same attention to the other. It's only when she's writhing, unable to stand still, that I kiss my way down her ribcage and belly before continuing my descent.

"So beautiful," I growl, lifting one leg around my shoulders so I can open her up completely. My tongue darts out to lap at her softness. "Does this gorgeous little pussy belong to me?"

Another whimper leaves her lips as she tilts her hips, as if trying to get closer.

Since that's not the answer I was looking for, I slap her clit with the tips of my fingers.

She squeaks, "You know it does."

I press a kiss against her mound before drawing her clit into my mouth and sucking gently. Even though her pussy was already drenched, it turns even creamier.

As rewarding as it is to score a goal—hell, three of them—this is what I take the most pride in—getting my woman off. Making her sob for me until the only thing that soothes her is the lash of my tongue or thrust of my cock.

When her muscles tighten and I know she's dancing on the precipice, I release her delicate flesh.

"You're right, I do. But I love hearing you say it. Your cries are sweet music to my ears. And they all belong to me."

From this angle, I'm able to see the glint of silver that winks at me from the plug I pressed into her ass before I left the house earlier this evening. It makes my dick throb a painful beat to know it's there. That she wore it throughout the game. Every shift of her behind had memories of when I fucked her this afternoon flooding her brain. After giving her a delicious orgasm, she knelt on the bed and allowed me to play with her gorgeous little rosebud. I primed it with lube and my fingers before finally pressing the plug deep inside her until it was seated perfectly between her cheeks.

As I nibble her delicate flesh, my fingers gather up some of her honey before slicking it around the base of the plug. Her cheeks tighten as I grip it and carefully twist and turn the metal, loosening it until it moves with ease. Only then do I slowly slide it from her rosebud.

Her breath turns labored as I continue eating at her. As the wide portion pops free, a sigh of relief escapes from her. Before she can get too used to it, I slip it back inside her ass. She squeaks as the plug slides home, her anus swallowing it up. There's nothing sexier than when she allows me to play with her backside.

To give her pleasure.

I fucking love it.

"Please, Mav," she cries. "I need you."

My tongue darts out to swipe her clit. "I know exactly what you need, baby. Don't you ever doubt it."

"I don't."

When I've tormented her ass enough, I slide the plug firmly into place between her cheeks. Tonight, after we get home, I'll have her kneel on the bed again and I'll give her another orgasm for being such a perfect girl before finally pulling the plug from her ass.

If I'm lucky, she'll allow me to fuck it afterward. Watching my hard length disappear in her pretty back hole is a turn-on like nothing else.

I want to own this woman.

Every single piece of her.

And in return, I shower her with more pleasure than she knows what to do with.

Her hands continue to grip the pipe high above her head as I press one final kiss against her swollen pussy. She's so ready to come.

One stroke of my hard length and she'll shatter.

I rise to my feet and, in one quick movement, slide deep inside her shuddering softness. I flex my hips, grinding my pelvis against hers. And just like I suspected, it doesn't take long before she's screaming out her orgasm. My name is a reverent chant that falls from her lips.

As soon as her pussy clenches my cock, I follow her over the edge. My own release has me seeing stars behind my eyelids.

Her body shudders around mine, milking me until there's nothing left to give. Every time we fuck, it feels like her inner muscles are strangling the life out of me.

Best.

Damn.

Feeling.

In.

The.

World.

And one I'll never grow tired of.

Once the final shudder racks my body, I huff out an exhausted breath and bury my face in the delicate hollow of her neck.

"I love you, sunshine."

A contented chuckle escapes from her. "I love you too."

I pull away enough to search her heavy-lidded eyes. "You know you're it for me, right?"

Her lips quirk. "Just like you are for me."

Satisfied with the answer, I nip her plump lower lip. "You ready to head home?"

"Yup." There's a pause. "Can we stop on the way and grab something to eat? I'm famished."

"I think that can be arranged." I give her a little wink. "After all, you're going to need your sustenance for round two."

Her sleepy eyes widen. "There's going to be a round two?"

One hand slips around her body to brush against the plug.

That's all it takes for her pupils to dilate and her breath to catch.

"Let's make it an energy smoothie instead."

"Done." I give her ass a little smack, knowing there'll be more of that on the agenda for tonight. "Now, let's go, before I decide to spread you out on the bench and fuck you senseless."

Her lips quirk. "It wouldn't be the first time."

With that, I give her a quick kiss before nabbing her fingers and pulling her into the locker room to get dressed.

And then we get the hell out of there and go home.

Where I make good on my promises.

But not before buying my sunshine an extra-large smoothie.

The End

Thank you so much for reading Mine to Take! I hope you enjoyed reading Willow and Maverick's story as much as I loved writing it.

Want to read the next book in the Western Wildcats Series?

One-click Break my Heart now!

After my life imploded last year, Dad decided that a change in scenery was necessary and moved us across the country. I've done the one thing I never thought I would—leave the competitive skating world behind in the rearview mirror.

It hasn't been easy.

Especially when the person buried in my past no longer wants to stay there.

Ever since stepping foot on campus, I've gone out of my way to avoid the hockey players that strut around like they're God's gift to the female species.

There's a reason for that.

My father is Reed Philips, head coach for the Western Wildcats. The number one rule in our house has always been that I keep a healthy distance from his players.

That's never been a problem.

And it's not necessarily one now.

Except...

I've just had a major run in with Hayes Van Doren.

One that includes me walking in on him freshly showered in the locker room and him thinking I was there to deliver a special birthday present by dropping to my knees.

Oh, trust me...he got a treat all right.

One that left him singing soprano.

I might have spent most of this year flying under the radar where Hayes is concerned, but that's no longer possible.

Everywhere I go, there he is.

Forcing his way into my life.

He's a complication I don't need.

Or want.

Except...

He's determined to change my mind about that.

The question is—will I let him?

Did you know that Elle and Carson have their own story? Turn the page for an excerpt of Campus Hottie!

Want to read Coach Philips's story?
Check out Just Friends now!
It's one of my favorites!

CAMPUS HOTTIE

ELLE

T he TA avoids all eye contact as he sets my paper facedown on the desk before moving on to the next row.

Crap.

The knot in my belly tightens as I realize that's probably not a good sign. What I can't afford is to barely scrape by on yet another test or quiz. I'd rather drop out of college than retake this class. And just to be clear, my mother would kill me if I actually did that.

Someone needs to explain what statistics has to do with being a theater major anyway. How is this supposed to assist me in pursuing my dream career as a stage actress?

The short answer is that it won't, which is exactly why I made a last-ditch effort to persuade my advisor on the third day of class that I should be given an exemption from Western's graduation requirement. His response was to sigh heavily as he removed his horn-rimmed glasses and pinched the bridge of his nose before effectively telling me to suck it up, buttercup.

So I'm stuck for the duration. A puff of air escapes from me as my shoulders slump. Failing this class is not an option.

"Aren't you going to look?" Mike asks from the desk parked next to mine.

I scrunch my nose and give my head a few violent shakes. "If it's bad, it'll ruin my entire day." And that's the last thing I need.

He rolls his hazel eyes before pushing his sandy-colored hair away from his face. "God, you are *so* dramatic."

A reluctant smile tugs at the corners of my lips. "That's what you love about me."

He tilts his head as if seriously considering the statement. "Hmmm...is it?"

I give him my most winsome smile before batting my eyelashes. "Yup, pretty sure it is."

"Maybe," he admits before pointing to the paper. "If you won't do the honors then I will."

The thick ball of tension that has taken up residence in the pit of my belly turns painful. "Stop trying to peer pressure me into doing something I'm not ready to."

His eyes ignite with humor as he elbows me. "Come on," he cajoles, "do it or I won't be your friend."

With a frown, I smack his shoulder and shift on the chair. "You're such a jerk."

He shrugs, looking unaffected by the insult. "Never said I wasn't."

When a few seconds trickle by, he raises his brows expectantly.

Ugh. I can already tell he won't drop the topic until I show him.

"Fine," I grumble. Air gets wedged in my throat as my heartbeat picks up tempo. I do a silent countdown before quickly flipping over the paper and staring at the number circled in red ink in the top right corner.

Sixty-five.

Shit. That's worse than I'd assumed it would be. My lips sink at the edges as my eyes widen. It's official, my Friday has just gone down the tubes.

"Sorry," he mumbles, looking equally surprised by the dismal score. "I really thought it would be better. We spent a ton of hours studying last week."

My hand drifts to my right temple where a headache is beginning to brew. This class will be the death of me, I just know it. All of my other courses are going great. Since day one, statistics has been a gigantic pain in my ass. No matter how much time I spend preparing for the tests or slogging through the daily assignments, I can't seem to wrap my mind around the concepts. I have some kind of mental block when it comes to math. It's always been a struggle, but I've usually been able to pull off a C. I would be thrilled with that at this point. We're talking happy dance and everything.

All of the red check marks decorating the page blur before my eyes until it looks like the paper is bleeding and should be promptly put out of its misery.

"Good morning, everyone," Dr. Holloway greets with a cheerful smile from behind the podium at the front of the room. "It's Friday, so I'll attempt to make this as painless as possible. Sound good?"

Ha! It's much too late for that.

His comment is met with a lone grunt or two that echo off the walls. By the blurry-eyed expressions filling the packed lecture hall, my guess is that most of my fellow students decided to jumpstart their weekend early. If they're expecting this material to do the trick and bring them back to life again, that won't be happening. Even though our professor does his best to breathe life into statistics, it's still dry and tedious.

Not one to be put off by the unenthusiastic response, he claps his hands together. "Excellent. Let's dive right in, shall we?"

Precisely forty-eight minutes later, my brain is on the verge of exploding from information overload. Statistical confidence intervals and the difference between populations swim around in my brain. If I'm not careful, the material will leak right out of my ears and onto the floor in a gooey mess.

As soon as he glances at his silver wristwatch and dismisses class for the day, everyone perks up and comes alive as if a switch has been flipped.

"Oh, I see how it is. Now you've all got something to say, huh?" Professor Holloway shakes his head as if disappointed in the caliber of student who populate his lectures. "Maybe I should assign a few pages to complete over the weekend."

The room erupts into noisy protests.

"Yeah, I didn't think so." He waves a hand in mock irritation. "Get out of here before I change my mind." His gaze travels over the sea of students loading up their bags before homing in on me. "Except you, Ms. Kendricks. Would you mind sticking around for a few minutes?"

Great.

"Sure." It takes effort to lift my lips into a smile.

Mike leans toward me. "Ohhh, the sexy professor wants to speak with you all alone. Lucky girl."

When I glare, he waggles his brows. "Give me a break," I mutter. "We both know he wants to discuss my dumpster fire of a grade."

Mike's gaze shifts to our instructor, who's shuffling around paperwork as undergraduates flee his classroom like rats from a burning building. "I'd be more than happy to have a little private tutoring from the likes of him."

An unwilling smile quirks my lips. This isn't the first time Mike has made just such a remark. "Something tells me the private tutoring you're looking for isn't in math." Especially since the big jerk received a ninety-three on his test.

A ninety-three!

That's the kind of grade I can only fantasize about.

His eyes turn dreamy as he leans his elbows on the laminated desktop before resting his chin on clasped hands. "I'll take whatever that man is willing to give me."

A chuckle bubbles up in my throat as I glance at our professor. I totally understand what Mike is saying about Dr. Holloway. He's good looking with dark hair and blue eyes. If I had to guess, I'd say he was somewhere in his early to mid thirties. The man obviously takes care of himself. Beneath his sport coat and khakis, he's lean and muscular.

Once I've packed up my belongings, we rise to our feet and move to the center aisle of the large space.

"All right, girl. I gotta get moving. I'll see you at three for rehearsal."

"Yup, I'll be there."

I live for play practice. It's what makes everything else in life bearable. Even statistics. I've been involved in the theater since I was a kid, and it's what I channeled all of my grief into after Dad died four years ago. I'm not sure I would have gotten through the loss of him without it. Instead of being constantly steeped in grief, I was able to escape, at least for short bursts of time, by pretending to be someone else.

With one final wave, Mike takes off and I turn, moving down the staircase to the front of the room where Professor Holloway waits. As the last student heads out, a heavy silence falls over the space. I clear my throat and hitch my backpack higher onto my shoulder.

"You wanted to see me?"

He glances up from the handful of papers he's in the process of organizing. "Yeah, thanks for sticking around. I was hoping we could touch base. I noticed you didn't do so well on the last test."

That's something of an understatement, and we both know it.

My grimace has the corners of his lips bowing up. Straight white teeth flash through the artificial light filling the room.

As he shifts his stance, his blue blazer falls open, revealing a perfectly pressed white button-down. "Oh, come on now. Is it really that bad?"

I huff out a breath as my shoulders loosen. "I know it doesn't look like it, but I'm actually trying. I studied for this test with Mike, and he got a ninety-three."

A thoughtful expression crosses his face as he nods. "Mike is doing well in this class. He seems to have a firm grip on the material."

I shoot him a sour look. "Unfortunately, his knowledge doesn't seem to be transferrable."

"In this particular case, I would agree with that statement," he says easily. "I wanted to mention that I have office hours every Tuesday and Thursday from four to six. You should stop in early next week, and we can spend some time going over your test and rework the problems you had trouble with."

"That would be all of them," I admit.

"Luckily for you, Ms. Kendricks, I just so happen to have a Ph. D in Applied Statistics. With a little one on one attention, I think we can get that grade up before the end of the semester. Right now, you're sitting at a D. And contrary to popular belief, that doesn't stand for 'darn good.' More like 'danger zone.' I don't think either of us wants to see it drop any further."

I suck in a sharp breath before blowing it out and jerking my head into a tight nod. With the upcoming production on campus, my schedule is jampacked, but there's no other way around it. I need help. And Dr. Holloway is offering it.

"Thank you. I'll plan to stop by on Tuesday."

"Excellent. You'll see, a little extra help will go a long way."

He's being really nice about this. Even though I loathe stats with the passion of a thousand burning suns, I'm appreciative of the lifeline he's throwing me. Plus, I can rub the fact that I'll be spending a little time alone with our sexy professor—as he likes to refer to him—in Mike's smug face.

"You obviously don't understand how terrible I am at the subject," I joke.

"Have a little faith, Elle. With enough hard work, nothing is impossible."

It takes effort to rein in my snort.

I certainly hope he's right about that. Or I'll be suffering through this class for a second time.

One-click Campus Hottie now!

JUST FRIENDS
REED

With a sigh, I collapse onto the couch in the living room of the house I share with a couple of guys from the hockey team and pop open a can of cold beer, guzzling down half of it in one thirsty swig.

Goddamn, but that hits the spot.

Know what else would hit the spot?

Yeah, you do.

It's the second week of September, and Coach Richards has us skating two-a-days, lifting weights, and running five miles for extra cardio.

As if we need it.

Oh…and he added yoga to this year's regimen.

Fucking yoga.

Can you believe that shit?

Let me be perfectly clear—I'm not into contorting my body into a pretzel and breathing deeply from my diaphragm. Sure, I get it. He wants us to work on our flexibility. And I'll do it, but that doesn't mean I have to like it.

Coach R is a total masochist.

Or is it sadist?

I can never keep those two straight.

No matter. Whatever kind of *ist* he is, the man thoroughly enjoys working our asses over. The only amusement I get is from listening to all the incoming freshmen piss and moan about what a tough schedule we have.

Welcome to Division I hockey, boys. Buckle up, it's going to be a bumpy ride.

Pile on fifteen credit hours and I don't have time for much else.

"Reed, baby, I've been waiting all night for you to return."

A curvy female drops onto my lap like an angel falling from heaven before she twines her slender arms around my neck and pulls me close.

I stand corrected. There's always time for *that*.

Hell, half the time, *that's* what gets me through the grind. Sex is an amazing stress reliever, and don't let anyone tell you differently. I'm way more chill after I've blown my load. And if I'm fortunate enough to do it twice in one night, then it's like I've slipped into a damn coma.

Pure bliss, baby.

Luckily for us, the Red Devils hockey team has its fair share of puck bunnies on campus who are always willing to provide some much-needed stress relief on a regular basis. God bless every last one of those ladies. They have no idea how much their *team spirit* is appreciated.

That being said, there are always exceptions to the rule.

And the girl currently cozied up on my lap is exactly that.

Megan thrusts out her lower lip in a sexy pout. "How is it possible that we've never hooked up before?"

The answer is simple. I go to great lengths to avoid her like a particularly nasty case of crabs.

She flutters her mascara-laden lashes and tilts her head. Her voice becomes lispy and toddler-like as she twirls a dark curl around her finger. "Don't you think I'm pretty?"

Pretty?

No, Megan is flat-out gorgeous.

Her long, black hair is as shiny as a crow's wing as it floats around her shoulders in soft waves. She has dark eyes that are tipped at the corners. And her skin is sun-kissed all year round. And if that weren't enough to have any guy giving her a full-on salute, she's also got gravity-defying tits and a nice round ass.

Have I imagined fucking her from behind and smacking that bubble butt a few times before blowing my wad?

You bet Megan's perfectly round ass I have. The girl is a walking wet dream.

And from what the guys on the team tell me (because they're a bunch of loudmouth assholes who like to brag), she can suck a dick like nobody's business. That being said, I won't be finding that out firsthand anytime soon.

I've made it a point to steer clear of Megan because every time I look at her, I see Emerson.

And imagining that I'm nailing my best friend is a definite no-no.

When I don't immediately respond, Megan grinds her bubble butt against my junk—which is something I really don't need, because just the thought of Emerson alone is enough to have me popping wood.

It's a messed-up situation.

One that Em is blissfully unaware of. Which is exactly the way it needs to stay. She can't find out that I've got the hots for her. Emerson Shaw is one of the first friends I made when Mom and I moved to Lakefield the summer before freshman year of high school. And we've been tight ever since.

While I enjoy having a casual, friends-with-benefits relationship with a number of girls on campus, I've never considered sleeping with Em.

Okay, maybe I've *considered* having sex with her. It would be hard not to imagine stripping her naked and getting jiggy with a girl who looks like that, but I've never done anything about it.

I've screwed too many women not to know that getting naked changes a relationship. And I like Em way too much to risk sleeping with her. She's the one person who has always had my back. And let's face it, I can be a hell of a lot more honest with her than my teammates.

Can you imagine me baring my soul to those assholes?

Exactly. I'd never hear the end of it.

My friendship with Emerson also gives me all this insight into the female psyche that I wouldn't otherwise be privy to. It's like taking a peek behind the magic curtain. I'm not willing to throw that away when there are plenty of random chicks I can get my rocks off with.

Moral of the story? Friends are a lot harder to come by than hookups.

"Reed?" Megan nips my lower lip between her sharp teeth before giving it a gentle tug and releasing it.

I blink back to the girl wriggling around on my lap. "Yeah?"

Her hands flutter to my shoulders before settling on them. "You're so tense."

Damn right I am. All I can think about is Emerson, and that's all kinds of wrong.

"Let's go upstairs." Her tongue darts out to moisten her lips as she whispers, "I know *exactly* what will fix that."

If any other girl were making the offer, I'd already be dragging her up the staircase to my bedroom. But that's not going to happen with Megan.

I just can't do it. Maybe I'm not *technically* doing anything wrong, but it still feels like I'm breaking some kind of friendship rule. Emerson may not realize I'm thinking about her like that, but I do.

And that's all that matters.

Guess I'll have to find a different girl to get busy with. Preferably a flat-chested blonde with big blue eyes who doesn't resemble Em. Or maybe a redhead, just to mix things up a bit.

Megan's eyes light up when I set my beer down and wrap my hands around her waist, until I carefully remove her from my lap. "Sorry, sweetheart. I've got homework to finish up for tomorrow." I tack on the lie to soften the blow. "Maybe another time?"

Her face falls. "Sure, no problem."

Before she can pin me down on a time and place, I beat a hasty retreat from the living room and head upstairs. Once I've taken refuge in my room, I fire off a text to one of my go-to girls.

Fifteen minutes later, my booty-call for the evening strolls through the door.

Know what I like most about Candace?

The girl gets right down to business. There's no need for small talk, and that I can appreciate. I'm in the mood to fuck, not debate world politics or climate change.

The door hasn't even closed and Candace is already shedding her clothes. Since she hasn't bothered with a bra, her titties bounce free as soon as her shirt is discarded. Her nips stiffen right up when the cool air hits them.

It's a beautiful sight to behold.

Except...

Nothing stirs south of the border. Not like it did when I was thinking about a certain someone downstairs who shall remain nameless. But I'm not concerned. I just need to harness my mental capabilities and focus on the task at hand. Which is getting my dick to work properly.

I yank off my T-shirt and toss it to the floor as Candace flicks open the button of her teeny-tiny shorts before unzipping them. With her gaze locked on mine, she shimmies out of them.

And wouldn't you know it...

No panties in sight.

Just a gloriously bare pussy.

Works for me.

Well, that's what *normally* works for me.

At the moment, limp dick-itis has set in.

Once Candace has stripped down to her birthday suit, she struts her sexy stuff toward the bed where I've made myself comfortable. Her eyelids lower as a knowing smirk curves her red-slicked lips. I rake my gaze over her toned body.

The girl is absolutely perfect.

"I've missed you." She crawls across the mattress until her hands are resting against my bare chest. "I'm glad you texted."

She says that now, but it probably won't be the case when she gets her hands on my junk.

What the hell is wrong with me?

I thought this kind of thing only happened to older dudes. I'm way too young for Viagra. I've seen first-hand how that shit can mess you up.

As a joke last year, one of the jackasses on my team got his hands on a couple of those little blue pills and slipped them to one of the freshman players. The poor guy was sporting wood for days. Unfortunately, a trip to the emergency room became necessary. When Coach R was apprised of the situation, he reamed our asses good and threatened to bench the entire team for the season. We skated suicides until our legs practically fell off.

No, thank you.

Candy trails her purple-tipped fingernails down my chest before pushing me against the mattress and straddling my torso. Then she leans over and licks a wet trail down my body until reaching the waistband of my athletic shorts. This encounter is going to nosedive real quick if I can't get it up in record speed. Not knowing what else to do, I squeeze my eyes tight as an unwanted image of Emerson pops into my head.

Dark hair, lush curves, bright smile.

Candace chuckles as she pulls my hard length from my boxer briefs like it's a much-anticipated Christmas gift. "There's my big boy!"

I groan.

I am *so* screwed.

One-click Just Friends now!

MORE BOOKS BY JENNIFER SUCEVIC

<u>The Campus Series</u> (football)
Campus Player (Demi & Rowan)
Campus Heartthrob (Sydney & Brayden)
Campus Flirt (Sasha & Easton)
Campus Hottie (Elle & Carson)
Campus God (Brooke & Crosby)
Campus Legend (Lola & Asher)

<u>Western Wildcats Hockey</u>
Hate You Always (Juliette & Ryder)
Love You Never (Carina & Ford)
Always My Girl (Viola & Madden)
Dare You to Love Me (Stella & Riggs)
Never Mine to Hold (Fallyn & Wolf)
Never Say Never (Britt & Colby)
Mine to Take (Willow & Maverick)

<u>The Barnett Bulldogs</u> (football)
King of Campus (Ivy & Roan)
Friend Zoned (Violet & Sam)
One Night Stand (Gia & Liam)
If You Were Mine (Claire & JT)

<u>The Claremont Cougars</u> (football)
Heartless Summer (Skye & Hunter)
Heartless (Skye & Hunter)
Shameless (Poppy & Mason)

Hawthorne Prep Series (bully/football)

King of Hawthorne Prep (Summer & Kingsley)

Queen of Hawthorne Prep (Summer & Kingsley)

Prince of Hawthorne Prep (Delilah & Austin)

Princess of Hawthorne Prep (Delilah & Austin)

The Next Door Duet (football)

The Girl Next Door (Mia & Beck)

The Boy Next Door (Alyssa & Colton)

What's Mine Duet (Suspense)

Protecting What's Mine (Grace & Matteo)

Claiming What's Mine (Sofia & Roman)

Stay Duet (hockey)

Stay (Cassidy & Cole)

Don't Leave (Cassidy & Cole)

Stand-alone

Confessions of a Heartbreaker (football)

Hate to Love You (Hockey) (Natalie & Brody)

Just Friends (Hockey) (Emerson & Reed)

Love to Hate You (Football) (Daisy & Carter)

The Breakup Plan (Hockey) (Whitney & Gray)

Collections

Claremont Cougars

The Barnett Bulldogs

The Football Hotties Collection

The Hockey Hotties Collection

The Next Door Duet

ABOUT JENNIFER

Jennifer Sucevic is a USA Today bestselling author who has published twenty-four new adult novels. Her work has been translated into German, Dutch, Italian, and French. She has a bachelor's degree in History and a master's in Educational Psychology from the University of Wisconsin-Milwaukee. Jen started out her career as a high school counselor before relocating with her family and focusing on her passion for writing. When she's not tapping away on the keyboard and dreaming up swoonworthy heroes to fall in love with, you can find her bike riding or at the beach. She lives in Michigan with her family.

If you would like to receive regular updates regarding new releases, please subscribe to her newsletter here-
Jennifer Sucevic Newsletter (subscribepage.com)

Or contact Jen through email, at her website, or on Facebook.
sucevicjennifer@gmail.com

Want to join her reader group? Do it here -)
J Sucevic's Book Boyfriends | Facebook

Social media links-
https://www.tiktok.com/@jennifersucevicauthor
www.jennifersucevic.com
https://www.instagram.com/jennifersucevicauthor

https://www.facebook.com/jennifer.sucevic
Amazon.com: Jennifer Sucevic: Books, Biography, Blog, Audiobooks, Kindle
Jennifer Sucevic Books - BookBub